DESIGNED
to death

The Faith Hunter Scrap This Mystery Series
by Christina Freeburn

CROPPED TO DEATH (#1)
DESIGNED TO DEATH (#2)
EMBELLISHED TO DEATH (#3)
(*coming April 2014*)

DESIGNED TO DEATH

"Battling scrapbook divas, secrets, jealousy, murder, and lots of glitter all make Designed to Death a charming and heartfelt mystery."

–Ellen Byerrum,
Author of the Crime of Fashion Mysteries

"Read this fun book and you will never think of Washi tape in in quite the same way again, I promise. Christina Freeburn's second installment in her scrapbooking mystery series is full of small-town intrigue, twists and turns, and plenty of heart."

– Mollie Cox Bryan,
Agatha Award Finalist, *Scrapbook of Secrets*

"This is a fun series with very likable characters you will want to visit with again and again with every new book. Even if you are not a fan of scrapping (and I'm not – it's about the only craft I never got into) you will enjoy the series as it is not heavy with information about the hobby – as some hobby series can be. And if you are into the hobby, there are hints at the back of the book."

– Kate Shannon,
Rantin' Ravin' and Reading

CROPPED TO DEATH

"Christina's characters shine, her knowledge of scrapbooking is spot on, and she weaves a mystery that simply cries out to be read in one delicious sitting!"

— Pam Hanson,
Multi-Published Women's Fiction Author

"This was a great read that had me reading non-stop from the moment I turned the first page. The author did a good job in keeping me in suspense with plenty of twists and turns and every time I thought I had it figured out, the author changed the direction in which the story was headed...The writing flowed easily and I liked the cast of characters in this charming whodunit!"

– Dru Ann Love,
Dru's Book Musings

"Witty, entertaining and fun with a side of murder...When murder hits Eden, West Virginia, Faith Hunter will stop at nothing to clear the name of her employee who has been accused of murder. Will she find the real killer before it is too late? Read this sensational read to find out!"

–Shelley Giusti,
Shelley's Book Case

"A cozy mystery that exceeds expectations....Freeburn has crafted a mystery that does not feel clichéd or cookie-cutter....it's her sense of humor that shows up in the book, helping the story flow, making the characters real and keeping the reader interested....And she promises more Faith Hunter books—I hope she writes fast!"

— Cynthia McCloud,
Scrapbooking is Heart Work Blog

DESIGNED
to death

A Faith Hunter Scrap This Mystery

CHRISTINA FREEBURN

HENERY PRESS

DESIGNED TO DEATH
A Faith Hunter Scrap This Mystery
Part of the Henery Press Mystery Collection

First Edition
Trade paperback edition | September 2013

Henery Press
www.henerypress.com

Copyright © 2013 by Christina Freeburn
Cover art by Fayette Terlouw
Author photograph by Megan Freeburn

ISBN-13: 978-1-938383-52-6

Printed in the United States of America

*To my mother-in-law, Cathy, who always believes
the books I write should be on the bestseller lists.
Having your support and encouragement
means the world to me.*

ACKNOWLEDGMENTS

A big thank you to the people of West Virginia who've done what they could to help this become home. We moved here ten years ago and one of the first things I did when moving to WV was find a new CM consultant. I knew if I wanted to meet some new friends, I needed to find a crop to attend and finding a consultant was the first step.

The next thing was looking for a writing group and/or organization. The internet is a wonderful tool as I stumbled across West Virginia Writers, Inc. Not only did I discover I could do things I didn't think I had the knack for (accounting) but I also "found" kindred spirits and "my sister".

I also want to mention that while scrapbook message boards can be filled with drama and angst, these boards also build long-lasting friendship and allow a part of "home" to travel with you.

A big thanks to all of those who participate on scrapbooking message boards...large and small...who not only share their life, projects, and musings but take time to share in the lives of others and offer words of encouragement and a hand of friendship when needed most.

ONE

I plucked a copy of the special issue of *Making Legacies* magazine from the stack on the cropping-turned-signing table. *Introducing the New Divas* was emblazed across the front in a bold, bubblegum pink font. The heavier cardboard style cover of the issue kept the magazine firm as it rested on my palm. I ran my hand over the slick surface and hoped having an official Life Artist Diva in residence would help bring fans to our store in Eden, West Virginia.

A basket of black cats, witches, and ghouls of various sizes and levels of scary was shoved behind the table into the corner. I had spent the morning taking down all of the Halloween decorations from the walls and doors, rearranging products so the focus of the store was no longer Halloween, which was two weeks away, and instead had a general scrapbooking theme. We changed the decor so it didn't compete with Belinda Watson's signing...as requested by her mother, Hazel.

Tonight, I'd have to put all our decorations back up and shuffle the inventory again. If we didn't get the new Halloween lines sold in the next few weeks, we'd end up discounting them when Christmas came. We couldn't keep money tied up in old inventory. Customers expected the latest and greatest at all times and seeing "stale" merchandise would have them turning to online sites for their scrapbook shopping needs.

"Pick up the pace, Faith." Grandma Hope scooted behind me and placed an array of acid-free markers on the table. "Restlessness is settling in."

The women with tickets for the class, and those who had pre-purchased books, waited in the store while the rest of the customers snaked down the sidewalk in front of Scrap This, stomping their feet and huddling together to ward off the chill. The line extended from our store all the way past Home Brewed.

I watched Dianne and an employee of hers walk down the line to take orders. Grandma Cheryl hustled outside with a calculator and her credit card ready iPhone to ring up purchases for the special issue of *Making Legacies.*

"Isn't this thrilling?" A woman sidled up to me.

"Absolutely. I can't wait for Belinda to start teaching."

Leslie Amtower's, editor-in-chief of *Making Legacies,* blue eyes shined as she gazed at the women clamoring for her magazine. She looked every inch the part of a creative vision. She wore a nicely tailored suit in grays and creams, the current color trend, and her long blonde hair was arranged on top of her head in artistic curling tendrils. A gray and cream scarf, shot through with a bold pink fuzzy fiber, completed the outfit.

"Am I mistaken..." Leslie pointed toward the cash register, her pink-tinted lips twisting unattractively, "or isn't that the murderer?"

No sound could be heard but the whoosh of all the women's necks rotating from Leslie, to Marilyn Kane, and back to me. Not this. We had finally shaken off, or at least I thought, the store's recent scandalous past and now Leslie lobbed it at us.

Marilyn froze with a finger above the total key.

I dropped a stack of books onto the table and reminded myself I didn't use the particular words bouncing around in my head. At least not out loud, and in front of my grandmothers. "No. Her husband was a murder victim."

Leslie flipped the ends of her scarf over her shoulder. "I could've sworn I saw her picture in the paper."

"Being suspected of something doesn't make a person guilty," I said. "The police found the real murderer." With my help. I kept that tidbit to myself, not just from not wanting to seem like a braggart, but to keep Leslie from remembering my picture had been in the paper for the same crime but for aiding and abetting the accused. I called it reluctant amateur sleuthing.

Scrap This had gained some notoriety because of the murder. I had hoped having a Diva in our midst would get our reputation back to revolving around scrapbooking.

A woman in line used her cell to snap a picture of Marilyn Kane. "Can I get one of us together?"

"Today's focus should be on Belinda. Not your employee." Leslie crossed her arms and glared at Marilyn.

I remembered my manners, refraining from pointing out *she* was the one who brought it to the customers' attention.

Marilyn yanked her purse from under the counter.

"Trust me, Marilyn doesn't want any of this attention," I said.

Grandma Hope raced over to the register. I hoped she planned on smacking the "paparazzi" lady, and convinced Marilyn to stay. We needed all employees on deck today. We didn't need shoppers to decide to look here then buy online because of long lines.

"Just make sure Belinda is the focus of this day." Leslie glided into the crowd, soaking up the hero worship bestowed on her by the croppers who recognized her from the picture included on the "Letter from the Editor" page.

Women squealed and reached out to stroke their fingertips on the scarf floating behind her, as if one touch transferred the "greatness" from her to them.

A camera flash went off. I turned around and saw reporter extraordinaire Karen England, looking very bored, standing in a corner while a man snapped shots with a Nikon D800.

My heart pitter-pattered and I felt a swoon coming on. I was in love. One day I hoped to afford the "love of my life." Until then, I'd covet from afar. The ruggedly attractive photographer in his forties saw me looking at him and brought the camera down, a mix of confusion and concern flashed on his face.

I pointed at the camera, then placed my hand over my heart.

He grinned and raised the camera up like a mock salute.

He understood the love affair I wished to have with his camera.

Karen narrow-eyed me and jabbed her elbow into his side. The photographer got back to work.

"I'll finish up here." Grandma Hope shooed me toward the classroom tables. "You go make sure everything is ready for the class."

"I'm on it." I scurried the few feet from the signing area to the class area.

I morphed into my role of special events coordinator. Who would've thought Belinda Watson, local Edenite would become a L.A.D.—a Life Artist Diva—on her first try. Scrapbook designers from all over considered being named a L.A.D. as "the shining moment" and first step of launching a design career. Belinda had never shown an interest in it, though her cousin Darlene had.

I shuddered. I hoped I didn't just Beetlejuice the woman by thinking her name. Darlene had been scary quiet the last few months since Belinda's name was announced. You would've thought she'd exhibit a little happiness for her cousin. Then again, she was Darlene so not much of a surprise.

I counted the chairs, then the class kits. I double checked my list. One cancellation. Not a problem. It would be snapped up once I made it known.

Someone cleared their throat.

I carefully flipped through the magazine, trying to find the page which showcased the layout using the technique Belinda planned on teaching today. It wasn't every day when a teacher requested we order pounds of glitter, pink boas, nails, hot glue sticks, cardboard, and hammers.

The person repeated the grating noise.

Holding in a sigh, I closed the magazine and looked toward the sound.

Annette Holland stood in front of me, a sheet of paper clutched in one hand. The other hand patted the back of her infant son who was attached to her front with a backpack style holder. The strap of a green fabric tote with Eden County Library screen printed on it slipped from her shoulder and now hung from the crock of her elbow.

Some customers shot an irritated glance her way. If there was one thing mothers didn't like it was for other mothers to bring their children to an event when they found a sitter for theirs.

"Going to start scrapbooking?" I smiled at Annette.

The paper trembled in her hand. This wasn't the strong, confident young lady I met a few months back. Then again, her life had changed drastically since she had an affair with Marilyn's husband Michael. She'd been a suspect in his murder, the grieving girlfriend, the town's black sheep, and now a single mother trying to raise her child on her own.

"You aren't letting children in the class, are you?" A customer glared at me from her place in line.

Behind Annette, Sierra clutched a stack of promotional flyers and leveled a hard stare at me. She switched her gaze to Annette and shook her head.

My co-worker and friend Sierra, or former friend if you asked her, glared at me. Sierra wanted the mom and baby gone before a mutiny happened. I felt myself digging in my proverbial heels. I had no intention of letting Annette into the class, but I couldn't remember if I specifically stated no children.

Sierra tucked the flyers under one arm then scribbled in the class book. "I've been dying to take this class. I hope it's okay I'm signing up. I didn't want to do it early as I figured we should give our customers a chance first. Unless *you* have a problem..."

I heard the sighs of relief from the customers who waited for the arrival of the diva. The book signing was scheduled first but the class attendees had arrived also, each hoping to get one of the three coveted chairs in the front row.

Annette thrust the paper at me. "Could I sign up for this?"

It was a print out of our Halloween crop. I checked out the last lines. Relief swept through me. I did mention no children at the crop. At least I wouldn't have to wage that battle after the fact.

"Sure."

Annette pointed at the salutation and then a section in the middle of the email. "I wasn't sure because of this and this."

I read the email I thought I knew by heart.

Hello wonderful croppers! Get those calendars out and mark this date! As a thank you to our wonderful customers, we're having an Eve Before Halloween Crop. This is a free crop for all of you! So get those sitters lined up or have those hubbies at home and come join us for an evening of cropping, snacks and special scrapping treats (no tricks, we promise).

From your friendly Scrap This employees and owners!

I cringed. Wow, a little exclamation point happy. Besides that, I didn't see any problems.

"I'm not a wonderful cropper, nor have I shopped here." The baby fussed. Annette bounced up and down. "So, I wasn't sure if you meant me. I figured you must or you wouldn't have sent me the email…"

Here I thought I did a good job in conveying our message. I spent two hours composing it. Just what I needed in my life…an email analyzer.

"If you received the email, you're invited." I handed the print-out back.

"Oliver said the invitation was specific." Annette tried hoisting the library bag back up her arm.

I lifted the strap and placed it on her shoulder, spotting a book about beginning scrapbooking. We needed a less nosy librarian. "Oliver didn't write the email, so what does he know."

"He knows that invitations specifically worded are meant for the ones invited not just anyone." Oliver White's know-it-all voice broke into the conversation.

I wanted to smack the guy. The county hired Oliver White as the new library director a few months ago. He was the straight out of college nephew of the retiring library director, and seemed to be following in his aunt's footsteps of becoming the town's Miss Manners. Originally, he had wanted to be a police officer. Some medical issues made it hard for him to pass the physical so he turned his interest in policing onto a different path.

"You're invited, Annette. I can't wait to see pictures of your little cutie. If you need help with your layouts, pick a spot by Gussie. She doesn't do much scrapbooking but loves baby pictures."

Annette crinkled her nose and fired off a "so there" comment with her eyes at Oliver.

"Words are important." Oliver held a copy of *Making Legacies* tightly in his hands. "You might not respect them—"

"I respect them all right. It's why I'm careful not to make someone feel unwelcome." I glared at Oliver. "I meant everyone and anyone who'd like to crop is welcome. Besides, it's none of your business who we invite to our events."

"Invite whoever you want," Oliver said. "But the proper use of language is my business. You should have written what you just said so it would've been clear."

"The line's getting long. You might want to go stand in it." I widened my eyes and smiled sweetly. "Was that clear?"

"Customer service isn't your forte."

The buzzer by the employee door sounded then stopped. After a gun-carrying criminal surprised me a few months ago, my grandmothers had Steve Davis add a security system by the back door. If the code wasn't punched in quick enough, a warning alarm went off at the police station and in the prosecutor's office where Steve—my grandmothers' appointed knight-in-shining armor for me—worked.

"Belinda must have arrived," I said.

Oliver drew in a breath and quickly rushed toward the front of the line.

"The end," I called out to him.

I watched one of our customers snag Oliver's arm and draw him to her side. They stood shoulder-to-shoulder and flipped through the magazine. No one else in line seemed to care so I'd let it slide, and Belinda had promised not to leave until every magazine was signed.

Cold wind snaked through the building and I fought back a shiver. October could either be an extension of a warm fall or the beginning of a cold winter. Two years in a row, trick-or-treating had to be postponed because of snow. The October breeze swirled around the room and I scrambled to grab the class schedules and other advertisements that tumbled from the heavy plastic tables.

Belinda waltzed into the store, waving like a teenage girl crowned Homecoming Queen. My grandma Cheryl followed after her, doing her best not to roll her eyes. A few customers began whispering, straining their necks to get a good look at the newest Life Artist Diva.

"Please don't let this title go to her head," I muttered.

"Belinda, look over here! Over here!" A customer jumped up and down, holding her cell phone out as she tried to snap a picture.

"Belinda, the library thanks you for the generous gift." Oliver waved his copy in the air.

"I must speak with Faith first." Belinda gave another queenly wave, blew a kiss at Oliver, then headed for me.

When she spotted Karen and the photographer, she froze for an instant. In that moment, I saw uncertainty cross her face. The shy woman, who needed her mom to book her signings and appearances, shone through the new confident, "celebrity Belinda."

"Belinda," I almost screamed her name to draw her attention, "can you give me some pointers on the class?"

Belinda shook her head. "I can't give out any secrets. Only those who paid for the class will get to learn this technique. I hope you have some way of making sure those who haven't purchased a spot don't get a free lesson."

Did Belinda expect us to empty out the store when the class started? Or put up a huge partition? I cast a glance over at my grandmothers. Hope looked confused by the request and Cheryl beyond annoyed.

I was both, considering I had to figure out how to incorporate this new demand from Belinda. "I'm not expecting any secrets. I just want to know which layout is the inspiration for your class."

Belinda wagged her finger at me. "No sneak peeks. Not even for you."

I heard Karen's unladylike snort from across the room. I refrained from giving her the evil eye, and also swatting Belinda with the magazine.

Yesterday alone, I had spent three hours on the phone making sure everything was just the way Hazel's "baby" needed it. Talk about helicopter mom. I had been instructed on the noise level permitted in the classroom area, the temperature best suited for Belinda's creativity, and how instructions couldn't be included in the class kit because Belinda feared her idea would be distributed without her permission.

Neither my grandmothers nor I liked the last rule but we went along with it.

When Belinda was named a L.A.D., scrappers within a four hour drive-time radius began calling, asking if we had any classes taught by Belinda on our schedule. Everyone considered Scrap This her home store, so they contacted us first and we didn't want to disappoint them.

"Hard to set up the class properly without the instructions." I picked up a copy of the magazine featuring Belinda and flipped through it. There couldn't be too many designs that needed glue, boas, glitter and a hammer.

Gazing at my hands, Belinda offered me a smile and patted me on the shoulder. "Silly me, I should've guessed. Of course I'll sign a copy for you. Would you like me to personalize it?"

I stopped my eye rolling in mid-roll when I noticed Sierra leaving her spot for the class and coming toward us.

Belinda whipped out an acid free bubblegum pink pen from her bubblegum pink and lime green Vera Bradley purse. The sleeve of her oversized coat covered her hand and hid the pen.

"Would you like me to take your coat?" Sierra asked. "I brought a quilted hanger today just for you."

"How thoughtful of you, Sierra." Belinda beamed at her and held out her arms, waiting for Sierra to remove the garment.

With only a slight hesitation, Sierra slipped the beige coat with a chocolate brown faux fur collar from Belinda's shoulders.

I pressed my lips together to stop from gaping at Belinda. I was a pink loving girl, but even for me this was overkill.

Belinda's purse was the perfect color match to the bubblegum pink and lime green t-shirt she wore which had "Life Artist Diva" embroidered across her ample chest. The tiny rhinestones strained to pop off. She paired the shirt with a pair of bubblegum pink jeans with tiny lime green scissors embroidered all over the legs and backside of the denim. Belinda pulled out a tiara made with lime green and bubblegum pink stones from her purse and delicately placed it on top of her head. The tiara was almost hidden by her mass of dark-brown curly hair.

Leslie stared at her diva with a look of utter amazement...and not the good type of amazement.

Sierra hid a snicker behind her hand cupped around her mouth.

"Faith..." Belinda cocked her head to the side and looked at me. Confusion twisted her features as she stared at the magazine I still held.

"Yeah, sure. I'd appreciate it." I held the magazine out to Belinda.

Belinda gently placed her hands beside mine and lifted the pristine issue of *Making Legacies* from my hands as if we transferred a baby between us. With careful turns of the glossy pages, Belinda stopped at the section that highlighted her artist biography and displayed a large glamorized photo of her. The right-hand side of the feature article showcased a featured artwork of hers.

The layout was breathtaking. As the magazine order had only arrived that morning, I hadn't had time to look at the pages featured in the special issue. Belinda surprised me. The introduction layout of hers had layers of embellishments artfully arranged around an Andy Warhol style portrait of Belinda.

A monochromatic color scheme of green circled the picture and helped pop the picture from the page. Usually, a large amount of embellishments overpowered pictures but Belinda's design of keeping the decorative elements in a muted shade of beige helped keep the focal point on the beautiful photo.

"This is great, Belinda." I tapped the photograph of her work. "I didn't know you'd been working on changing your style."

Belinda blew on the inscription and handed me back the magazine. "It's always good for an artist to test their skills. I never would've been inspired to stretch my creative wings if it hadn't been for your classes."

"Thanks." I peered at the note Belinda wrote. *To one of my favorite scrapbook store employees. Keep encouraging the love of art to all those who wander into the store.*

One of. Well, I guess if Sierra flipped through my copy and read it, Belinda didn't want her to think I was the favorite.

A thump sounded at the backdoor. I shot a look at my grandmothers. They both frowned. The thudding grew louder.

Belinda sighed. "I guess my mom is finally here. She promised to come and be my page turner."

"Page turner?" Did I really want to know the answer?

Belinda nodded, arranging ten bubble gum pink acid-free markers on the signing table and shoving off the ones my grandmother had placed there earlier. "My mother said the line would go quicker if she turned to the correct page and all I had to do was sign."

Cheryl paused at the maroon curtain that separated the store area from the stock room and flicked a glance over her shoulder. I knew that look. It had been given to me quite a few times growing up...the girl-needs-a-reality-check stare down.

Tapping an index finger on her bottom lip, Belinda studied the placement of the signing table. "Should my back really be facing the large picture windows? Passersby might be interested in stopping to get a quick peek at a celebrity."

Hazel rushed past the rows of pattern paper and beelined to us. She had bought, or made herself, a similar outfit to the one Belinda wore. Instead of bubblegum pink being the major color it was lime green with the pink shade as the accent, and her claim to fame stated "Mother of Life Artist Diva."

"This won't do." Hazel tsk-tsked. "The lighting here is too harsh for Belinda to deal with all morning. The table should be angled away from the windows. This just won't do at all."

I was wondering how our attendees would feel having to look at lime green and bright pink all day. "It will be hard for the students taking Belinda's class to follow along if they have to twist their necks to watch the demonstration."

Hazel looked at me as if I was a simpleton. "Are these tables bolted to the floor?"

I frowned. "No."

"Get a move on then. Start rearranging." Hazel swished her hands in a go-away-little-doggie manner. "My daughter is the most important person here."

Belinda had the good graces to cringe at her mother's words. One attendee hustled over to the register and I heard her ask for her class fee back.

Annoyed murmurs erupted from the rest of the class. A few women discretely, and some not so, placed their copy of *Making Legacies* they had intended to buy back onto the pile.

Leslie started tapping a stylus onto the screen of her iPad, a frown marring the pleasant expression her tattooed eyebrows and eyeliner attempted to give her. The editor-in-chief didn't appear pleased with the diva's behavior.

This was going to be a long day.

TWO

"Next," Hazel announced, holding out her hands for an issue of *Making Legacies* to slide in front of Belinda.

Two more stragglers raced into the store, grabbed a magazine, and jumped into the back of the line. I looked over at Belinda. This time, she nodded yes to my suggestion of closing off the line. The signing should've ended an hour ago, but Belinda hadn't wanted to turn away any of her fans, and neither did Leslie Amtower. She cared about the books being sold, not the class.

I, on the other hand, had to balance both. I thought making the class attendees wait for an hour was more than long enough.

The women poised at the cropping tables as if preparing for battle, one hand hovering over a hammer and the other over the wide range of tin sheets, finally smiled. For over an hour, they waited for the diva to begin the class. With one word from their idol, they'd grab the hammer, a pin, and snatch up the nearest color of thin sheets of aluminum to start poking the metal into creative submission.

I had yet to figure out how the boa came into play.

Hazel slid another copy of the magazine over to Belinda. With a flourish, Belinda signed the copy and handed it to the waiting groupie. The class attendees' arms quivered in anticipation, two more signatures and then they'd be on their way to the fame of being part of the first class taught by Belinda.

"What product did you use on this layout?" A young woman with hopeful eyes asked, tapping a design with stacked flowers on the corner of the photo. "I love these shapes and haven't seen them before. This would be great for my engagement photo."

Belinda queen-waved off the young lady. "I have a class to teach. No time for questions right now."

"I'm sure there's a supply list included." Hazel beamed at the young woman.

"There's not." The woman remained glued to her spot, staring at Belinda. "Don't you remember what product this is?"

Hazel looked pointedly at me.

Holding in a long-suffering sigh, I smiled at the girl. "Leave your email with one of my grandmothers and I'll locate the supplies for you."

"Thanks." The girl beamed and skipped toward Hope.

I was surprised *Making Legacies* hadn't included a product list with the layouts. It was standard for the items the designer used to be listed either alongside or underneath the layout. Was this a way for the magazine to get more readers to check out their blog and increase their number of hits?

The last autograph seeker made it through the line. Hallelujah. The students flexed their fingers, anticipating the first words from the newest scrapbooking It-Girl.

Gathering up a set of tools for Belinda, I raced over to the table and arranged them for quick and easy access. Hammer. Check. Different size nails. Check. Different color tin sheets. Check. Protective mat for the table. Check. Hot glue gun. Check. Glitter. Check. Pink boa. Check.

"Do you need anything else, Belinda?" I hoped for a no. The table was running out of room.

She glanced at the items and pointed at the hammer, nails and tin. "If you don't mind, can you scoot those over toward my mother? She's doing the hands-on portion while I read from my notes." Belinda reached into her expensive bubblegum pink leather artist portfolio and pulled out a stack of paper.

I stepped closer to Belinda and lowered my voice. "These women paid a premium price to take a class taught by you."

"I am teaching it." She waved the pages under my nose.

"Teaching as in demonstrating. If they just wanted to read the instructions, they could have done that at home."

Belinda laughed. "These instructions haven't been published yet. They are the first to be learning this technique. You should be pleased I'm debuting this class at Scrap This. I could have gone elsewhere."

Right now, I wished she had. The paying customers took this class under the belief the creator of the technique would demonstrate it, not have her mother do it while the diva read the instructions aloud. Granted, maybe her hand was tired from writing but then a short break was in order, not substituting another instructor at the last moment.

"This will be a problem." I crossed my arms and tried to keep my voice even, neutral and low. "For us, you, and the magazine. These women will talk. And don't forget the editor is watching. If word gets out a class taught by you isn't really done by you, you're done as a diva."

Not to mention another hole punched into the reputation of Scrap This. We already had a murder to live down, now we'd have to add an expensive class taught by a flaky teacher. Though I had a feeling the customers would be more willing to forgive the murder.

Tears glittered in Belinda's eyes and she lowered her gaze to the ground. The papers in her hand trembled. "This is my first class. I'm not the best at public speaking. I'll get confused. That's why I need..."

My heart went out to her. There had to be some way to help Belinda with her anxiety, give the customers what they paid for, and not have Ms. Amtower bad-mouth the store. I'm sure she'd place the blame on us and not in her choice of diva.

I flipped through a bunch of scenarios in my head. No. No. Possibly.

Wait. That one would work. I grinned. "How about your mom reads the instructions while you demonstrate? You can then add in some anecdotes here and there."

In the back of the store, Karen leaned against the wall, half-asleep. She was probably wondering what she ever did to get this assignment. The adoption day at the animal shelter was probably more exciting than a book signing and a class at a scrapbook store.

The photographer took a couple of shots of the paper racks, stickers, and the curtains blocking off the storage area. At least he appeared busy and interested.

Belinda chewed on her lip. "I'm not sure."

"It'll be fabulous. The women will understand someone will be reading the directions so you can concentrate on showing them how to create the actual project."

"Well..." Belinda looked at the women who were waiting with bated breath for their illustrious teacher to begin. The hero worship in the students' eyes must have gotten to her because she perked up and then motioned for her mother to take over as the reader. "We must give the public what they want."

Thankfully, egos always overruled fear.

Holding in my breath of relief, I wandered to the edge of the open classroom area to observe. If needed, I could step in to help some of the struggling students.

Cheryl rang up purchases while Hope helped other unhappy scrapbookers discover what products were needed to reasonably duplicate the pages in *Making Legacies'* newest edition.

The bell jingled. I kept my eyes on the class.

"I forgot. The new wonder girl is making her first appearance today." Darlene Johnson, self-proclaimed professional life artist expert and Belinda's cousin, sidled up to me. "How quaint. She can't talk and demonstrate at the same time."

The photographer went to snap a picture of the class. I held my hand up and all he got was the back of it.

Darlene picked unseen lint off the sleeves of her dove gray shirt and slipped the strap of her silvery-blue leather Coach bag further onto her shoulder.

"Let him take pictures. Belinda's style is, shall we say, so 1999."

"Jealous much," I muttered under my breath. It had to wound Darlene that Belinda won a major design contest on her first try, while Darlene still struggled to even have one layout published after a decade of submitting.

Not to mention the two cousins had been competing against each other since they left the womb. Darlene's mother, Eliza, considered it a victory her daughter was born on Halloween, fitting when one thought about it, while her sister Hazel popped out her child on November first.

There was no doubt in anyone's mind why the fathers-to-be bolted soon after the pregnancies were announced. Neither man was heard from again, a fact that didn't seem to bother or even interest either the wives or the daughters. The men had sent the child support and alimony checks on time so they were happy.

"Sorry, but the class is booked." I smiled at Darlene. "If you'd like, you can sign up for the Halloween Eve crop. Belinda will be attending it."

"She's teaching." Darlene flipped her expertly cut brown hair off her shoulders, forcing the word "teaching" past her lips as if it was distasteful. With two fingers, she picked up a copy of the magazine a class attendee had placed on the edge of the table and laid it on her palm. She dusted her fingers together and then made a production of wiping the appendages onto her pressed dress pants.

I pocketed my fists and reminded myself I was raised to be polite, kind, and not start fights. No matter how irritating and deserving the person happened to be. I prayed I kept my temper.

"Of course artists should support each other, even if it is just a small contest sponsored by *Making Legacies*. Belinda should get some accolades. This publication is all about being trendy and being an artist inside the box." Darlene shuddered and flipped through the magazine. Light bounced off her red glossy nails.

"This is the most sought after title in the scrapbook world." I looked at Belinda and hoped Darlene's words weren't heard by the instructor or the students. The ones in the back of the class arched their necks back to catch the venom Darlene spewed.

By the pinched look on Hazel's face and the shaking of Belinda's hands, the "hope ship" had sailed away without my wish on it.

"When you're trying to create out-of-the-box artistic work that isn't just like all the other famous scrapbook page designers, then there's—" Darlene stopped talking, pulled in a breath and released it as a hiss.

THREE

I watched in rapt fascination as Darlene's complexion changed from alabaster white to cherry red. The magazine fell to the floor. I looked down. Belinda's smiling face stared up at me. It was a great photograph of Belinda and I felt a smidge of jealousy that I didn't photograph as well.

Releasing a screech that shook the building and rattled the windows, Darlene ran straight for Belinda, arms outstretched and hands moving like a claw machine going for a prize. Open and close. Open and close.

Straight for Belinda's throat. I ran forward.

From the corner of my eye, I saw Karen come to life.

"Faith, stop her!" Hope's cry galvanized me into action.

Darlene made an amazing leap. Tin sheets and the front row students scattered as her body grazed over the tabletop heading for her cousin. Red painted claw-like nails aimed for Belinda's throat.

I weaved through the class attendees who were scuttling backwards, away from the wrestling match about to go down. I shouldn't have turned down Officer Conroy Jasper's offer of volunteer security guard. At the time, my main concern was Conroy trying to pick up a hot girl or two at the event, not a reenactment of a battle scene from a Twilight movie.

Belinda stood frozen.

Hazel answered Darlene's battle cry with one of her own. The shrieks shook the rafters. Hazel tossed the instruction sheets and went for the hot glue gun.

Women paused and focused on the brawl. Apparently, they just realized the great gossip potential of a good catfight. Who wanted safety when the best scandal to hit the town in months was being displayed right in front of their very eyes? A few moved forward, clutching their cell phones and holding them out at arm's length.

Wrapping my arms around Darlene's waist, I tugged. She reached back with one hand and clawed at my face.

"It's mine! She stole it!" Darlene lashed out with her legs. One hand tightened on Belinda's handmade t-shirt. "It's mine!"

"Let go of my daughter!" Hazel squeezed the trigger of the glue gun. Hot liquid glue dribbled from the nozzle and splattered on Darlene's hand.

Darlene snarled and hissed in pain but kept hold of Belinda. I tightened my grip on the raging scrapbooker and pulled.

A cloud of blue, yellow and green dust attacked our eyes. Hazel wielded the glue gun in one hand and a plastic jar of glitter in the other.

Was she trying to brand us?

Darlene twisted and turned her hips, killer heels jabbed into my legs. I hung on for Belinda's dear life.

Rip. I cringed. Underneath us, paper crinkled. Profits destroyed. I wanted to plead for help but was afraid my grandmother Cheryl would jump into the mix. I just needed to restrain Darlene for a little longer. Grandma Hope was probably on the phone right now arranging for either Steve or Ted, the detective who I tried to get along with for the sake of staying on his good side, to come as my back up.

As the specks of color continued to rain down on us, Darlene twisted her head and started blowing in Hazel's direction while continuing to kick at me.

"My eyes!" Hazel screeched.

The color bombardment stopped. The container clattered to the floor. Though, unfortunately for me, Darlene persisted in attacking me with her heels.

Where in the world was Steve—or Ted—when I really needed their help? There were times I didn't want to be totally self-reliant and capable. Where were these knights now?

Darlene's grip relaxed. I yanked her from the table and we both splattered to the linoleum floor with Darlene on top of me. Darlene grabbed a pot of glitter as we fell, whipped off the top and heaved it at Hazel and Belinda. Both covered their heads and screeched as the color figments coated them.

"That's it! I've had enough of you." Belinda screeched and kicked off her kitten heels. Things were about to get real ugly now.

"Faith, do something!" Sierra shouted.

What in the world did she think I was doing? I didn't wrestle as a pastime. Belinda wasn't the only one who'd had enough of this nonsense. I tightened my grip and rolled over. I pinned Darlene, face-down to the floor.

"My necklace." Belinda pummeled my back with a container of glitter. Specks of gold, rose, and Christmas green fluttered over and around me. "She took my necklace."

How in the world did I become the punching bag? Thankful Belinda hadn't grabbed the hammer and nails, I ignored the blows and kept hold of Darlene. An elbow jabbed into my stomach. I sucked in a breath, pressing more of my weight onto the life artist gone berserk.

Darlene grunted and squirmed.

Snap. Snap.

Flashes went off. Just what we needed, layouts of a brawl in Scrap This. It's what one always looked for when looking for a place to shop and crop. I hoped this didn't show up on the community blog or in the church's newsletter as I saw Frieda joined in documenting the moment. Pastor Evans was having a hard time explaining to his mother-in-law that God didn't need, nor want, any help in having "sinful behavior" brought to His attention. One day I wanted to add a picture of her taking a picture of others to the newsletter, but copy-catting bad behavior to point out bad behavior never worked out the way one intended.

Karen's photographer moved in closer, aiming the lens of the camera I thought I might be falling in love with at me. I wasn't so enamored with it anymore.

"Some help instead of taking pictures." How could the photographer stand there and take photos at a time like this? I guess not all men were helpful in a brewing crisis.

I heard Hope ushering some of the onlookers outside as Cheryl herded some to the back. Customers expressed their disappointment at being denied the opportunity to witness the hostility.

"The cops are on their way." Sierra pulled and pushed Belinda away from Darlene and me.

"Good." Darlene muttered from under me. "That thief needs to go to jail."

"Thief! How dare you...you...twit!" Hazel charged forward, high heels clacking on the linoleum floor.

I braced myself for impact. After a frustrated scream, the sound of heels stopped. I turned my head to peek at Hazel. She paced a few feet away, trying to get past my grandmothers who turned themselves into a human barrier.

The front door yanked open and the bell jerked back and forth, adding a hectic musical track that went well with the current situation of the class morphed into a public brawl. About time. I glanced over to let the police know what happened. It wasn't the police.

Standing before me was Gussie Buford and her two brawny sons, Wayne and Wyatt. Gussie stood with feet planted and a take-charge expression engraved on her face. Wayne and Wyatt looked perplexed and hesitant, their usual expression when facing any circumstance.

"Boys, you get in there and settle those women down." Gussie pointed to Hazel, Darlene, and then me.

"I'm not doing anything wrong." I sat up, still keeping Darlene pressed to the cold floor. "I'm maintaining law and order. Or trying to anyway."

Wyatt snorted.

I launched a glare at him.

Gussie swatted the back of her son's head. "If Faith says she's not part of any wrongdoing, then she's not. Gentlemen do not...ever ...call a lady a liar."

"Sorry, ma'am." Wyatt looked at the ground then peeked at me. The grin on his face said he knew I wasn't an innocent damsel.

Normally, I did have some part in creating my own problems but this time, well this instance, was all Darlene.

"Momma, you said it ain't right for us to go around manhandling women." Wayne shifted from foot-to-foot. "And considering one of them is elderly."

I winced. Wayne wasn't the brighter of the two brothers. Hope and Cheryl reddened and stepped back, giving Hazel a clear shot of Wayne.

Normally, Wyatt and Wayne stuck together like glitter to glue. For better or worse, they were victors together or went down for the count together. Except in this occasion.

Wyatt—the smarter brother—rushed toward the back of the store, putting plenty of distance between himself, the insulted woman, and his brother.

I didn't blame Wyatt one bit.

Darlene wiggled underneath me, pushing and bucking, trying to throw me off.

"Stay still."

"I can't breathe right." She hissed out.

I didn't want to smother her. "Okay, I'll let you sit up, but if you try to stand or crawl, I'll let Sierra's boys come over and play cowboys and bank robbers." A game Harold, Henry, and Howard— the Hooligans—would relish. Darlene would make a mighty fine bronco to tame.

Sierra flipped open her cell phone. "One button is all I have to push. Hank wouldn't mind bringing the boys down."

"I won't move," Darlene said, propping herself off the floor with her elbows, "if you ensure that Belinda doesn't leave."

Seemed like a fair and stupid request. Darlene assaulted Belinda. Why would she want to leave before the police arrived?

"Fine." I stood up and dusted off my hands, wishing I got rid of this situation as easily as the small particles of glitter on my palms.

Belinda shuffled toward the door in her bare feet, pressing a shaking hand to her throat. A neck no longer decorated with the Diva necklace. "I don't want to stay here. I just want my necklace back."

"It's mine." Darlene clutched the jewelry in her fist, pressing her hand into her dove gray shirted-cleavage. A sliver of the beaded silver chain trailed from between her index and middle fingers.

"Let me have the necklace." I held out my hand.

Darlene shook her head and glared at Belinda. "It's mine. I earned it. Not her."

Had Darlene lost her mind?

Belinda swiped at tears and took a few steps backwards. My grandmothers blocked the front door to make sure no one escaped.

The bell rang and all heads swiveled toward the door. Detective Ted Roget walked inside followed by Officer Conroy Jasper. Ted scanned all the women in the store and then focused his intense green eyes on me.

My knees shook. There was no reason for my nervousness of police to rear up with Ted, especially since I wasn't causing the commotion this time. He knew my darkest secret and wouldn't use it against me. If he were inclined to let my skeleton out of the closet, he'd have done it months ago when I interfered in a murder case by starting my own investigation to prove he was the murderer.

Ted yanked the cord of the glue gun from the wall. "Someone care to explain what is going on?"

Was I mistaken, or had his gaze lingered on me for a moment longer than anyone else, a hint of appreciation in those cool green eyes?

I glanced down and saw my shirt had ridden a few inches up and exposed some of my stomach. I tugged it down and narrowed my eyes on Ted. A gentleman kept his wandering gaze to himself or made it not so obvious.

Disappointment flashed across his face.

I wanted to continue the stare-off, but Ted's attention left me and was now fixed on Darlene and Belinda. His eyes widened for a second when he took in Belinda's attire.

Darlene jumped to her feet and jabbed a finger, not one of the ones holding the diva necklace hostage, toward Belinda. "She stole from me. I demand retribution."

Belinda whimpered and huddled against her mother. The women almost blended together with their similar style and almost matching outfits.

Matter-of-fact, Hazel and Belinda looked way too much alike. I hadn't really paid attention before but now side by side I saw Hazel had added some extensions to make her hair style, which last week was at her chin, to shoulder length. And her previously dark brown hair with gray shot through it was now dark brown and curly with red highlights. Just like her daughter.

Since Belinda didn't seem fazed by her mother morphing herself into her twin, it wasn't my concern. No matter how odd—or creepy—I found it.

Hazel wrapped an arm around her daughter's shoulder. "Don't worry, baby. Mom won't let that witch hurt you."

Ted sighed and pulled a notebook from his pocket. "Officer Jasper, start interviewing some of the other women."

"She tried to kill me." Belinda sniffed as fat tears rolled down her rouged cheeks. "I didn't do anything to her."

"Liar!" Darlene made a sudden movement forward.

Ted made an equally sudden movement toward where he kept pepper spray and his gun.

I snagged Darlene and halted her progress. I really didn't want to see anyone get shot — even Darlene. "It's better to stay put."

She threw a glare at me. I aimed my gaze at Ted's side. Darlene switched her attention from me to the object I looked at. Darlene nodded and dropped her hand to her side.

Ted pointed at Wayne and Wyatt. "Collect up anything that could be used as a weapon. Have Mrs. Hunter and Mrs. Greyfield lock the items up somewhere." He pointed at my grandmothers.

"Yes, Sir." Wayne and Wyatt said in unison. Gussie beamed.

Great. There went our scissors again, along with our trimmers, glue, and glitter as Darlene and Belinda showed how they could be used as a method of attack.

"I just wanted to give him the proof." Darlene pointed to the stack of *Making Legacies* magazines.

"The special issue?" I looked at my grandmothers. Both shrugged and eyed Darlene with wariness. Had Darlene's competitive scrapbooking spirit finally cracked her?

I smiled, hoping it portrayed warmth and understanding, not the fact I thought she was a few foam stamps short of a complete alphabet set.

"Look at her..." Darlene nearly strangled on the pronoun, "...layouts."

I picked a copy on the table and flipped through it, stopping at Belinda Watson's section. I turned the magazine face out, flashing the pictures to Ted like we are at a story time hour in the library.

He squinted and looked at the photos. "What am I missing? I'm not an expert."

I sort of was and still didn't know what Darlene meant.

"Give me that." Darlene snatched the magazine from my hand and rested a manicured nail on top of the layout. "This design. It's mine. Belinda submitted my work under her name."

Women inched forward. Eager ears and even more eager mouths waited. I swore a few rubbed their hands together in glee.

"You're a liar." Hazel started toward Darlene. She stopped and screeched, swatting at Wayne who knelt at her feet, one hand on her ankle and the other on her high heel. "Stop fondling me!"

Wayne pressed his lips together and tugged Hazel's leg up, tilting the woman to the side. I reached out to steady her before she fell to the ground in an inelegant and unladylike heap.

Gussie blanched and covered her face with her hands.

Karen scribbled furiously into her notebook. The photographer disappeared somewhere, probably back to the news station to start going through pictures of the brawl.

"I have proof." Darlene crossed her arms and tilted her chin up.

"Wayne, what are you doing?" Ted's expression was a mix between revulsion and confusion.

"He's assaulting me!" Hazel hit Wayne again.

Wayne was unfazed. "Now, ma'am. I'm just following orders. Detective said to get anything that was a weapon. Now, I've been kicked by shoes like these. They sure do hurt."

Wyatt nodded in defense of his older brother. "Me too. Like heck."

Ted rolled his eyes. "Don't worry about the shoes."

Wayne shrugged. "Okay, Detective, it's your investigation but don't say we didn't try to help."

"I'll take my chances." Ted centered a look on me and kept it there.

I squirmed under his gaze. What did I do now? I was being helpful. Matter-of-fact, I put myself in the way of harm to stop Darlene from committing a crime. Ted continued staring at me.

I had enough. "What?"

"Why are you sparkling?"

I glanced at my arms. Gold, green and red glitter clung to my skin and clothes. I shook my head and a rainfall of sparkling dust floated around me. "The top wasn't on when Belinda clobbered me with the glitter."

"Why did Belinda go after you?" Ted scribbled something in his notebook.

Was that suspicion in his eyes? I refused to allow my imagination and conspiracy notions to run away with me. Again. "She meant to nail Darlene with it but her aim sucks."

Ted turned to Belinda.

The woman blanched. "Mom!"

"Faith! That language." Hope glared at me.

Hazel, still wearing heels, ran over to her thirty-five year old daughter and took her in her arms. "How dare you bully my child? She's the victim here. That horrible woman attacked her."

"I retrieved what she stole from me." Darlene wore the coveted Diva necklace.

Tears streamed down Belinda's face. "That's my necklace. It was sent to me. I'm a Life Artist Diva. Not you."

Ted held out his hand, palm up and then curled his fingers up and back down. "Give it up."

"No." Darlene pressed her hand to her throat, protecting the symbol of divahood.

"I have a jail cell I can house you in," Ted said. "I might have to keep you there overnight. It will take a long time to interview every single woman in this room."

Apparently, Darlene believed the words were a promise and not a threat because she handed the necklace over. "The toggle is still intact so I didn't rip it from her neck. She wasn't hurt. I took it off. Nicely. Admirable of me, considering..."

"Yes." Ted's voice was still in neutral. "I'm sure that's your recollection of the incident."

Jasper walked over, exasperation clear on his face. "Detective, I'm not getting anywhere. Every woman has a different story on who started it, what happened, and even the time. Some say the fight started when the doors first opened this morning."

"That's not true." I crossed my arms and glared at Jasper. "Everything was orderly, maybe feisty on occasion, but no violence whatsoever until Darlene arrived."

Jasper frowned. "Faith, I'm only repeating what was told to me. I'm not saying you or your grandmothers stood by as women conducted a boxing match in the store."

"I'm sorry." I shoved my hands into the back pockets of my jeans. "I don't like anyone lying about my grandmothers."

"Now you know how I feel." Hazel rubbed her daughter's back. "Darlene is lying about my daughter."

"No." Darlene slapped her hands against her legs. "That's how I feel looking at the magazine. Belinda lied when she sent in those layouts. Those are mine. She stole them." Darlene pointed at Belinda. "I will prove to the scrapbooking world that you are a fraud."

A gasp came from behind me. I turned. Ms. Amtower stood with a hand pressed to her chest.

Belinda wailed and dropped her head to her mom's shoulder. "Why is she doing this? I didn't steal them. She gave them to me, so I submitted them."

Gave them to her?

"Gave them?" Ted scribbled something in his notebook.

"I need to call my lawyer." Ms. Amtower pulled an iPhone from her purse and scurried toward the door. "This is not good."

"Wait!" Belinda made a valiant but failed attempt to grab the editor-in-chief's arm as the woman hightailed it out of there. "Darlene said she didn't like the pages so I could have them as my own."

"For you to put the photographs of our mother-daughter cruise on, you idiot. Not for you to say you designed and send them in for a contest." Darlene clutched the magazine to her chest. "We were working on my mom's birthday present. I never would've given you permission to submit them to a contest."

"You gave them to me. That makes them mine. You said they weren't contest worthy," Belinda shot back. "I wanted to prove you wrong. And I did."

"You cheated! You could have at least scraplifted the design instead of actually using my pages. I even paid for all those supplies!" Darlene tossed the magazine. It smacked Ted in the chest. "You just wait until I post about this. The chat board will eat you alive."

"That's enough, Miss Johnson." Ted narrowed his gaze and this time directed it at Darlene.

"You're a fraud." Darlene swung back around and jabbed a finger at Belinda.

"Do you want me to call your mother?" Ted asked.

"No!" We all shouted. We had to teach Ted how the mom-threat worked around here and who to use it on.

Usually the threat of calling a parent, especially a mother or grandmother, had "children" of any age behaving, but not so with this crew. Wyatt and Wayne...yep. The Hooligans...yep. Darlene...nope—especially when it came to a fight between her and Belinda. Hazel and Eliza were not only bitter rivals like their daughters, but had spent their whole lives trying to outdo the other. Throwing Eliza into this hot bed of emotions would create a brawl any Real Housewife would envy.

"Call her." Darlene smirked.

I stood beside Ted and whispered. "Hatfield and McCoy battles are tame compared to Eliza and Hazel fights."

"Why don't we just take it outside?" Gussie said. "Fill up a pool with some mud and let the girls wrestle it out."

Wayne and Wyatt looked over the candidates and cringed. I felt the same way. Besides, we were a store dedicated to promoting and encouraging preserving family memories, not feuds.

"There will be no more fighting." Ted announced and fingered the handcuffs attached to his belt. "Is that understood?"

Grabbing her daughter's hand, Hazel stalked out the door with her crying daughter trailing behind her. "We're not taking any more of this. Darlene is just jealous she can't take wonderful pictures. She said those layouts were yours, there's nothing she can do about it."

"Watch me." Darlene crossed her arms over her chest.

FOUR

The cell phone squawked from the bedside table. I rolled over, tugging the extra-plump pillow over my ears. After the horrible morning and afternoon, I called it an early night. Now someone wanted to ruin my sleep.

"Answer me. Answer me." Its mechanical voice screeched.

I had gotten rid of the landline to cut down my expenses, but now wished I had kept it. My mind was conditioned to respond to the classic ring of a phone but had the ability to shut out other ringtones, unless they were highly annoying. The problem with highly annoying was the mood I found myself shoved into. Like now. I wanted to flush the thing down the toilet or throw it through the window. Thankfully, the costs of the repairs stopped me from acting on impulse.

The electronic parrot voice repeated the phrase. "Answer me. Answer me."

Resigning myself to fate, I pushed the pillow from my head and groped around until the offending device was in my hand. The need to silence the grating voice was more dire than going back to sleep...the reason I picked the ringtone.

"What?" I said, blinking at the clock a few times before it came into focus, eleven at night.

"I'm taking that means you haven't seen the message boards." Sierra's aggravated tone cut through the haze of lingering sleep. "Good thing your grandmothers put you in charge of monitoring it."

Ignore. Ignore. Ignore. I wanted to slap the be-nice-voice in my head silly. The disharmony between Sierra and I was lasting much longer than I, my grandmothers, and Steve predicted. We were now going on over six months and the iciness Sierra directed at me was colder than the early winter we were experiencing. I kind of had it coming. I did think she was related to a murderer. But everyone made mistakes now and then. Hopefully with Christmas around the corner, Sierra would allow the spirit of the season to fill her heart with some forgiveness for me.

Of course, I could help it along with volunteering to babysit the Hooligans, Harold, Henry and Howard, while she went Christmas shopping for her sons. But I wasn't sure I wanted to be forgiven that badly. And there was the little, tiny fact that I wasn't the one in the wrong.

Or not totally in the wrong.

"Imagine that. You have nothing to say."

I had plenty to say but most of it was better left unsaid. Forgiveness was something I was to give, regardless, even when it was hard. Like now. I leaned my head against the wood headboard and silently forgave Sierra's attitude. "I don't search the web when I'm asleep. Sorry my sleep schedule doesn't match yours."

"What an exciting single life you lead. In bed by eleven."

"It's my life. I like it." I ignored the twinge in my heart.

Okay, not like but accept. I had made choices in the past requiring my quieter lifestyle if I wanted the past to remain deep in my background. I had at one time behaved as a young woman with "no cares in the world and no one to answer to" and it wasn't all it was cracked up to be. I ignored and mocked my upbringing and reaped some huge soul-battering consequences for pretending I was someone else.

"I was browsing some of the scrapbook message board sites and found—"

I took the abrupt end of the sentence as my cue to fill in the last part. "That most people on those boards talk about scrapbooking but don't actively do it. Shopping carts must always be placed into the corral or else you are the worst type of human being. Shopping on Black Friday, or on Thanksgiving, is proof you hate people and are consumed with greed?"

"Aren't you amusing today?"

"I was today, but tonight I'm irritable." I didn't handle being woken up well. A truth my grandmothers could attest to. While I had no trouble getting up on time when I was in the Army, I didn't enjoy it, but being a rule-abiding girl with a guilt complex, I never complained. Out loud.

Sierra sighed and was probably counting to ten like she did when dealing with a temper tantrum by one of her elementary school-aged boys. "Darlene started her campaign against Belinda and Scrap This. She's trashing both on her blog, and also on the most frequented scrapbooking boards."

I groaned. We *so* did not need this right now. Well, not ever. But definitely not when Scrap This had just gotten past a scandal.

"Is Belinda responding back?" I tossed off the covers and reluctantly left the warm bed. I padded down the hallway to my office.

"Not that I can tell. It's just gearing up."

"I'll take care of it."

"As you should have been," Sierra said, getting in the must-have last word.

Turning on the monitor, I plopped into the burgundy leather office chair then opened up the browser. I clicked on the first website and with one eye closed, scanned the topics on the front page of the number one scrapbooking website.

I wanted—needed—to look at the train wreck before me, but still wished I could avoid the view.

Darlene made sure the title of the post was dramatic and attention grabbing.

Making Legacies Contest A Fraud. My Work Stolen By Them!

I also loved the addition of quite a few angry icon faces. I clicked on the message and mentally braced myself for the bashing to commence.

I am livid. Darlene started the thread.

At least she didn't use all caps.

Today I went to support one of the new Making Legacies Life Artist Divas at her first signing and demonstration. I was so happy for her!

Yeah right.

I got there a little late and needed to wait for the class to end before I got my copy of the special issue. I decided to chat with the assistant manager who was watching the class.

More like making snide comments about the magazine and the newest diva.

I looked at the first layout of this so called Diva. It was mine! I looked at the next. Mine! All twelve of her layouts were designs the LAD cased from me. I went to talk to the thief, and you will not believe what happened next. The assistant manager ASSAULTED me...

When she wanted to lie, she brought out the all caps. I also liked the little redesign of the story she told Ted. I copied and pasted the thread into a word document, and took a screenshot so it showed the time, to be on the safe side.

The assistant manager didn't want me to talk to the Diva. Maybe I should have waited for the class to be over, but

Belinda Watson—that's right—the come out of nowhere It-Girl (no surprise now about how she just popped onto the scene...she swiped another artist's hard work) is a FRAUD.

Responses siding with Darlene stacked up. A few posters even suggested banding together to start sending emails to the magazine, the store, and Belinda's blog to let them know she was a fraud.

Not that I don't believe you, a poster responded. *But how would Belinda have stolen your design? I've thought a few times that someone "copied and stole everything" from me but there was no way. It was just a coincidence. Sometimes ideas happen at the same time.*

Other posters agreed with the calm voice in the sea of anger. I heaved out a sigh of relief. It looks like the rant would be seen as what it was...jealousy, plain and simple.

Darlene defended herself:

We live in the same town and crop at the same store. We hang out together all the time. Think it's still such a coincidence? I let her use them for an album she was working on. I had no idea she'd submit those ideas and create classes and 'teach' them.

Someone with the screen name of Little Lamb posted:

I'm starting to wonder if the whole truth came out last spring about the murder. Wasn't the assistant manager wrapped up in that?

Leaning forward, I gripped the arms of my office chair. My fingers itched to jump into the conversation but defending oneself never worked out well on message boards.

You mean, Faith? You think she had something to do with my layouts being swiped?

Little Lamb replied:

Maybe in that, too. Was submitting something Belinda usually did? If not...

Who in the heck was Little Lamb? And what in the world did they have against me?

I know she doesn't like me. And Belinda never cared about contests before so you might be on to something. I could see Faith wanting to ruin me. I'll have to think on this for a while. Darlene added an angry face icon to the end of her post.

Butterflies fought in my stomach. Darlene was just revving up. The gauntlet was thrown. Could I get Ted to have the site owners shut this thread down as he was investigating who started the fight this afternoon? I doubt he'd appreciate a call from me at midnight whining about mean things people said on the internet.

Now, Steve, he wouldn't mind. He'd even come to my defense. Or else, he'd tell me that I found enough trouble in real life and didn't need to go jump into web based drama. Defending oneself on the web, or having others do so, always made a person look guiltier. And I already had enough instances in my life where other people's actions nearly landed me in jail.

The best way to handle it was to keep quiet and allow Belinda and Hazel to tell these women the truth. Or at least their version of the truth.

A board regular popped into the conversation:

Why wasn't all this information about you two cropping to-gether included in your first post? Sounds like someone has the bitters.

Darlene fired back:

Why would I be jealous of someone whose only talent is be-ing able to scraplift and mail out someone else's design?

And the reply:

Prove it!

Another poster entered the conversation but only contributed a smiley icon holding a bag of popcorn and munching on kernels. While a buttery treat sounded good right now, I didn't want to leave before the thread slowed down. No sense joining in the merriment when I wasn't sure if the store—or me—were in the clear.

Darlene typed:

I took the password off my layout gallery. Check there.

A first-time poster calling themselves JealousMuch entered into the cyber conversation.

Who's to say you didn't scraplift Belinda?

I guessed Belinda. I didn't know why Belinda thought she'd get away with submitting a design of her cousin's without getting called out on it. But to use a dozen layouts all by Darlene was over the top. And what pride and pleasure would Belinda get from using the work of others?

Of course, the glee might have come from annoying her cousin.

Because I didn't. Darlene responded.

Well, that cleared it up.

Hmmm... JealousMuch started her next reply. *I took a look at the time stamp for the upload. You just did that a couple days ago. Maybe you got a sneak peek of the magazine. Maybe one of the employees gave you a little looksee.*

Caught. The next person replied.

A long time poster joined in the fray:

I knew there was something odd going on. That's why I didn't join the pile-on. It always happens with these contests. Some self-proclaimed artist doesn't get chosen and decides to destroy one of the winners.

And Darlene bit back:

I did not copy her. She CASED me. Belinda Watson is a no talent hack.

Personal attacks were not going to go over well. Darlene had a large post count on this particular board, she knew how it worked.

JealousMuch added unnecessary fuel to Darlene's raging inferno and the two went on from there:

Ho hum. So, two of your layouts are similar. Stop being a baby and deal. I bet you entered and lost.

I did not! I had no interest in submitting anything to Making Legacies!

Then why do you care? Sounds like a case of 'thou doth protest too much.'

Because it is my work. My creative endeavor not hers.

Again, prove it!

I frowned. Where did Little Lamb go? I would have thought they'd have jumped right in to defend Darlene and throw suspicion back onto me conspiring with Belinda. That user seemed to have vanished right out of the conversation, though. But, Darlene kept going:

Belinda stole the design from me during a crop at Scrap This. Just take a look at Belinda's layouts in the gallery. What is posted in the magazine is so beyond her capabilities.

JealousMuch posted:

You are a real witch. Trying to ruin this woman's happiness. You suck.

Darlene defended again:

The assistant manager sat her by me...

A different long-time member popped into the thread.

Same crap different day. When it starts not going your way, you add more details. What's next? 'All these people private messaged me and said they agreed with me. They just won't say it on the board because of all the bullies.'

Snickering yellow heads filled up the first row of the next response. Even those mocking faces didn't quiet Darlene.

Believe what you like but I know the truth. Belinda swiped my designs, my pages, and submitted them as her own. I bet the manager convinced Belinda to do it. She doesn't like me. See if I ever go to another crop there.

Could I get that promise in writing and notarized?

Gee, I wonder why. JealousMuch shot back.

I've always tried to be helpful to her but she's so insecure, any woman stronger than her is a threat. The girl ran home to work with her grandmas because she couldn't hack it in the military. And when I asked some simple questions about a store contest, she had to get her grandmothers. I mean really. Not to mention the whole crime thing ...

Tears sprang to my eyes. I expected some anger but this type of character-assassination spewed by Darlene slammed my heart.

Not too long ago, I relaxed rules for a contest so that Darlene could keep her ideas protected and now she claimed Scrap This—I —helped Belinda Watson steal her layouts.

JealousMuch asked:

I bet this is some little game between you and Belinda to drum up blog hits. Hoping for a book deal also?

I drew back from the screen. Had Belinda and Darlene created some elaborate drama so they both gained fame and notoriety? I wouldn't put it past Darlene. Belinda, on the other hand, I wasn't sure about. Thinking back on the brawl, the only one who seemed surprised about all of it...besides me, my grandmothers, and the class attendees...was Hazel. The necklace did come off pretty clean from Belinda's neck. Almost like someone undid the clasp rather than ripped it off.

What was so important about this title that Darlene and Belinda went through so much trouble for Belinda to win, and then for Darlene to announce the truth?

It made no sense. Darlene was the one who coveted a title in the scrapbooking world, not Belinda. Why would Darlene give up her dream for her cousin? If those two plotted this out, there was something bigger and more important going on than being labeled a Life Artist Diva by a scrapbooking magazine.

Something involving the store and me. Otherwise, why bring the murder up if it didn't play into their scheme? Were they trying to bankrupt the store? Take it over?

My breath locked in my throat. A deep rage built in my chest. I clenched my hands, releasing the pressure the moment my nails dug into the skin of my palms.

They wanted our store. My grandmothers store. If they wanted a fight—

No. I slapped the thought away. Not going there. Not this time. The last time I speculated about people, I nearly got myself shot and risked Ted losing visitation time with his daughter. I was not going there this time. A little gossip would not have me opening up another of Pandora's pretty decorative boxes again.

But, I wasn't stupid enough not to get some "protection" for my grandmothers and me. I took a couple more screenshots and saved them to my hard drive. One never knew when they needed a just in case pile of hard truth.

FIVE

"Answer me. Answer me." My phone squawked.

I lifted and dropped my head against my pillow a few times. Not this again. With kids, you'd think Sierra would go to bed at a decent hour. She bashed me about not having a life, how about her spending her nights on the computer rather than with her husband.

I burrowed under the blankets, taking the pillow with me so I could muffle out the sound. Whatever new tidbits of trouble Darlene or Belinda...or Darlene and Belinda...were creating could wait until I felt like getting up. Nothing would get me out of the bed until noon. One eye opened a fraction and focused on the clock. Two in the morning. Sierra wouldn't be calling me now.

I bolted upright and snatched the phone. My heart slammed against my chest. My grandmothers! Please God, let them be okay. I glanced at the number on the screen. No name registered in my head.

"Hello," I croaked out. Calls at this hour from unknown people usually brought grief, or started crime and horror novels.

"This is Nancy from Sound the Alarm. There has been a disturbance registered at Scrap This."

"What happened?" I shoved my feet into sneakers.

"Our system doesn't indicate details, just that the motion sensors and alarm went off. Should I notify the police?"

My mind focused on the ugliness being said about the store on the internet. "Yeah."

"Yes, ma'am. Please stay on the line—"

I ended the call. Now wasn't the time for the reminder of how lucky I was to have their service followed by a request for a customer service survey. I learned about their "good-bye" spiel when we first contracted for the service. It took about a week for us to remember we had an alarm.

I raced down the stairs. Yanking open the door, I grabbed my jacket and car keys from a hook by the front door. I was a woman who learned lessons. There was no way I'd show up at Scrap This alone. But there was also no way I'd sit at home waiting for the police to tell me how my grandmothers' store was vandalized and our livelihood destroyed.

Haziness coated the sky and left the night a mix of inky blackness with wisps of white. The mist coated my skin with dampness. I flicked on the small flashlight attached to my key ring and ran across the front yards. My shoes squeaked on the dewy grass.

I slipped and shot my arms out to keep my balance. I made it to Steve's house and pounded on the door. Sometimes having a wannabe knight-in-shining-armor living two doors away worked in a gal's favor.

"Come on, Steve." Cold air slapped at me. I wrapped my arms around myself and bounced up and down, hoping to get some blood and heat flowing. After a few seconds, I went to beating up the door again.

It flew open.

My closed hand rested on the muscular — and naked — chest of Steve Davis. An anime-style angel decorated the upper half of his left forearm. Something coiled inside of my stomach and blocked my vocal cords. On its own accord, my hand opened. The warmth of his body slowly worked its way through me. All I could do was stand and stare. I'm sure my expression matched the wide-eyed, disbelief playing on Steve's face.

Steve stood in front me bare-footed, bare-chested, and wearing tight jeans. His hair was mussed. A protective and angry expression replaced the shocked look. He wrapped an arm around my waist and drew me inside.

"What's wrong?" One strong arm cradled me to him; the other hand stroked my hair. His warmth and care wrapped around me.

I leaned into his embrace. Savoring and falling into the moment. My eyes drifted closed. Why had I been fighting this for so long? This felt right. I sighed.

"Is it Hope? Cheryl?" Steve tipped my chin up. His worried gaze took me in.

Hope? Cheryl? Rational thought returned. My grandmothers. The store. The alarm.

"Someone broke into Scrap This. Or is." I forced myself from his arms and grabbed his hand. "We have to go."

"Call the police."

"The security firm did." I tugged at him. He didn't budge an inch. "I need you to come with me."

He sighed. "I'm not going to talk you out of this am I?"

"No."

I turned and ran behind him. A good shove in the back should get the man moving. My splayed hands roamed up and down his back as I tried to move him out the door. Another part of my treacherous mind said I was shoving him in the wrong direction with the wrong motive in mind. I ignored my basic instinct. I listened to it once and found myself in a heap of trouble I, with my bordering on conspiracy theory mindset, couldn't even have conjured up on my own.

"Give me credit for coming to get you," I said.

"All right. I'll come." Steve held his hands up in surrender. "Can I at least put on shoes and a jacket?"

Shoes and something to cover his muscular chest would be good. I didn't want any distractions and needed to quash the giddiness rising up in me. I was way too interested in what Steve was or— in this case—wasn't wearing.

"You sure you don't want to change first?" he asked.

I glanced down.

Drat. I was wearing my turquoise flannel pajamas emblazoned with the phrase *I'm Scrappy and I Know It* across my torso and only the word scrappy across my derrière. I tugged down the hem of the shirt, hoping it covered the word.

I zipped up my jacket. "I'm ready. The longer we wait the more damage they'll do to the store."

Steve yanked on some running shoes and a leather jacket. He took hold of my hand. "Let's go." He herded me toward his car.

I balked, nearly tripping me and Steve.

"I thought time was of the essence." He let out another of those impatient sighs I heard a lot when he was around me.

"It is." I allowed him to lead me to his car.

I didn't like giving up control, or totally relying on someone else. I did it once and it ended my life...so to speak. I liked helping people but wasn't fond of accepting it. I knew I could trust Steve, but didn't want to have to trust him.

The locks on the door clacked as Steve reached for the driver's side door. "Jump in."

I raced over the passenger side and slid in. I kind of expected Steve to open the door for me, but the man knew I craved independence and was trying to stand back and give me the space I told him I needed.

Poor guy. I still could not figure out why he didn't run in the opposite direction. He wanted a real relationship while I was content with banter, flirting, and just knowing Steve cared about me.

I glanced over at him. The lights from the streetlamps played across his strong profile. Stubble dotted his cheeks and the top of his head. My hand itched to feel the texture.

I knotted my hands and pressed them into my lap. He'd do anything for me and that reality terrified me because I could easily see myself reciprocating. I could never put myself in the position again of giving my all to another man.

Not after Adam. The man I married 'til death do us part, which turned into until he accused me of a murder that he committed, and I got an annulment to set me free. If not for one MP who believed me when I said I was innocent, I'd be sitting in jail instead of Adam.

No one but Ted knew about my sordid past, and I planned on keeping it that way.

"You all right?" Steve threw me a quick glance.

"Yes," I said through my clenched teeth.

He cast another look in my direction. Nervous. His gaze wandered to my fists. "You sure?"

I flattened my palms onto the soft fleece of my pajama pants. "Yep." I grinned.

"I'm sorry."

"For what?" Maybe I should've driven as Steve seemed half-asleep.

He shot another look at me. "You keep staring at me and it usually means you want to say something but are censoring yourself."

Just admiring. I kept the thought to myself. Now wasn't the time for any confession, mundane or common knowledge. "Wondering why you keep your tattoo covered up."

"I'm a prosecutor."

"It's not like the angel is naked. She's wearing pants and a long sleeved shirt."

Steve's jaw tightened.

Was he afraid others in the community might think of him differently? Some could be a little high-strung and a breath away from the line of holier-than-thou. "It's tasteful. Beautiful. Maybe the sword might not be so good when you're trying cases but—"

"It doesn't lend to a professional appearance."

"So you don't flash it at work. Interesting, I've never seen it up close before now."

"You've always had the option."

That shut me up.

"Someone is trying to break into the store. How about we concentrate on that instead of the other topic?" Steve flicked on the blinker.

"Other topic? You can't even say tattoo."

"Drop it, Faith."

What in the world was going on with him? Why was this off-limits? "What is with you?"

"Long story." There was a gruffness to his voice I never heard before.

"You won't tell me."

"Not a story for now." Steve pulled into the back of the shopping complex and headed for Scrap This. The employee parking lot was in the back lot and where we had the motion detectors.

I placed my left index finger on the button to undo the seat belt and my right hand on the door handle.

Steve's headlights flashed onto a figure crouched by the door. "Don't get out of the car."

Anger flipped through me at the order. "I'll do what I want."

"Faith—"

I shoved the door open and bolted from the car. "The police are on the way!"

The figure didn't budge at my threat. Good or bad, I wasn't sure. I took a few steps closer.

The motion detectors sprang on. Dark hair tumbled over the woman's face. Limp hands rested by pants decorated with pink scissors. What was Hazel doing at the store so late at night? And why was she cuddled up to the door? Was she drunk? Hazel had been known to overindulge on occasions.

I knelt down and shook her shoulder. "Hazel..."

The head lolled to the side and I got a clear view of the person's face. Blood coated the side of Belinda's face, streaking down from a large gash going from temple to her cheekbone. What was she doing here? This time at night? Tears filled my eyes. The scream I wanted to release came out a gurgled sound of pain.

A hand gripped mine. "My phone's in the car. Call an ambulance."

"But—"

"Let me do this." Steve's gaze met mine.

"It's my grandmothers' store. Mine." I squared my shoulders bracing myself for what I needed to do. See if Belinda was alive.

Steve rested a hand on the small of my back.

My hand shook as I went to place my fingers on the pulse point on Belinda's throat.

Steve drew in a sharp breath. A whispered curse told me Steve knew what I did.

What I learned when I finally registered Belinda's wide and unblinking stare. She was dead.

SIX

Hazel's heartbroken wail tore through the emergency room waiting area. I cringed and pushed myself back into the hard plastic chair. Why couldn't the hospital get more comfortable seating? People didn't come here to lounge around. They were either sick, injured, or with someone who was one of the two.

Or dead. I shivered and tears burned my eyes.

Steve reached for my hand. I shoved it into my pocket.

He sighed.

I know he wanted to offer me comfort, but I wasn't good at accepting it. I didn't want to need anyone. Couldn't. Especially now I knew Steve held something back that shouldn't be a big deal. I ignored those moments with Adam. I wouldn't do it again.

Then again, what right did I have to total honesty when I refused to give it?

Hearing Hazel's heart breaking made me remorseful about my standoffish ways. My grandmothers wouldn't be around forever and then I'd be left with no one. I shook my head and cleared out the self-pitying thoughts. This wasn't about me. It was about poor Belinda and Hazel. The closest mother-daughter combination I knew. What would Hazel do without her daughter?

I swiped at the tears trickling down my cheeks. Steve deliberately ignored my movements and looked away to give me the independence I demanded at pretty much all times.

Why had Belinda decided to show up at the store so late at night? I didn't know what was so important she couldn't wait until

Monday morning when we reopened, or ask us today at church if we could let her into the store.

An evil thought slithered into my mind and I tried to stop it. I really did. What if Belinda had snuck over to do something that would hurt the store or my family? What if the cousins had decided to open up their own store?

Then why ruin their reputation by having the truth known about Belinda's cheating in such a dramatic fashion?

Cold air rushed through the waiting room. Karen England pranced through the emergency room door. Her boots clicked across the linoleum as she made a beeline to the nurse's station. She licked her lips, eyes growing wide as she craned her neck to catch a glimpse of whoever sobbed.

Karen pointed to the examination rooms. "I'm here to see a friend."

The nurse glared at Karen. "Your friend's name."

"I hear her." Karen dabbed at her cheeks with the ends of her silk scarf. "Please, she needs me."

So, Karen knew something happened tonight but not the actual what. Steve had only said there was an injured person behind Scrap This. He deliberately gave sketchy details knowing too many people found a way to monitor the dispatcher's calls.

"Her name and yours." The nurse rose and pressed her hands on the counter. The nurse stood at almost six-feet, lithe, and had well-defined muscles.

Karen drew back and flicked a glance in my direction. Her eyes narrowed.

I hope she didn't think I was honing in on her territory and trying to get into the news business. She hadn't realized yet I wasn't the story kind of gal. Once you had been "a story" you weren't so keen on creating any for someone else.

At least not deliberately.

"I'm Karen England. I demand you let me go and comfort my friend." She prepared to charge forward.

"And I'm telling you to sit in the waiting room."

Karen swept her hair over her shoulder and tilted up her chin. "Or you'll call security to throw me out?"

The nurse looked Karen up and down, an I'll-love-doing-this smile stretching her model perfect lips. "I don't need security."

"I should go offer some help." Steve slapped his hands onto his thighs then stood.

Drat. I'd rather he let the women work it out. I was rooting for the nurse.

"May I be of some assistance, ladies?" Steve walked smoothly between the two women and offered both a smile.

The nurse narrowed her eyes on Steve. "I don't need a man to handle this problem for me."

I liked her. I wondered if she'd think it was weird if I asked for her name and phone number. My grandmothers didn't think I hung out with friends often enough and this woman sounded like someone I'd get along with really well.

"I'd love your help Assistant Prosecutor Steve Davis. This nurse doesn't understand how important it is I go back there." With each word, Karen walked her fingers up from Steve's stomach to his nose. She ended the sentence by bopping her finger on his nose.

I gripped the armrests on the chair to stop myself from walking over and bopping Karen on her own nose. I watched Steve's reaction carefully. Was he as offended as I was by Karen?

He had his "courtroom" face on. My stomach clenched a little. I didn't know if that was good or bad. Was Steve hiding his reaction from me or Karen? Which one of us was he afraid of ticking off?

The nurse rolled her eyes. "I don't care if he's the governor of West Virginia. Only family and friends who the patients have requested will be permitted in the back."

"Steve?" Karen batted her eyelashes up at him.

"Those are the hospital's rules. They must be followed." Steve said. "If you must speak to someone, you can either wait..."

I cleared my throat, trying to get Steve's attention. *Please don't do that to Hazel.* The last thing she needed was Karen the vulture-reporter hovering around her.

Steve didn't hear me, but Karen did. She lasered a glare over at me. The words in those evil eyes rang in my head loud and clear. Stay. Out. Of. This.

Not. Going. To. Happen. I responded back with a look of my own.

"Let me drive you home." I heard someone say as Hazel's muffled cries came toward Steve and Karen.

Karen's eye brightened and she swiveled.

"Steve..." I didn't have to give the warning cry. Steve already positioned himself to block Karen from the grieving mother.

Officer Conroy Jasper held onto Hazel's arm and led her from the examination room. Hazel, pale and wide-eyed, stumbled even with Jasper's help. She barely noticed the six-foot tall female nurse, Steve, Karen, or me.

"Why did it happen? Why?" Hazel repeated the questions over and over again. "One wrong step? That's it. Just one?"

"I'm so sorry, ma'am. Sometimes these things just happen. Belinda must've tripped in the dark." Conroy wrapped an arm around Hazel and pulled her tighter to him, settling a warning look on Karen.

Hazel looked over her shoulder and ground to a halt. Her blue eyes snapped and I swear fire shot out from them. One of us enraged her with our presence. And from the hatred in her eyes, I hoped it was Karen.

"How dare you come here!" The brittle words shook from Hazel's throat as she pulled away from Jasper and charged over toward us.

Toward me more specifically.

Karen grinned and slipped a small notebook from her pocket. It looked like I was about to become a story. Again. At this rate, Karen should just follow me around. I'd give her enough ideas to fill at least one column a month.

I braced myself. Keep calm. A grieving mother deserved some leeway. Belinda's parade had been rained on at Scrap This. Belinda's last moment of happiness. I had been in charge of the signing and class. I guess I should've used some of the decorative duct tape we had gotten in to seal Darlene's lips.

Hazel trembled from head to toe. She clenched her fists and her breaths came out in angry spurts. "You...you..."

I took a tiny step back. I *knew* I didn't do anything but Hazel sure felt I did, and whatever it was made her want to throttle me.

"Show up here after killing my daughter!" Hazel raised her bunched fist.

Jasper raced over.

Steve stepped in front of me.

Karen yanked her high tech cell phone from her bag. Probably preparing to snap a picture of the punch, nothing made a story better than a photograph.

"What?" It was the only word in my befuddled mind. Kill her daughter? Of all things I imagined she'd be angry about, I never considered that one.

"Let's get you home, Hazel." Jasper offered me a sympathetic smile and carefully placed an arm around Hazel's shoulders.

"You might think she's innocent but I know the truth." The words "Mother of a Diva" across Hazel's more than ample chest quivered with her rage. The glittery claim caught the lights and caused shimmers of light to float around.

"What happened to Belinda was a terrible accident—"

The hatred in Hazel's eyes dammed the rest of the words I was going to speak.

"It wouldn't have happened if you hadn't asked Belinda to go to the store." The pronoun hissed out between Hazel's clenched teeth.

I had enough. It was one thing to be understanding and another to stand by with mouth closed when accused of a crime — especially murder. Been there, done that once and it didn't get me anywhere except to a jail cell and a loss of a career, even though I was proven innocent.

"That's a lie, Hazel." I crossed my arms and fired off a glare of my own.

"Faith, take it easy." Steve placed a comforting hand on the small of my back.

I stepped away from it and shook my head. "No way. I'll stand here and take a lot of stuff, but I refuse to allow even Hazel to spread a rumor that I murdered Belinda. I'm not going to jail just so I can be polite and behave in a socially acceptable manner toward a grieving mother."

"No one's going to jail." Jasper once again tried leading Hazel away.

"Don't you go lying to me, girlie." Hazel snapped her fingers very close to my face.

I gritted my teeth and clenched the hem of my jacket before I reacted in a stupid way and gave Jasper a reason to haul me off to jail.

"I didn't say you murdered her but you did kill her." Hazel clarified. "You told her to go out there in the middle of the night to meet you. Why your grandmothers couldn't meet me at a more reasonable hour, I'll never know. I told Belinda I'd get it for her. If Hope or Cheryl had met me, and you didn't tell Belinda—"

Now she wanted to bad mouth my grandmothers. It. Was. On. "You're a liar."

"Come on, Faith. Let's go home." Steve grabbed hold of my hand.

Frowning, Karen jotted down notes.

Jasper stepped into the spot of the floor separating me and Hazel. "Now I'm going to officially say to break this up. I know you're upset Hazel, but Belinda died from a slip and fall. It's not Faith or her grandmothers' fault. I can't let you go around accusing people of a crime."

"But she asked..."

"No, I didn't," I said. "The police can check my phone records or you can check Belinda's phone. I didn't call her tonight."

"I will." Her voice wobbled and she allowed Jasper to take her home.

"You know she just needed someone to lash out at," Steve said.

"Lashing out I'd accept, being accused of killing someone I won't."

"What in the world is Hazel going to do now that Belinda's gone?" Karen dropped her phone and notebook into her purse.

A deep ache settled in my chest and tears pooled in my eyes. The fight left me as quickly as it entered. The world was cruel sometimes. No rhyme or reason. No warning. Tears slipped down my cheeks as I watched Jasper lead Hazel to his squad car. I felt a strong arm go around my shoulders. This time, I accepted Steve's comfort, burrowing into his side and resting my head on his shoulder.

How would Hazel get over her daughter's death? Belinda was her life. Her purpose. I stuck my hand into my coat pocket and reached for my cell phone. Should I call my grandmothers? Having lost their only children also, they might have the understanding arms and tears the grieving mother needed.

SEVEN

I turned on the Keurig and peered into the tote I filled with investigating supplies. Phone, notebook, pen, magnifying glass, my small camera, and a change of clothes suitable for church. Everything I needed. A heavy day stretched out before me. I had to get to Scrap This and find out what Belinda had been up to.

I hated thinking ill of the dead, but I could not think of any other reason for Belinda to be at the store except for creating mischief. After I took a quick look around the store, I would need to change and get to church. I could just call my grandmothers and let them know I wasn't going, but that required too much of an explanation.

The coffee stopped brewing and I transferred the hot liquid from the ceramic mug into my stainless steel travel cup. I needed to find a smaller size that fit into my machine. One day I'd burn myself pouring from one cup into the other. Or else spill it all over the floor and defeat my purpose of leaving quickly.

I got into my car as the sun peeked over the mountains. As long as nothing unexpected happened, I would be able to accomplish my mission and get to the church service on time. Only a clueless person walked into church late when Gussie was opening with a solo. And if one did, you did it once and never again.

Slowly, I backed out of my driveway and crept down the street, throwing a quick glance at my grandmothers' house. All was quiet and still. I knew I'd have to explain one day, probably tomorrow when the full news hit the newspapers, but not today. I wasn't ready to face questions from them, or have to tell my grandmothers Belinda died at our store's back door.

My heart and thoughts drifted away from me and to Belinda's mother and what the poor woman was going through. Maybe I should tell my grandmothers and not wait for them to hear it at church or through the grapevine. They knew the pain Hazel was experiencing and could be a solace to her. My mother and father died in an airplane crash when I was an infant. My grandfathers and grandmothers raised me, living side-by-side in the townhouse complex they still owned. The last unit had been my parents and had been left vacant until I moved back home.

A car was parked a few feet behind the employee parking spaces of Scrap This. My heart thudded. I slowed down. I snagged the strap of my purse and tugged it toward me. Digging around in the tote for my phone, I scanned the area. The trunk of the four door sedan was opened. A person wearing jeans and a nylon jacket was leaning into the compartment, rooting around for something.

My breath caught in my throat. Why was someone here this morning? Were they also looking for something left behind? Maybe Belinda hadn't arrived at the store by herself, or even at all when she was alive. Jasper had said Belinda tripped because it was dark. The security lights would have clicked on and allowed Belinda to see the two small concrete steps.

Drawing in a deep breath and shutting up the annoying conspiracy theory voice, I grabbed hold of my cell phone and dropped it onto my lap. One closer look before I made a drastic call and announced Belinda's death was really a murder and the culprit returned to the scene of the crime. I hooked my arms around the steering wheel and leaned closer. The horn bleated. Not a great spying tactic.

The person jerked upright and spun around, nearly hitting their head on the open trunk. Ted.

What was he doing here?

Ted rolled his eyes then returned his attention his car. He pulled out a large tub and plastic gloves.

Was he gathering evidence? I pressed a hand to my mouth. Was it murder? What other reason would he have for being at the store? The police wouldn't have had time to collect everything last night or complete a thorough investigation in the dark. What looked like an accident in the night screamed murder in the morning.

I had to know what was going on. I got out of my car and went and stood beside him, peeking into his trunk. A large brown box was shoved in the back next to a green garden hose.

He slammed the trunk. "Do you mind?"

"If you're taking evidence from the store, I have a right to know."

Ted gave me an odd look. "Evidence?"

Drat. I swallowed hard and tried to think of a good reason I used that particular word. Thinking of nothing good, I went with the truth. "You're a homicide detective. I figured you were here because of Belinda's death. How could she have tripped because it was dark when the security lights turned on?"

Ted frowned.

"That's something to consider. Right?" I rocked on my heels.

"Maybe they didn't go off."

I shook my head. "Nope. Steve and I drove over here when the alarm company called me. When I approached the back door, they turned on."

Ted's frown deepened and now his eyes tugged down.

I probably should really shut up now. I had a bad feeling I was doing the law enforcement equivalent of sticker sneezing and creating a mess instead of an eye-pleasing layout.

"So you're here investigating a possible crime?" Ted crossed his arms over his chest.

"Of course not. I'm not a detective. And there hasn't been a crime committed."

"Hallelujah." Ted raised his hands in the air like he was praising. "She finally figured out she's not a cop."

"You're hilarious."

"I'm not being a jokester." He grabbed the tub and gloves and headed for the employee entrance.

"You are looking for stuff."

He plopped the large tub by the back door and scanned the wall.

I watched Ted. What did the man plan on doing?

He rested his hands at his waist and took a few steps back, examining the back of the building.

Curiosity got the best of me. "Something in particular you're looking for?"

"A faucet."

"A faucet?"

Ted nodded. "The thing that water comes out of and you can attach a hose to it."

I glanced in the tub. A scrub brush, detergent and bleach were nestled inside. My heart pitter-pattered. Ted had come to clean up. "Thanks."

Ted jerked his head and stared at me with wide eyes and a hint of an interested smile.

Ugh. The simple word came out breathy. Not what I intended. I pointed to the left. "It's at the far corner."

"I don't know if my hose will reach."

"We have one in the backroom. I can get it. If it's okay."

"If it wasn't okay, I wouldn't have been out here to clean up."

The warmness in my heart got a little cold. I pressed back a relieved smile. Just like Ted to change my opinion of him in a heartbeat with an annoyed comment. I was amazed this man even thought I was capable of planning a crime, much less committing one, as he seldom gave me credit for anything.

Except for getting into trouble and on his nerves.

"I'll be right back." I unlocked the back door and marched into the store with my head tipped up. Ted's attitude wouldn't bother me at all, or at least not enough for him to get a reaction out of me.

Before I reached the hose, my foot snagged the edge of a box. An involuntary screech flew from my mouth as my body pitched forward. My hands shot forward to break my fall. Fortunately, in front of me were more boxes so I landed on cardboard filled with packs of paper rather than the cement.

"What's wrong?" Ted was at my side, gun in hand.

"I tripped." I pushed myself up from the boxes with only a twinge in one wrist. I rotated my left hand, hoping to work out the kink. I grimaced.

Ted holstered his gun. "Let me see."

"It's nothing." I tried to hide my hand but Ted was quicker.

Gently, he touched and examined every inch of my wrist, lingering a little too long on my pulse.

"Told you. It's fine." I croaked out.

Ted's gaze locked onto mine. I saw the heat in his green eyes. My heart rate picked up speed. I didn't want him looking at me like that.

Oh yes you do.

Ted raised my hand, never taking his eyes off of me. "A kiss to make it better."

No. No. No. Even as I screamed the words in my head, and told my body to tug my arm away, another part of my brain shut me down. My knees quaked and I held my breath, yearning to feel his lips on my wrist. I shouldn't listen to the part of me begging for the simple act of tender care from a man who should be off limits.

Another man I shouldn't have in my life.

The word "another" was like a cooler full of cold water being dumped over my head. Rational thought returned. Along with guilt and something that almost felt like betrayal. For a woman who swore off romance, and vowed she'd be single for the rest of her life, I sure did have one too many options tugging at my heart.

I yanked my hand away. "I see the hose."

"I'll get it." Ted said, the words almost sounding like a growl.

I waited for him to drag it outside before I followed. No way was I taking the chance of tripping over the hose and falling into him. I didn't know if I could defeat temptation twice in less than two minutes.

Why should you?

The pout entered into my head. It was a good question. Why should I feel like I was betraying Steve? Steve and I weren't officially dating. Then why did I get so bent out of shape—jealous—when Karen touched him. Was it because it was Karen, or because someone treaded where I thought only I belonged? And if I felt that way, why did I insist on keeping Steve at arm's length?

I shook my head. I needed to get out there and help Ted not ponder my love life, or my determination not to have one. I could be here for days, months even, before I came up with an answer that made sense.

With Ted's help, this chore would be done sooner and I'd get to church without my grandmothers knowing something was up. Until they read the newspaper, or Ted stopped by and asked them questions. I wondered if I could get him to hold off until tomorrow. The last time he questioned someone on the Lord's day, Grandma Cheryl threatened to call Ted's "real" boss...his mother...instead of Chief Moore. I bit back a smile and almost skipped outside.

Ted narrowed his eyes. "Do I even want to know?"

"Not likely."

"That's what I thought."

Ted tugged on a pair of gloves and held out another pair. He either expected me or always came with a backup.

I took the gloves and put them on. "Where do you recommend we start?"

"I'll take care of the door and the wall. How about you scrub the parking spaces and wipe down the dumpster. Blood can splatter."

His no-nonsense tone left me cold. "Okay."

Ted cringed and stopped me from walking by with a gentle hand on my arm. I jerked away as his fingers sent a shockwave through me.

"Faith, I'm sorry." Ted caressed my arm once then removed his hand. "I shouldn't have said that. Belinda was a friend of yours. This has to be upsetting."

"I know you didn't mean to upset me. Reality just sucks some-times."

We both knew then it was time to stop talking and work. For whatever reason, we brought out the worst in each other. A tension always seemed to hover over us and neither of us knew how to van-quish it without reacting to it for a bit first.

After filling up the containers with water and soap, I carried the bucket over to the dumpster and left the heavy tub with Ted. I noticed the small metal door was opened. I frowned. I knew it was closed when I left last night. Feral cats wandered all over town and if we didn't keep the dumpster shut tight, we'd have a few taking up residence. I'd hate for a cat to get stuck in there and the waste man-agement guys not notice before it was too late.

Did someone throw something away? Belinda? Why would she come to Scrap This to throw something away? Especially in the middle of the night. Cold pinpricks attacked my scalp.

I shot a glance over at Ted who was putting a lot of elbow grease into the bricks near the employee entrance. Would he find it suspicious that I brought up the possibility again of Belinda's acci-dent not being an accident? But, what if there was something in there that told me why Belinda came here alone last night. Maybe she was dumpster diving and when she tried getting out she slipped and hit her head.

Taking in a deep breath, I placed my scrubber into the pail. I tugged the handle. It squealed.

"What are you doing?" Ted asked his most often asked ques-tion.

"The door on the dumpster is open." I yanked harder.

"It's broken. Noticed that last night." Ted dunk the brush into the sudsy water then went to town scrubbing down the door.

"You were here last night?"

Ted nodded. "There was a death here. I needed to come..."

He continued talking but I had stopped listening. Broken? I wandered back over and examined the door. It looked in working order to me. Though, the bolts holding the sliding panel looked newer than the rest of the dumpster. I guess our trash company worked even on Sundays when a complaint was made. That explained it being open.

"I should tip those guys at Christmas. They've already fixed it."

Ted jerked upright, spun around and faced me. "What guys fixed it?"

"The waste management company. New door, or at least bolts, already installed. Thanks for calling them."

Ted tossed the brush into the tub. "I didn't call anyone."

My insides tightened and my stomach went on a roller-coaster ride. Someone else who knew the door was broken called the trash company, or else fixed it themselves.

A person who needed Belinda's accident to be the accident the police believed it was. I might be right about Belinda's death being a murder.

I wanted to throw up.

Ted retrieved another set of gloves. This pair was thinner and a murky white. "Do me a favor and call the station. Tell them I need an officer sent here ASAP."

I wanted to argue but the intense look on Ted's face stopped me. Sometimes it was best to listen and not push an issue, especially when a person didn't have a good reason to argue.

I pulled out my cell phone and made a quick SOS call to the police station. As often as I'd been calling it the last few months, I should put it on speed dial.

I hoped and prayed my suspicions were wrong. Maybe Belinda went to throw something away and the door handle broke while she tugged on it and that caused her to lose her balance.

I tucked the phone into my pocket and walked back over to Ted who was halfway inside the dumpster. "An officer is being sent."

Curses floated into the air. A moment later, Ted emerged shaking his head a few times.

I edged closer. Wanting and not wanting to see what caused him to use those particular words. One thing I knew about Ted, he used profanity when he was angry. And the anger always stemmed from people being hurt by others.

"Faith..." Ted twisted, blocking my view of what he held.

I hated that warning tone people turned my name into. I crept closer. In Ted's hands was a copy of the latest *Making Legacies* magazine. Across Belinda's face was the word LIAR in black letters. Tiny splats of a reddish-brown color looked out of place on the shiny, pastel colored cover.

I said the first thing that popped into my head. "I didn't do it."

"The right to remain silent, Faith. It can actually be a good thing."

The ember of guilt mixed with self-righteousness inside of me burned bright at Ted's words. "So you think I had something to do with it?"

"Not currently. But I'm sure you'll find a way into it."

I wanted to continue feeling outraged but I kind of had a history of making an investigation a little harder when he looked for evidence.

"There's one question running through my mind right now." Ted placed the magazine into a brown paper bag. "Why would Faith have thought Belinda's death was a murder?"

I shrugged.

Ted narrowed his eyes. Apparently, he didn't like that answer.

I shrugged again and added a smile this time.

His eyes closed even more, only a tiny slit of green showed.

"You were the one who told me I should remain silent."

Ted rolled his eyes. "Now you decide to follow rules rigidly. Figures."

"Am I free to leave or would you like to shove me in the back of your cruiser? Or do you plan on interrogating me here?"

Ted sighed. "Are you done yet with the dramatics? It was a simple and reasonable question. What made you start wondering about Belinda's death?"

"I don't really think I'm dramatic."

"No. Of course not."

"You accused me..."

"I didn't accuse you of anything. You assumed that I did. Assumed the worst. Something I shouldn't be so surprised about."

I shot him a triumphant smile. "You should know. You do the same thing."

"Faith..."

I was testing his patience, and loving every minute of it. Served him right. "You're assuming the worst about me, by assuming that I assume the worst. Something you believe is a character flaw. So, pot meet kettle."

Ted looked a little shell-shocked, concerned, and confused. He shook his head. "Let's stop with the assuming and just go with straight-forward. 'Cause I don't know what you just said."

Truthfully, I wasn't sure about what I just said either.

"I'll just go straight to the question I really want answered. Who hired you?" Ted stressed the word hired.

Hired me? For what? I groaned and smacked my palm to my forehead. Ted thought I decided to give amateur sleuthing another try. Not going to happen. I learned my lesson last time I used my fledgling legal experience to help a friend beat a murder rap.

"No detective work for me," I said, crossing my heart.

Ted groaned. "Please, stay out of this. Don't make me shove you in a cell for your own good."

Now I was getting offended. "Didn't I just say I was staying out of it?"

"I've seen that look on your beautiful face before. What you say you'll do isn't compatible with what you plan on doing."

Ted's warning went into my brain and then right back out. But, the fact he called me beautiful made itself at home.

EIGHT

The late afternoon sun drifted through the windows in my crafting area. My grandmothers sat across the table from me, attempting to work on my pages, but like me, their hearts weren't in it.

An array of scrapbooking items littered the table and floor in my craft area. I never did make it to church, though the news of Belinda's accidental death now being a murder had worked its way through the congregation.

My grandmothers decided it was a good day for an impromptu cropping session at my house, telling me the sad news about Belinda made them want to focus on something happy. I think they wanted to keep tabs on me.

The last time a murder struck our town, I ended up inserting myself right into it.

Our cropping plan wasn't working for any of us though. For the last two hours, we sorted through pictures and changed the focus of our session three different times. We went from catching up on holiday pages, to putting page kits together as giveaways at the Halloween crop, and now we moved on to layouts for the store. My mind kept returning to Belinda's death. Why had she been at the store? I feared my grandmothers would somehow get caught up in this problem.

I arranged and rearranged the pictures on the white cardstock I wanted to use as my background. No matter where I placed the photos, nothing worked. It all looked out of place. Maybe it was the smiling faces from Marilyn's birthday crop. Maybe it was the fact the image showed the very area where the signing was held, the event that might have been the catalyst for Belinda's murder.

I shoved the pictures off the page and into the square fabric tote beside me.

"Which one of these pictures do you think I should use of Steve?" Grandma Hope held up two photos of Steve taken at our last singles crop.

I barely glanced up from the two pictures I snagged from Cheryl's pile, "The one on the left."

In one of the photos, Steve pretended to work on a layout and tried ignoring the young woman vying for his attention. I couldn't remember the woman's name who worked with Annette. In the background, Darlene shared a table with Oliver, Wayne and Wyatt. Darlene looked compressed. Her elbows held tightly against her body and all of her supplies in a one-foot diameter, almost like she was creating a wagon-circle around herself.

Wayne and Wyatt only came because their mother made them. It was a compromise. She'd stop asking about grandchildren and interviewing potential daughter-in-laws, if they attended the once-a-month singles crop. The brothers agreed. While they upheld their side of the promise, Gussie hadn't. At the last crop, she walked around and handed out questionnaires to all the women.

Except for me and my grandmothers, everyone else was fair game.

Oliver White started coming a few months ago. He was more interested in getting some of the experienced scrapbookers to help him put together a grant proposal slash scrapbook about the library rather than finding himself a woman. His seat of choice was always near Darlene. It kept all the women away and gave him access to peek at her layouts. To shut him up, Darlene had "helped" him a time or two.

Hope shoved Steve into my face. "Are you sure? He looks a little angry in that one."

I piddled with the pile of brads dumped out in front of me. "I'd say he's more moody than angry. Women like that."

"Then I'll save this picture for you." Hope put it off to the side.

"I'll blow it up to a nice five by seven size." Cheryl pulled out her iPad. "I have it on here. I'll just run upstairs and use Faith's printer."

"Why not download the photo to Faith's computer?" Hope placed the other picture of Steve onto her background page. "Then she can also have it as a screensaver."

"Even better." Grinning, Cheryl rose.

I didn't clear the history from my computer last night. I didn't want my grandmothers seeing the message board and what people had been saying about our store. Or more likely, my grandmother seeing the image of the screen shot in my photo folder when she put Steve up on my screen.

I pushed back from the table and reached for the iPad. "I'll do it."

Cheryl twisted, putting her device halfway behind her back. "I'm quite capable of transferring the picture."

"I know that. I just want to do it." I smiled big and bright. Big mistake.

Hope and Cheryl exchanged a look. I knew it well. It was the secret look they shared when they both thought I was hiding something and they were debating with their eyes on which one of them should confront me.

What excuse would they buy and I wouldn't forget? Whatever I said, I knew my grandmothers would bring up later. A Christmas present was the perfect cover-up for why I didn't want them on my computer...besides the truth. I hated lying to them, but the truth would hurt them so much more than my small covert operation. And it wouldn't be an out and out lie as I intended to make them a gift using my computer...maybe a calendar with monthly crop dates.

I forced out a pout. "It's just that I have a project on my computer. A surprise."

A soft smile emerged on Hope's face. Cheryl still seemed skeptical. One grandma out of two wasn't bad.

"If you want to ruin your gift..." I trailed off. I started to increase my pout but stopped. If I got too dramatic, I'd sway Hope over to the side of doubt.

Cheryl sighed and handed over the iPad. "Fine. But I want to see the screensaver."

I hurried upstairs and went into my office, making sure to close the door. I didn't want to lock it because that would set off warning bells and flares in my grandmothers' minds. Having them sneak upstairs and peeking at the computer wasn't a good idea either. While Grandma Hope loved surprises, she also had some snoop in her.

I turned on the computer. After a few minutes, it was up and running. I had a little time before my grandmothers came looking for me. First things first, I got Steve transferred from the iPad to the computer.

It really was a great picture of Steve. I wouldn't mind staring at him every time I worked or scrapbooked on my computer. I was trying my hand at digital scrapbooking. I loved paper scrapbooking but was enjoying the process of learning a new technique, and digital scrapbooking would be easy to do on the road. Once I got a laptop. Lugging around a desktop wouldn't be easy.

I took a flash drive from my desk drawer and transferred the screenshots of the message board threads I took last night. I wasn't sure if any one of them would come in handy, but there might be something in there. I leaned forward and scanned the comments again. Nothing hinted at the horrible events that would take place.

Or did they? I slowed down and read them again. My heart raced. I read one section again. And again.

You mean, Faith? You think she had something to do with my layouts being swiped?

Maybe that, too.

What had Little Lamb meant by that comment? Was she referring to me being in cahoots with Belinda and helping her "steal" Darlene's pages? But, this person had also mentioned the last murder.

I shuddered. *Last murder.* Now we had two. Did I really want to get involved in this again? Wasn't I already? This person mentioned me. Mentioned that case. Why would they unless they wanted to point the finger at me? Did they kill Belinda and wanted the focus off themselves?

No. Belinda was still alive when this person posted. I didn't get a call from the alarm company until a few hours later.

I didn't like this one bit.

"Faith? What are you doing up there?" Grandma Cheryl's voice carried up the stairs.

Darn it. I lost track of time. Okay. No jumping to conclusions. Close everything down and go back to scrapbooking. Digging up information on the internet led me to a wrong suspect last time. Besides, as I told Ted, I wasn't investigating. I tried my hand at sleuthing and it didn't work out well.

Okay, a little well as Marilyn was home with her family instead of in prison, but my investigation ruined a lot of relationships.

"Faith." There was an edge to Cheryl's voice.

Quickly, I deleted the history then logged off. I took the flash drive out of the USB port and shoved it into my pant pocket before my grandmother poked her head into the room.

"Do you need *my* help?" she asked.

"Nope. I have everything under control." I smiled and turned off the monitor. "All done."

She frowned and looked at the printer tray. "Why did you turn off the computer? I wanted to see Steve. And where's my print?"

Good reason. Come on brain, spit one out.

"Out of ink. I was trying to eliminate a distraction. Seeing Steve's picture made me think that he probably got called into work and will be eating a frozen dinner. I'm thinking I should bring him something to eat."

Cheryl smiled. "A splendid idea. Let's go see what we can rustle up in your kitchen."

I mentally went through my cupboards and refrigerator. Cheese. Eggs. Bread. Peanut butter. Frozen chicken.

Grandma Cheryl linked her arm through mine and pulled me from the office. "Don't worry, honey. Grandmas got themselves a feast just waiting to be prepared at their house. A nice lasagna, salad, and apple cobbler is just what that man needs."

NINE

I drummed my fingers on the steering wheel. The blinker clicked and clacked as I waited for a green light. I should have snuck through the red light so I wouldn't be facing this choice. I had intended on taking Steve dinner. The lasagna, salad and dessert were in matching containers snuggled inside a wicker picnic basket. The smell of toasted, melted cheese, oregano, and garlic bread rumbled my stomach.

My grandmothers had decided Steve needed company so they packed up my share also and sent me on the way. I had wanted to eat first but they insisted I get the food straight from the oven to Steve.

Now, I sat at the intersection contemplating a little detour. Turn left and I'd be heading toward the courthouse and Steve. Turn right and I'd be at the store.

Steve or store? Store or Steve?

My head and heart warred with each other. My head said Steve. Less chance of danger. Less chance of getting in trouble. Less chance of being accused of interfering in a police investigation. My heart said the store. I missed something last night. Something important. Something the police needed to know...before I once again became a prime suspect.

A horn tooted. I should drop it. Really I should. But I couldn't. Someone murdered Belinda at the back door of my grandmothers' store.

The horn behind me sounded again.

I turned right. My heart cheered. My head groaned. The last time I ventured into amateur sleuthing it hadn't worked out quite the way I planned. And that time I had a good reason for doing a little detecting work on the side.

This time, the reason was plain and simple nosiness coupled with anger of someone using our store as the place to commit the heinous crime. Not that I wanted Belinda murdered anywhere, it's just that I didn't like it literally at our back door. I had no indication anyone suspected me of the crime beside a cryptic message on a chat board made by someone who named themselves after a creature who followed Mary to school.

We opened tomorrow. I had to make sure the police hadn't missed anything. It's not that I believed Ted didn't know how to do his job, or I knew how to do it better, it's just I'd know what was out of place.

Of course, searching in the dark wasn't the best time but there was no way I'd come out in daylight. Police officers were still out gathering evidence this afternoon and there was no way I'd let them know what I was up to. Especially Ted, who despite my words to the contrary, probably thought I was looking for a way to involve myself into his case.

He didn't understand I had no interest in detecting, but just in finding an answer that pointed away from Scrap This and my family as the reason for Belinda being there. Also, I didn't want a murderer showing up to reclaim something they left behind. If I found it first, I could hand it over to Ted and make sure the word got out about the discovery. I wanted my grandmothers safe. Who could fault me for that?

A name popped into my head and I kept it in there. I didn't really care what Ted thought. I'm sure he'd change his mind if it was his brother or mother in possible danger.

I dimmed my lights as I pulled into the back lot of the shopping complex where Scrap This, Home Brewed, and a nail place scheduled to open after the new year were located. Some of the guys in town started referring to our small area as gossip row.

I eased the car behind the stores. The quietness of the night unnerved me a little. I heard the tires crunching over some of the loose gravel and the low hum of the security lights. Every noise, including the thudding of my heart, seemed magnified. I swallowed and tried shutting off the Halloween images that popped into my head. Witches. Werewolves. Zombies.

I knew those things didn't exist, but a killer did. Women usually got murdered in movies by forgetting their brains at home and venturing out into dark places at night by themselves. Kind of what I was doing right now.

Sweat coated my hands. I clenched the steering wheel tighter and parked the car at the corner of Home Brewed.

I didn't want anyone spotting my car near Scrap This. No sense tipping off the cops or the person responsible for murdering Belinda. All I wanted was to find why Belinda found it necessary to come to the store, or anything the killer might have left that the police didn't realize didn't belong.

Time to get this over with. I took in a deep, steadying breath. The aroma of melted cheese and garlic filled me. My stomach rumbled again. A tiny taste wouldn't be so bad. If someone else showed up and I needed to hide, I sure didn't want my hunger to give me away. Fortunately, my grandmas put my dinner and Steve's into separate containers so I could nibble on my lasagna without Steve knowing I took a little detour.

Before I knew it, my little snack turned into a full meal. I wiped my mouth and crumbled up the napkin, depositing it into the picnic basket. I'd have dessert with Steve. Hopefully he wouldn't ask me why I brought myself dessert and not dinner. I didn't want to lie to him nor tell him the truth.

If I delayed any longer, he might find out what I'd been up to. Someone would spot my car in the parking lot and call the cops, especially since a crime recently occurred here. This area of town wasn't hopping on Sunday. Usually, the only reason for parking behind stores was teenagers engaging in an activity they didn't want their parents catching them doing.

My poor grandmothers would be so disappointed that I parked behind Home Brewed. My being up to no good wasn't the steamy kind of no good. They'd been rooting for Steve and me to move our flirting friendship to the next level, hoping they could "force" a marriage because of a "scandal." My grandmothers, and others in Eden, still had some old-fashioned traditions and standards.

Pocketing my keys, I slowly opened the door and left the safety of my car. I stood outside for a few moments and listened. Stillness. The night sky was clear and the stars created a soft glow around the area. It looked like the quintessential perfect night but I wasn't going to take any chances.

I popped open the trunk and retrieved a large, metal flashlight. The moon and stars gave me enough light to see without tripping so I kept it off. Clutching the flashlight to my chest, I made my way toward Scrap This. The flashlight was bulky and a little awkward to carry but if anyone tried anything, it would leave them with a heck of a headache.

The dumpster loomed ahead of me. Even up close and almost personal, the dumpster was a dark shape. There was no way I'd find a clue just using nature's light. Here went everything. I clicked on the flashlight and shined the bright beam onto the dumpster. Yellow crime scene taped winked at me. The tape stretched from one side to the other, right over the door. I wouldn't be looking in there tonight.

While I bent rules on occasions, I would never completely break them. It made me a little too antsy and my long-held guilt complex would eat me alive. I'd end up snitching on myself before anyone else did just to quiet the voice in my head.

Besides, having found the magazine in the dumpster, I'm sure Ted hauled away everything in there.

Hunching over, I moved the beam of light to the ground and moved it inch by inch. I hoped to find some clue easily overlooked in the daylight. It was easy to miss something when your eye focused on everything. If someone lost an earring, a button, anything small and easily overlooked, I'd be able to see it.

A hum of an engine broke the stillness. I bolted upright and turned toward the sound. A car pulled into the back lot. I couldn't make out the make and model. I clicked off the flashlight.

Too late! The car aimed right toward me, or at least in my general direction. I had no idea if the driver was gunning for me and I didn't plan on staying still and finding out. I gauged the distance of me to my car and the other car to me. I'd never make it. I could blind the driver with the flashlight. But, I didn't know who it was. It could be my grandmothers sent Steve looking for me. I couldn't risk it. I'd have to hide out until I knew if the person was friend or foe.

Frantically, I looked around for a place to hide. I shouldn't have parked my car behind Home Brewed. Like an idiot, I worried so much about Ted catching me poking around my own store, I never thought for a second the murderer might come back tonight. If it was the best time for me to snoop it sure was the best time for them also.

Reason one hundred and one I should never consider detective work as a way of making my livelihood.

Wait. I was smart enough to keep my car keys with me. I'd go inside the store. If it was a foe, I'd call the police. I was willing to give up an explanation for protection. I fumbled with my keys, nearly dropping them twice, before I got the door open. I stumbled inside and slammed the door shut just as a fist pounded on the door.

I breathed a sigh of relief and leaned against the door. Made it. Unless the person had a gun. I scrambled away from the door, heading toward the left side of the storage area and behind a few boxes. Better protection.

"Open up." An angry woman's voice drifted through the closed door.

For some reason, knowing it was a woman made my heart rate slow. I also wasn't quite as anxious to call the police. Not that I didn't think a woman wasn't capable of violence, just I'd have a little better chance going up against another woman and winning.

The voice was familiar. Very much so.

The woman pounded again. "I know you're in there, Faith."

Darlene? What was she doing here? On second thought, I would rather not know. I remained quiet, hoping she would get the message and go away. Real soon. Like before someone spotted her and called the police. I did not want to have to explain this visit to Ted.

"I know you're in there."

So?

"Or maybe I don't..." she trailed off.

Whatever she planned on saying next, I wasn't going to like it. There was too much glee in her voice. Darlene wasn't known for her helpfulness and thoughtfulness toward others. She was the biggest pain in pretty much everyone in Eden's derrière, except for those residents who listed the Hooligans in that particular spot.

"You could be a prowler." Darlene tapped on the door. "Or the murderer returning to the scene of the crime."

Yeah right. If she believed that she wouldn't be knocking on the door begging to be let in.

"I think I should—"

My patience left right along with common sense. I walked over to the door so Darlene could hear me better. "You're right. I'm in here. You can leave now."

"Not a chance. You're up to something." She banged on the door. "Let me in."

"I'm working."

"On a Sunday. At eight o'clock at night. And your car isn't parked here. Sounds suspicious to me. Maybe you're not Faith."

I snorted. "Right. You know it's me. That's not going to work."

"I know, I know. But will the police believe I'm calling to annoy you or because something is up?"

"If you call them, you're going to have to explain to them why you're here."

"And so will you." Triumph echoed in her voice.

Okay, she had me there. I didn't want to explain my presence here anymore than she wanted to explain hers.

Ugh! I was going to have to let her in. I opened the door a crack. "Fine. But keep it down."

Darlene squeezed inside. "What did you find?"

She wasted no time. "Nothing yet. What did you find?"

"Why do you think I'm here looking for something?"

"Because you don't work here. How did you plan on getting inside?"

"Who says I wanted to come inside?"

I rolled my eyes. "Whatever. How about we stop the games and just agree to get on with what we both had planned to do? Find whatever Belinda came here to look for."

She heaved out a huge sigh and stuck out her hand. "Deal."

We shook.

"Let's split up." I flipped the lights on, glad we had thick blinds to block any light from showing through the slats. "Chances are someone is going to notice your car and call the police."

"Don't worry." Darlene headed into the main part of the store. "I parked my car by yours."

"Like we're not going to have to explain that."

"I have one." Darlene threw a know-it-all grin at me over her shoulder. "I broke down and I called you to pick me up."

"And why would I do that?" I might as well find out from her, because I couldn't come up with a good reason.

"Because you wanted to know why I was here in the middle of the night."

In a weird way, it made total sense. "Okay. The second question would be why were you here in the middle of the night. Detective Roget is going to ask. I can guarantee you he'd be the one showing up."

"I'm sure you can."

I frowned. I didn't like that smug, high-pitched tone she used. Then again, there wasn't much I did like when it came to Darlene.

"I'll search around the table Belinda used and also check the class kits left behind. You can look on the tables the students used and also on the floor."

"Why do I have to crawl around?" Darlene smacked her hands onto her hips. She tapped her foot, the toe of her black leather boots making a soft clicking sound on the linoleum.

"I know what I put in the class kits, including Belinda's, so if anything extra is in there I'd know."

"What if Belinda came to put something back rather than take something?"

Interesting theory. "I'd know that also. Stop arguing and look. Someone is going to be knocking on that back door soon."

"Aren't you the bossy one?" Darlene tugged up the hem of her pants and slowly knelt on the ground.

I refrained from answering her question. Getting into a verbal war with Darlene kept us here longer. I, for one, did not want to be here any longer than necessary. And I had a bad feeling I was already pushing those proverbial moments. I went over to the table Belinda used and started going through the box of supplies. We never got around to doing the class so nothing should be gone.

There were pieces of the kit missing. A few of the tins, distressing ink pens, and also the special hammer Belinda insisted we have on hand. She didn't want to bring hers to the store, but had no problem taking any of the store's items home. Had Belinda been trying to return the items? Being accused of stealing product wouldn't look good for her on top of the accusation of stealing layouts.

No. Steve and I would have found something on her, unless the murderer took the items when they left. But why? Belinda stealing, or returning stolen merchandise, was a good reason for her to come in the middle of the night. She wouldn't want to walk into the store during business hours and give us the stuff she pilfered. Though I'm sure she'd have done it by accident, I mean it had gotten wild and crazy.

How did Belinda expect to get into the store? Did she plan on breaking and entering or had she borrowed a key from someone? I had mine. I doubted my grandmothers would've loaned out theirs.

Sierra? Possible.

I shuddered, envisioning how that conversation would turn out. Maybe I'd get Darlene to ask her. She wanted to do more than just crawl around on the ground.

No. Absolutely not. Asking Darlene to question Sierra meant we were working together on Belinda's murder. Partnering with Darlene wasn't on my agenda.

I glanced over at Darlene who crawled around on the ground, shining a small flashlight she had attached to her key ring. The only person I knew who'd been angry enough to attack Belinda was currently in the store with me.

Was Darlene looking for something that would prove her guilt beyond a reasonable doubt? Or had she planned on leaving something to give the police another suspect?

Darlene must have felt my suspicious gaze because she stopped scuttling around and turned her head to look at me. She frowned. "I didn't do it."

My famous words to Ted repeated back to me. "I didn't accuse you."

"You're not saying it but I can see it."

"You can see it?" I was intrigued. "Really? How?"

Darlene rolled her eyes. "Because you aren't as unreadable as you believe you are. Everyone knows how you feel about Steve...and Detective Roget."

"I like them so what."

"Give it up, Faith. It's more than like. You have the hots for both of them." Darlene stood and grinned at me. "Have to say I'm kind of surprised. I didn't think you had it in you to lust over one guy much less two."

"And what does that mean?" I crossed my arms. "I'm not lusting, as you so elegantly put it, over Steve or Ted."

A sharp pound on the front door had me yelping and Darlene squealing. Caught. I'd rather deal with the police than Darlene's interest in my possible romantic choices.

Not that I was looking...who was I kidding I was seriously thinking about breaking my vow of singlehood. Though, it wasn't a choice between Steve and Ted. It was a decision of actually wanting to start dating, have a real relationship rather than a heated flirtation with Steve.

The pounded sounded again. "Police."

It was Ted. I hoped Darlene's excuse worked. "It's show time."

I lifted up the corner of the blind and peered out, double checking that it was in fact Ted. I mean, I could be mistaken about who I heard and I should be safety conscious.

Ted narrowed his eyes and pointed at the lock. "Open up."

"I'm finishing up."

"Faith..."

Ugh...the warning tone. I wasn't a child needing a good scolding. Just for that, I wouldn't let him in. "Everything is fine here. You can go about your business."

"This is my business. Open up."

Gee, everyone sure was bossy tonight. I smiled at him sweetly and opened my eyes wide, the innocent damsel look. "I had no idea Hope and Cheryl brought in a partner. They didn't say one word to me."

"You know what I mean." Even in the dim light, I saw a muscle in his jaw twitch.

I looked over my shoulder. Wait a minute. Where's Darlene? If she snuck out the back door I'd never trust her again. Of course, I shouldn't have trusted her to begin with.

She used me to get what she wanted, into the store.

I unlocked the door and jerked it open. "Forget it. She took off and will never admit she came here."

"She who?" Ted lumbered inside and stared down at me.

This was why I should stay out of investigations. I didn't have to worry about anyone snitching on me, I snitched on myself. "Doesn't matter."

"I think we should finish this conversation at the station."

TEN

Once again I was in the police station, sitting in a tiny room, waiting for the police to interrogate—talk—to me. Anxiety raced through me even though I knew this time I hadn't done anything wrong.

Okay, maybe a little wrong as Ted...Detective Roget...had warned me not to get involved. I had told him I had no intention of doing so. I meant it. I really did. I had only wanted to see if I could discover why Belinda had showed up at the store. It wasn't my fault that Darlene had showed up and coerced me into letting her inside.

I pressed my hands onto my knees to stop my legs from shaking, afraid I'd be showing an admission of guilt to a murder. A murder I once again had nothing to do with, but somehow got wrapped into because I was conveniently at the wrong place at the wrong time. It was the convenient part that might end up getting me into trouble. How many people ended up being tied into a murder once, much less three times?

I watched Detective Ted Roget pace in front of the small window, hands gesturing in the air. I wasn't sure who he was yelling at, though I guessed Steve. My choice for the one phone call. My list of people to call in an emergency wasn't very extensive, and with this type of issue, I figured Steve was my best bet.

Darlene lied to me. She had the perfect plan and ran out when I needed her. I should've left her outside. I took a huge risk for nothing. No clue. No evidence. Nothing except for a trip to the police station.

Would I need bail money?

The door banged opened and I sat up straight, hoping to portray innocence and confidence.

"I thought you weren't getting involved in this investigation." Ted charged in and threw the question at me. He slapped a folder against his thigh.

I craned my neck, trying to spot Steve. Didn't he come here to save me, not leave me in the lion's den I had kind of willingly climbed into?

"I expect an answer, Faith." Ted pressed his hands onto the top of the metal table and leaned forward. His gaze drilled into mine.

"I'm not. Not really. I was curious on why Belinda decided to stop by the store. It's just weird she picked that time..."

"How do you know she went there at that time?"

"I..." I slapped my lips shut. I didn't know. I was pretty sure. The alarm would've gone off earlier. "Nancy at Sound Security called around that time. I wouldn't think they'd delay in calling me about a possible break in. Unless..." My stomach started churning, the yummy lasagna not feeling yummy anymore. "...Belinda was killed somewhere else and brought to the store. Why?"

Ted sighed and looked up at the ceiling. "I should've known. I should've known she'd turn that comment into a question."

"It's a good question." I crossed my arms and glared at Ted. Was Ted trying to trip me up? Get me to confess to the murder. Well, it wouldn't work. For one, I didn't kill anyone. Two, I wasn't *that* brainless.

"I'm the detective. Got it?"

I nodded. I knew how this little exchange went. He asked. I answered without words, the preferable method for Ted.

"Your actions tonight make it look like you're up to something."

"Up to what? I went to the store owned by my grandmothers which I manage and was going through the class kits. Things were left in a little bit of a disarray..."

Ted's green eyes narrowed.

I rolled mine. "...after the class turned into a brawl. Thanks to Darlene. I can't believe she snuck out. See if I ever help her again."

"Can I get that in writing?" Ted shoved the folder toward me and offered a pen.

I spotted Steve walking toward the room. I waved and smiled, which promptly fell from my face when I noticed Karen England and the photographer walking behind him. My grandmothers were not going to be happy to see me as the headline in tomorrow's paper. My only saving grace was I called Steve for help. They'd love the fact I turned to Steve when I found myself in a jam.

I, on the other hand, had a different feeling roiling through me. This funny, skittering kind of feeling ran along my nerves. And Darlene's words bounced in my head. Okay, I was having more intense emotions toward Steve. I was also now relying on him. Counting on him. Trusting him.

I wasn't sure I liked this new development. But I was sure I liked even less the look on Karen's face when she looked at Steve. That woman lusted after him. I clenched my hands, dropping them into my lap so Ted didn't see.

Steve tapped his knuckles on the small glass window. I stood and grinned. Freedom had arrived. I'd leave and not even stop to try and find out why Karen decided to visit the police station.

Hopefully, Steve kept this little incident between me and him. Though, with the addition of Karen, and Bobbi-Annie straining her neck to see what was going on, my grandmothers would know before Steve and I got to the parking lot. Gossip flew faster around here than glitter in a scrapbook store during a life artist cat fight.

"I do not need this." Ted stalked over and yanked the door open. "Davis, I've already explained to you..."

"Karen..." Steve began.

Burgundy red flashed in front of my eyes for a second. Karen? He was on a first name basis with Karen. *Get a grip.* Of course he had called Karen by her first name. She was in our age bracket and he knew her.

"...came by because she has some pictures you might find interesting, Detective Roget," Steve said.

"Unless it's related to my case, I do not have the time." Ted tried closing the door but Karen braced it open with her elbow.

"It is." Karen stepped into the room, dragging the guy with the camera with her. "This is Leonard Blue. He's a freelance photographer and has been working for the paper for a few months."

"This is somehow on my need to know radar because..." Ted's irritation came across loud and clear.

The man was testy. I hoped that whatever Leonard would either get me off the hook, or deserved the detective's ire more than me.

Karen sighed dramatically and arched backwards, leaning into Steve. "He's not a friendly sort is he?"

"I don't have time for this." Ted took hold of Karen's arm and hustled her toward the door.

In my head, I cheered, back flipped, and added a spiffy cartwheel at the end.

"You should." Karen pulled away. "If I was in charge of this murder case, I'd wonder why Darlene Johnson was lurking around Scrap This and then forced Faith to let her inside. I wonder what Darlene threatened to do."

Ted's expression went blank, but he motioned for me to hand him the folder and pen. I complied.

"Wouldn't put anything past a woman like that," Leonard said. "I was at the book signing and saw this Darlene woman attacking the victim. Pretty vicious."

As annoyed as I was with Darlene, I couldn't let Ted think the worst about her actions tonight. "She didn't threaten me. Not really."

Steve and Ted gaped at me for moment. Even Karen seemed a little shocked at my words. She had intended to dramatize the event to make herself look more heroic.

Steve moved away from Karen and paused near me. I saw the hesitation in his eyes. He wanted to show me his support and care but wasn't sure if I would appreciate it. I offered a soft smile and took a step closer. He placed an arm around my shoulders and I snuggled into his side.

Ted switched his attention to the photographer. "You have photos of the fight in the store?"

Karen fought a frown as her eyes turned into a sliver of evil on her face.

"A couple. Also got some tonight of Darlene forcing her way into the scrapbook store." Leonard stuck his hand into his front jean pocket. "I have the memory card with all the pictures on it. Karen said you'd need it."

"We were going to drop it off tomorrow after getting the shots we needed from it." Karen slid her gaze toward Steve. "When I heard about Faith being dragged down here like a criminal, I knew we had to turn it over tonight."

Right. I'm sure this was all about me, and had nothing to do with Steve. The woman actually had the gall to use helping me as a way to win Steve's affections.

Leonard held out a memory card. "Here you go, Detective."

Ted took the card. "Let me make sure I understand this scenario correctly. You happened to be behind Scrap This and saw Faith and then Darlene show up."

"Yes," Leonard said.

"That leaves me wondering what you were doing there." Frowning, Ted leveled a hard stare at Leonard.

The man snuck a glance at Karen. She licked her lips and nodded.

"No." Ted held up a hand and shook his head. "I don't want you telling me what Miss England told you to say. I want the truth."

"He is—" Karen began.

"Trying to confirm his truth with what you've told me. I saw the look," Ted said.

I volleyed my gaze back and forth between the three participants. Steve gave my shoulder a squeeze. I gave a quick, light sidekick to his ankle. I didn't need a reminder to remain quiet. For now,

I was off Ted's radar and I liked it. I enjoyed seeing Karen squirm. It was also fun watching Ted interrogate someone else for a change.

"He went on a job for me and was making sure he could tell you. Reporters do have their own private sources." Karen gave Ted a haughty look.

"Private sources." Ted stood directly in front of Karen and looked down on her. "So, someone has been feeding you information about the murder and you're keeping it quiet."

Karen looked nervous. "No, Detective that's not what I'm saying."

"Sounded like it to me."

Steve tensed beside me. His body grew rigid and his hand bit into my shoulder. I sucked in a breath. and he released his hold. Peeking up at him, I saw his intense focus on Ted and Karen. I wasn't sure if the anger was directed toward the detective or the reporter.

From the slight blush creeping onto Karen's cheeks, I knew she hoped Steve planned on defending her.

Not if I could help it. "You're having your photographer follow me around." I added as much shock and fear into my voice as I could. "Stalk me."

Karen narrowed her gaze at me. "Don't flatter yourself, Faith."

I gasped in mock indignation. "You think I want some man watching me."

"As most people know, criminals usually return to the scene of the crime," Karen said.

Blinking rapidly, I looked up at Steve. "They think I killed…"

Steve hugged me. "No one thinks you did anything to Belinda."

"Hazel thinks Cheryl had something to do with it. But I told her it wasn't true," Karen said.

"What?" Steve and I said in unison.

"Hazel said she called Cheryl and told her Belinda left her necklace at the store and needed it," Karen said. "Cheryl refused to go that night, so Belinda called Faith to help her."

Why did people keep saying that? "Belinda did not call me.

And I can't believe Hazel expected my grandmother to head out in the dark and cold to get the diva necklace."

Ted frowned.

She shrugged. "I'm only telling you what Hazel said. She called me because she feared the police wouldn't look into the matter."

Ted crossed his arms. "Hazel never mentioned any of this last night."

"She probably felt bad she didn't insist Cheryl go to the store instead of Belinda going to meet Faith."

"For crying out loud. Are you listening to me? Belinda didn't call me so I wasn't going there to meet her." Sweat coated my hands and a low buzz started in my head and ears. No. I couldn't. I wouldn't go through this again. I had nothing to do with Belinda's death. "Check my phone records."

Ted rested a hand on my shoulder as Steve tightened his hold on me. "You're not under suspicion Faith."

"That's why Hazel came to the press instead of the police," Karen said as she inspected her polish. "She knew the detective in town has a little bit of a crush on the most likely suspect."

"That's enough." Ted's clipped words put an end to Karen's conversation. "The only people who determine suspects are the police. And none of you are on the force. Am I making myself clear?"

We all nodded. Ted's patience had been tried and he was ready to convict and sentence us if we continued playing point the finger.

"I want the truth. Not allegations. Not assumptions. The truth as simple and plain as can be made. Leonard, you first." Ted pointed at him.

"Karen wanted me to hang around the store tonight and get pictures of anyone who came by," Leonard said. "Criminals usually come back to the scene. They either want to cover their tracks or else bask in their crime."

Karen nodded. "That's right. I've done a lot of reading about criminals and their thought processes. I figured if we got pictures of people hanging around the store, especially when it was closed, we'd find out who killed poor Belinda Watson."

"Just what we need in this town, more arm chair detectives," Ted said. "And did you ever think people might assume you two were involved because you are hanging around the store in the middle of the night?"

"I wasn't hanging around the store," Karen said. "Leonard was."

Ted fixed his gaze on Leonard. "Isn't that nice of you, Miss England? You send someone else to do your stalking so you couldn't be charged with anything."

"I wasn't stalking anyone," Leonard said. "I just went to get some pictures. Good thing I was there tonight so I could back up Faith's story."

"I don't need back up," I said. "And I don't have a story."

A story was something someone said as entertainment. Fiction. Made up. I was giving verbal truth. No embellishing.

"Since this has been cleared up as far as Faith is concerned, may she go home?" Steve started leading me out the door.

Ted nodded and motioned for us to go. "Make sure she gets home. She looks a little peaked. I think seeing Belinda like that affected her more than she wants us to know."

No. Seeing Karen make goo-goo eyes was churning my stomach. I kept it to myself. No sense letting Karen know how much her interest in Steve annoyed me.

"Faith doesn't want anyone to think she can't handle the weight of the world." Steve tightened his hold around me.

"Some women just aren't cut out for high pressure jobs." Karen grinned, an evil-queen twist of the lips.

Couldn't cut it? I'd show her who couldn't cut it. I wiggled from Steve's hold and headed in her direction. Steve tucked me back up against him.

Karen's eyes narrowed. I smiled and snuggled into Steve. Ha! Take that. She might have won the battle of the digs, but I won the war of who the man took home.

ELEVEN

There'd been little dialogue between me and Steve since we left the police station. I had tried a conversation a few times, but Steve wasn't in the mood. He pulled up beside my car parked at Home Brewed. I remained still, waiting to see if he'd say something. Even the obvious like "we're here."

More minutes ticked by. Okay. I got the point. He had nothing to say to me, or probably more likely, nothing nice to say so was refraining from talking. Well, I needed to talk.

"I appreciate you coming to help me out. Tonight and yesterday. It means a lot to me."

Steve nodded and stared out the window.

I expected my mini confession to get some kind of reaction from him. Okay, I needed to try again and harder. "I'm not setting out trying to find trouble. It just kind of keeps working out that way for me."

Steve lips turned up slightly. "I know this isn't my business, but my advice is don't trust Darlene again."

I let out an unladylike snort. "There's a warning I don't need."

"I'm thinking I should check your place tonight. I don't like knowing Karen had the photographer following you around."

This was one of my concerns of 'officially' dating Steve. He'd think it was his duty to protect me and look after me. I didn't need looking after, or being told what was in my best interest.

"She had him watching the store. Not me. I'll be fine."

Steve fought a frown.

I knew he meant well. And, I did like the fact he was annoyed with Karen. "It's nice knowing I have someone I can count on. I kind of feel like I'm using you and I hate it."

Steve faced me. "You can count on me. I'm here for you."

"I know."

Steve cupped my cheek. "That means a lot to me. I wish though you could trust me. I want the wall down between us."

"There's no wall." I inched back, hating breaking contact but also terrified of it. Butterflies had taken flight in my stomach and a heated feeling raced through me. Relying was enough at this point.

I fooled myself for over a year, believing my only interest in Steve was in admiring him. One unexpected and soul-shattering kiss from Steve during my last "investigation" had me reconsidering my stance on no romantic entanglements ever. I still found myself wavering between forever single or trying again. Every guy wasn't Adam.

"Don't lie to me. Or yourself. You don't mind talking as long as the conversation doesn't steer toward defining what we are to each other. "

"You're important to me. We're friends."

"I want more than just being your friend."

I knew that. So did practically everyone else. I wanted more but then I didn't. "You don't want to be friends?" I gave him an innocent smile.

"I'd like more than friends." Steve settled back into the driver's seat. "If friends are all we're meant to be, let me know. I'll respect your decision."

Why did I have to make a decision right now? I liked being friends and the flirting. Liked the will-we-or-won't-we become an actual item aspect of our relationship. How long would Steve keep waiting for me to make some kind of declaration? Did he want the type of relationship I was satisfied with? Were all my confusing signals fair to him?

Karen was making her intentions quite clear. So was Steve. He wanted a real relationship. Get married someday. Have children.

Steve was a great guy. Successful. Nice. Considerate. Honorable. Hot. I couldn't blame Karen. I'm surprised there weren't a few more women trying to win his heart.

He deserved more than my insecurities. Heck, I deserved more than my insecurities and allowing Adam control of my life. People made decisions all the time and changed their minds. I married Adam, realized the huge error of that choice, and got it annulled. If I could alter that, I could decide to edit my rule about no more romantic relationships ever. Life should be more than living from guilt. Everyone made mistakes and deserved forgiveness. Including forgiving myself.

I undid the seatbelt and gave into the impulsive thought zipping through my head. Kneeling on the passenger seat, I leaned over the console separating me from Steve. I placed my hands on his shoulder for balance and kissed him. Good. I wanted him to know I was interested. Very interested in him.

Steve's hand tangled in my hair, encouraging me. My blood was getting way too heated considering our location, a parked car near Scrap This. I did not want to be caught by Ted, or anyone else, making out in a car behind Home Brewed.

"Thank you." I whispered the words onto his lips before pulling back. "I should go."

I needed to tread carefully. Not for my sake, not because I viewed all men as untrustworthy, but I didn't want to break Steve's heart. He didn't deserve it. When I made a commitment to him, I wanted to jump into it with my whole mind, heart, and soul. Not holding anything back.

I scrambled from the car and quickly entered my own vehicle. The scent of garlic hit me. Steve's dinner. It was probably spoiled. No sense giving it to him. Plus, I didn't want to have to add this part of the evening into what happened tonight. He might think I planned on meeting Darlene at Scrap This and used him as a cover. I spotted a pair of headlights at the other end of the parking lot. Ted checking up on us. Me anyway. I don't think he had any reason to suspect Steve.

I thought about driving by the car and giving a cheerful wave, but toying with an already aggravated homicide detective wasn't a good idea. I left the parking lot and headed straight home, though the smell of the food was making me hungry. A slice of pizza with oozing cheese flashed into my mind. My last detour didn't work out for me, so I kept my intended destination and went home.

I pulled into my driveway. After slipping out of my car, I waved at Steve and made a show of rummaging around in my purse. I hoped he'd go in rather than wait for me to make it safely inside. I didn't want to explain the picnic basket. I snuck a peek. He went inside.

Good. I hauled out the basket and unlocked my front door, doing a quick check to see if Karen sent Leonard to follow me. I was alone. Thank goodness. I shoved the door open. The scent of garlic trailed after me. I threw out the food, not wanting to take any chances, and carried the trash bag outside.

I returned to the kitchen. The smell of the food clung to me. My clothes had absorbed the odor. I headed to the laundry room adjacent to the kitchen and stripped off my jacket, shirt, and jeans. I dropped them into the washer and closed the lid. I'd try and rustle up some more laundry tomorrow night and get the machine started. I hated running the washer when it wasn't full but I also didn't want the garlicky clothes sitting in their very long.

My cell phone rang from the washer. Ugh! Good thing someone called me this late or else I'd be buying a new one. I retrieved the phone from my jacket then dropped the garment back into the washer.

"Hello." I walked up the stairs.

"Tomorrow, I'll tell you our next step," Darlene's voice flowed over the line.

I hung up. There. I stayed out of it. Steve and Ted should be proud.

TWELVE

I scrambled inside the store Monday morning. I had fifteen minutes before my grandmothers arrived. I wanted to do a quick check before they or any customers entered the store. Flipping on the light caused a cascade of colors to glitter from the floor.

A quick vacuum job gathered up most of the glitter, and almost sucked up a heart necklace, a thin friendship bracelet and a library card. I snagged those items and tossed them into our lost and found basket. I'd work on locating the owners later.

I scanned the class kits and found nothing out of the ordinary or missing from the student ones left behind. It looked like the only one who took a little something was Belinda. I boxed up the kits and placed them into a corner behind the main counter. Some of the attendees might come back for their kit. Get something for their money.

I tugged open the blinds. Two pieces of cardboard were taped to the window. I unlocked the front door and walked outside. There was a tinge of cold in the air with a promise of some warmth later in the day. The beauty of October in West Virginia, one never knew if it was skiing or golfing weather.

One handmade sign had a hastily drawn skull with a red slash through it and the word "Danger" written in a shaky block style print was under the skull. The other sign said "Do Not Enter" and had a picture of Scrap This that had been in the newspaper. It also had a red slash going across it.

A horn tooted.

I turned. Hazel had parked facing Scrap This, her mammoth white truck taking up four spaces. She gunned her engine.

I gave her a half-hearted "I surrender" wave then took down the signs. I wasn't worried about obvious displays of crazy. From my past experiences, you had to worry about the people who didn't act like they were out to get you.

I flipped the open sign over. Tearing up the cardboard signs, I walked toward the storage area. I wanted to throw the signs into the dumpster so my grandmothers didn't see them.

The back door rattled.

I tossed the pieces of cardboard behind the boxes of the pattern paper we received. I needed to work on getting the merchandise out this morning. This way, I could hide the signs among the other cardboard going to the recycle center.

My grandmothers walked into the store.

I hid my hands behind my back.

"Busy I see," Cheryl said.

"I was vacuuming." I pointed into the main area.

Cheryl eyed the vacuum.

"The floor was kind of sparkly."

"Put it away before a customer trips over the cord." Cheryl brushed past me muttering under her breath.

What had made it into the paper this morning? Cheryl and Hope were usually morning people.

"I'm going to search on the internet." Hope headed for the small hallway leading toward the office and employee lounge. "I know there's going to be somewhere this talk started over the weekend."

"What talk?" I followed after Cheryl. Did they find out about Darlene's ranting on the message boards?

"I'm starting to think we need to take a seminar on damage control." Cheryl grabbed an armload of *Making Legacies* and placed them behind the counter. "Ms. Amtower called. There's some talk at the publishing company about recalling the magazines.

Their blog has been hit with thousands of messages regarding what happened here this weekend."

"The murder?"

Cheryl narrowed her eyes on me. "That Belinda admitted she stole those designs and now every designer in that issue is being accused of cheating."

"I guess it makes sense to recall the issue. Or at least not sell it anymore."

Cheryl's shoulders lifted and dropped as she drew in a deep breath then released it. "This whole fraud thing could bring down the entire magazine."

Wow. I knew it would be bad for them but not that bad. Had Belinda thought about that when she concocted her scheme? Brilliant idea the more appropriate term as Belinda wasn't much of a schemer.

I barely got settled behind the counter when the phone rang. I snagged the receiver. "Scrap This, how can—"

"I want a refund for Saturday's class." An irritable voice barked at me.

My heart dropped. I shouldn't be surprised about this turn of events. Of course, attendees would want their money back as there hadn't really been a class.

Normally, we don't offer refunds on the classes but this was a time to make an exception, and by the end of the day I'd probably make a lot of them. First, I'd try and see if we could switch her fee to another class or give her store credit.

"Would you like to transfer the fee to another class?" I searched through our ordering history, looking for some new products to tempt her with. Nothing exciting expected until the end of next week. The shipment we got in was a reorder of a line. "I have the class kit packaged up for you to take home."

"I want a refund. In cash, just like I paid."

"Normally, we don't offer cash refunds..."

"I don't shop at stores that breed killers. I'll be by this afternoon to pick up my refund and also return the magazine I bought."

"Magazines are non-refundable." I planted my elbows on the counter and leaned forward. This was going to be a long day.

"I refuse to pay good money for *Making Legacies* when the featured artist is a fraud."

"Our store had nothing to do with that. I'm sure if you wrote the company—"

"I bought it from you. You bought it from the publishing company. You should deal with them, not me."

The woman hung up. I had been tempted to ask her if the book had been written in by anyone, another reason to not offer the refund, but it would only have irritated the customer more. And, I'd have offered the refund anyway.

I made a note on the clipboard at the register so Marilyn and Sierra knew the refund had been authorized, and for them to go ahead and issue on to any customer that requested one. First, switch to another class. Second, store credit. Third, refund in method they paid.

I picked up the phone and dialed the extension to the small office in the back of the store.

"Scrap This—"

"Hi Grandma, it's me." I explained the situation and the decision I made.

"I'd have done the same thing."

"I didn't think it would be good to go back and forth with her." I made a note to send out an email about the found items. Maybe I should ask Oliver to read it over for content.

"Let's hope our other customers are a little more understanding about the magazine issue. The class I totally understand. Once Sierra gets in, see if you can brainstorm a couple of fun and unusual classes that might entice people to switch their fee over."

What would entice angry customers to take another class from us? Maybe one done by a hot guy. "I can see if Steve will give a photography class."

"Perfect! If the customers aren't interested in the topic, they might be in staring at the teacher."

Too bad, I couldn't figure out a way to get Ted to teach something. But the man didn't know much about scrapbooking and I didn't think crime techniques were something our clientele would be interested in. Though, with the ways things were going around Eden lately, a class on self-defense might be a good idea.

I drummed a pencil on the counter top. I needed some more good ideas before Sierra came in.

Not that I didn't think she couldn't come up with any, but I wanted to pass them on to grandma before Sierra shot them all down. This battle between us, that I didn't want to participate in, wore me down. Maybe I'd call Marilyn and see if she could stop by this morning and brainstorm. I needed a buffer between me and Sierra.

The most advance scrapbooker I knew, and who was on top of all the new trends, was Darlene. The problem was most locals would rather not know something then hand over some of their hard earned money to Darlene. Customers from outside of town might be interested. I'd have to run the idea by my grandmothers first. They'd be the ones to suffer through the complaints and fallouts of allowing Darlene to teach.

It was a shame Darlene's abrasive and know-it-all attitude preceded her. She'd make a great teacher if she wasn't so condescending and well...a know-it-all. Darlene had some great ideas and was good at explaining them...if you could get past the sighs and eye rolls accompanying the directions.

One more refund and two store credits later, Sierra arrived. I glanced over at the clock.

"I'm late. Want to make an issue of it?" Sierra shoved her purse under the counter. "It's not like it's busy in here."

"It would be nice to know if you're running behind," I said, keeping the majority of my opinion to myself.

"This wasn't a planned delay. Something came up." Sierra pulled the clipboard from the peg and started reading.

"Everything okay?"

"Like you really care."

I pulled the clipboard from her hand and placed it on the counter. Hard. "I do care. I'm sorry about what happened. I really am. For no other reason than it hurt you. But, I didn't just throw a dart at a wheel of suspects I keep in my house. I had reasons."

"You said he hurt you. Hank would never—"

I held up my hand and shook my head. "No, I didn't. Someone else told Ted that. Remember?"

I zeroed my gaze directly into hers, keeping contact and hoping she'd remember all the details of that horrific time. It wasn't fun for any of us having our friend and co-worker accused of murdering her husband. Heck, it wasn't fun for me since my investigation placed me into the path of the killer.

And on the radar of a very annoyed homicide detective.

Whether Sierra wanted to admit it, Hank crossed a line and deserved to be on the hook. Since Hank and I didn't have anything to do with each other, and there were no plans for us ever being friends again, I'd let it go to salvage a friendship with Sierra.

"You didn't tell the detective the information was wrong."

"At that time, all Ted believed about me was I was trouble. You think me vouching for Hank would've helped?"

Sierra smiled. "That is true. You weren't on the detective's list of favorite people."

"No kidding. I topped his most annoying and most likely to be shoved into a jail cell list."

The bell went crazy and the door nearly slammed into the wall. Leslie Amtower stalked into the store, papers clenched in her hand.

"Where are the owners?" She waved the stack of printouts under my nose, shaking them for emphasis.

"They're working in the office this morning," I said.

"I want to speak to one of them right now. If you think you're going to get away with this you're crazy." She pointed a trembling finger at Sierra. "Go get her right now."

Sierra slid an I-don't-think-so look toward me. If there was one thing Sierra didn't like, it was being bossed around. If this woman thought she could march into Scrap This and issue out orders like a power-tripping drill sergeant and have them complied with, she was the one out of her mind.

"I'm sorry, but you became my employer when?" Sierra crossed her arms and glared at the woman.

"I need someone to get her and I don't trust this one." Leslie now jabbed her finger at me.

This one? I didn't know if I should be more irate than curious. What had I done to upset the woman so much? Okay, the class didn't go off without a hitch on Saturday but that was more on her than on me. If anyone should be fuming, it should be me and my grandmothers.

I caught Sierra's eye and nodded my head toward the back of the store. She shrugged and went to get Hope or Cheryl.

"I don't have a clue what issue you could have with me...but we sure have one with you."

"With me?" Leslie sucked in a breath and placed a hand on her chest.

"Yeah, you. Your choice of one of the life artist divas has made a lot of our customers unhappy. They want to return the magazine."

Okay, one person so far but she didn't need to know that.

"You're going to turn that on me after what you did." Leslie planted her hands on her hips and glared at me. "Not going to happen, honey."

Honey...well, I could play this game also. "Listen, sweetie, you asked us to host Belinda and we were happy to do so since she was a local woman—"

"Ah ha!" Leslie grinned so broadly her face looked like it was splitting apart. "Local woman. That right there. She cropped here. Shopped here."

"She was mainly a home cropper."

"Don't mince words with me. She came here and so did her cousin. That awful woman Darlene."

I wouldn't argue with that assessment. "Just because they're both local women, doesn't mean I'm wrapped up in whatever happened."

"But all this points to it." She tapped the sheets.

I let curiosity get the best of me and looked at it. A stack of printouts from the message board. I scanned it. I felt the frown stretch my mouth down as uneasiness wormed through me. This wasn't the entire thread. Some posts were missing, plus a few had been changed.

"Anonymous posts on a message board." I shrugged. "Good luck in a court of law."

Leslie sneered at me. "What about public opinion?"

"That court will turn on you and *Making Legacies* faster than they will the store."

"That's what you're counting on. I'll put a stop to your plan." Leslie snatched the sheets from my view.

"What plan of mine? And why in the world would I want to harm you or your business, especially if it ended up hurting my grandmothers and their store?"

That caught her off guard. Confusion entered her gaze and she stepped back from me.

I fought back a smile. I shouldn't be amused, but the over-the-topness of her behavior poked at my funny bone. If anyone deserved a fit of self-righteousness, it was me. It was because of her poor choice of a 'diva' that we were out money.

"How would Scrap This, or I, profit from some scheme between Belinda and Darlene? If Belinda and Darlene planned this, why would Darlene throw a fit in the middle of the store for God and scrapbookers to see?"

Leslie shoved the papers into her oversized Coach purse. "Now you're trying to talk your way out of this. It's not going to work. You, Belinda, and Darlene tried to conspire against me and got caught. I will get retribution for this."

"Ms. Amtower..." Cheryl's voice carried from the hallway. "Please come to my office."

Leslie evil-eyeballed me. "You just wait until this gets out."

I shrugged. "I'd be worried, except I made a screenshot of the original thread."

Leslie's eyes widened.

I grinned.

"You bring yours. I'll bring mine." Leslie stomped toward the back. "We'll see who comes out the winner."

I'd bring it all right.

People walked by the store, slowing down to peer into the large front window. No one took one step inside, unless they came by for a refund. The lookie-loos sped up if Cheryl, I, or Sierra caught their eye. I anticipated a little bit of a slow down since the news of Belinda's murder was splashed all on the front page of the newspaper, but not a total stop.

I thought customers would at least come in to snatch up an issue of *Making Legacies* featuring Belinda as the drama surrounding it could make it valuable. Instead, most returned their copy. They didn't want to support cheating.

The only good thing that came out of the conversation between Cheryl and Leslie was the rest of the copies were returned—almost forcibly—to the editor-in-chief. Grandma Cheryl didn't appreciate her granddaughter being accused of being in cahoots with Darlene and Belinda to ruin the magazine.

Darlene and Belinda, partners in crime. Or so it appeared. Belinda wasn't the brightest person in the world, and also very shy. It wasn't in her nature to do something that would bring a lot of heat and attention onto her. I truly believed she thought Darlene gave her those layouts which made it okay to submit. Why Belinda decided to submit was a question with no answer. Submitting layouts wasn't something Belinda did. She considered her layouts to be nothing more than layouts, and not work. Entering into contests and trying to get on design teams wasn't part of scrapbooking to Belinda.

She loved the hobby aspect of scrapbooking, not the business cutthroat part of it. It was why she didn't crop at the store. She didn't like her pages compared to anyone else's and had no desire of "improving" or making pages others would ooh and aah over. It was all for her and her mother.

Did Hazel convince her daughter to submit? If Hazel saw those pages Belinda "made," I could see her wanting her daughter to submit them—or doing it for her. Hazel and Eliza had turned one-upmanship into a lifestyle. It was *their* hobby. Hazel would want her daughter winning a title like "Life Artist Diva" before Darlene, especially when it was something her sister's child wanted so much.

If anyone was conspiring with Belinda it was Hazel. The back door buzzer hummed through the store.

"Sorry I'm late!" Marilyn called out.

"No problem. We're not really hopping here." I returned my attention to rearranging the Halloween product line as Sierra put all the decorations back up. At least it gave us something to do.

"I don't want Sierra late picking up the boys." Marilyn scrambled behind the counter to put away her stuff.

Sierra smiled at her and gave her a one-arm hug as she snagged her purse. "If they get into any trouble, I'll be able to blame you. Did the cat get out again?"

"I'll deal with anyone I have to. The cat remained in." Marilyn gathered up her hair and knotted it behind her neck. "I just couldn't pull myself together today. I've been dragging all morning."

I slid a glance over at Marilyn. The talk of Belinda's death likely brought back her husband's murder and the effect it had on her family. The Kanes had been slowly recovering, and trying to move on with their lives without having to leave the town they loved.

Grandma Cheryl stormed from the storage area and headed for the front door. Her cell phone clutched in her hand. "If she wasn't grieving..."

Darn it! I forgot to get rid of the signs. I flicked my gaze to the window. Thankfully, Hazel decided to end her spying attempt on the store. One, she wasn't good at it. And two, I don't know if I could hold Cheryl back from throttling the woman. But I had to try. Cheryl was headed on a woman hunt.

"I'm going with her." I pointed at my grandmother.

Marilyn nodded. "Hurry."

I raced outside and caught up with Cheryl. "Grandma, where are you going?"

She came to a full stop and spun around. "Young lady, you go back to the store right now."

"I wanted to make sure you're okay."

"I'm fine. I need you back in there managing things."

"Marilyn can handle it. You're upset." I placed a gentle hand on her arm. "I need to make sure you're okay.

Cheryl closed her eyes and muttered numbers under her breath. "I'm angry. That doesn't mean I need my hand held. Really, Faith, I will be fine. I can handle this issue."

"What issue?"

She said grieving woman, which meant Hazel so the problem had to do with Belinda's murder. Or rather Hazel's reaction to it.

"I really don't want you involved with this."

I linked my arm through my grandmother's. "We're family. Whatever is your problem is mine."

"Now you believe in that."

Heat skittered along my cheeks. I knew my grandmother was referring to the fact I refused to tell them what happened in Germany that caused me to run back home, withdraw from everyone, and push away a great guy.

"Is Hazel telling more people Belinda's death is our fault because Belinda came to the store for her necklace?"

Cheryl's face turned crimson.

Fear and shame flashed through me. My grandmother was going to have a heart attack because of my big mouth. "Grandma—" My voice trembled and tears filled my eyes.

Her expression softened. She patted my hand. "Honey, don't worry about me. My temper gets the best of me but never controls me. How in the world did you hear about that? I told Hazel Saturday night none of us would waltz over to the store in the middle of the night to get a silly necklace. If she called you..." She clenched her fists.

"No. No one called me except—" I changed direction of the conversation. Almost slipped and told her about my "meeting" with Darlene. "Karen England mentioned it last night at the police station..."

Cheryl's eyes narrowed and her grip on my hand tightened.

Drat! I hadn't meant to say that either. I walked out of one verbal slipup straight into another one. Well, might as well get the rest out. "I went to the store last night to try and find out why..."

"Faith! What were you thinking?" Cheryl screeched. People on the other side of the street paused and stared at us. Cheryl sent a glare at them and had them scattering.

I shook my head so hard, the rest of my body moved like a dog drying itself off. I hoped those people weren't thinking I just confessed to the murder.

"I wanted to know why Belinda showed up at the store the night she was murdered."

"You lied to us. You told me and Hope you wanted to take Steve dinner."

"I didn't lie." I swallowed the lump in my throat. "I had meant to take Steve his dinner. I did. The light turned red at the intersection and I ended up going to the store."

"Your car just turned that way." Cheryl narrowed her eyes. I knew she was wishing I was young enough to ground or turn over her knee.

I needed to get to the end of this story and give as little detail as possible. "Detective Roget came by and made me go to the police station. Karen was there and told him what Hazel was saying..."

Cheryl wasn't looking any happier.

"I called Steve for help. He came and got me out of there."

"Steve knows about your little shenanigans." The fire in her eyes fizzled a little.

I said the one thing I knew would get me out of any degree of hot water. "I kissed Steve to thank him for his help."

Cheryl grinned. "In that case, I think I'll take you with me. Maybe you can get some information out of Steve."

Now my grandmother was getting involved in the case? Oh, I didn't think so. I dragged my heels. "I think we should both go back to the store."

"Not until I find out if the police are taking what Hazel is saying seriously."

"I'm sure they're not. Steve would tell us."

Cheryl nodded once. "Absolutely. That's why we're going to his office right now and finding out for certain. No sense waiting and wondering all day."

With arms linked, Cheryl and I made our way to the courthouse. A slight chill to the wind had me wishing that I had brought my jacket. I remained quiet knowing if I complained Grandma would send me back to the store. There was no way I wanted her wrath unleashed on Steve without him having backup. The poor guy deserved some consideration after all he had done for us, for me.

The courthouse was a brisk walk from our store. It was located at what had once been the center of town before the growth spread in a rectangular instead of a square shape. Main Street was now at the far end of the town with the courthouse acting as the beginning. The police station sat at the very end of the street, one block over and at the end. What had once been a prime location for the heart of town was now an inconvenience. Most of the storefronts and homes on that side of Eden were vacant.

We passed by the small side road leading to the park and the "fancy" restaurant in town. It was a Victorian style house converted into a small romantic dining place serving crab cakes, shrimp, and steak. They also carried three different kinds of wine: red, white, and zinfandel. Their dessert was to die for in a figurative sense while some claimed the seafood they served was to die for in the literal sense. I didn't know either way because I hadn't had the occasion for a romantic dinner since I moved back home.

We went up the concrete steps leading to the old brick courthouse building. Metal detector archways, new additions to the building, greeted and said goodbye. I kind of understood wanting to make sure no one entered the building with firearms, but was curious why the county thought people would exit with them.

I guess a gun-toting criminal wouldn't be concerned about entering through the proper door.

Fortunately, the air outside cooled Grandma down before we got to the courthouse. She was still determined to get her information but no longer looked like she wanted to hurt someone. We headed straight for the receptionist area. How did Mrs. Alwright feel about being the first line of defense if someone entered the courthouse with evil intentions?

She was like the cruise director of the building, the one who directed people to the proper area. Filing a document, go to the left. Participating in a court hearing, bear to the right. Here to see a prosecutor, right side also. Need to pay a parking ticket. Wrong building, you needed the police department down the road and one block over.

Mrs. Dawn Alwright looked away from the computer screen. She smiled at me and Grandma, a quizzical look on her face. If it had just been me, she'd figure I came to visit Steve, but with Grandma tagging along she'd have no idea what the visit entailed.

"How can I help you ladies?"

Grandma hustled me down the hallway. "We're going back to visit Steve. No need to call ahead, it's a surprise."

Mrs. Alwright's eyebrows shot up.

I grinned at her and waved, nearly tripping when out of the corner of my eye I spotted Leslie Amtower in the section of the building reserved for filing petitions and requests. Had she decided to "bring it" using the court system?

We made it to Steve's office. With a soft knock that didn't qualify as even a tap, Grandma twisted the doorknob and stepped inside.

Steve nodded at Grandma. He didn't look surprised. I had a feeling Mrs. Alwright sent him a warning message.

I took a look around Steve's office. Still disorganized in a mad scientist kind of way, much unlike his house which was so orderly it caused me anxiety issues. I noticed a few new additions to his toy collection. Along with his paddle ball and the handheld video game there was a Rubik's cube and an Etch-a-Sketch. I stared at it. I wondered if layouts could be designed on it, like a primitive tablet.

Grandma Cheryl drew in a deep breath. What did she see? I knew that sound. It was her way of voicing disappointment and horror at a poor choice. I followed her gaze.

I saw what brought about the shock, Steve's collection of assorted no-need for refrigeration microwavable dinners. I knew the microwave wouldn't bother Cheryl, but knowing the man survived on prepared food when she and Hope had an open door policy for him to join us for dinner would.

Steve caught my eye. I jerked my head a couple of times in the direction of his food of choice.

He went with the smart choice and picked his own topic of conversation.

"To what do I owe the pleasure of this visit?" He ended the question with a bright, welcoming smile as he shoved a folder into his desk drawer.

The man was good. I doubted he really appreciated our interruption but he played it off and looked happy to see us. I smiled back.

"Do the police believe the nonsense Hazel is saying?" Grandma asked.

"I don't know the police's thoughts on any matter." Steve's expression and tone remained pleasant.

"Don't you sass me, young man." She scowled at him. "You know exactly what I mean. Do the police really think the store had anything to do with Belinda's murder? That we sent her there Saturday night?"

"I'm not at liberty to say." Steve leaned back in his chair.

I wasn't sure if he did it out of habit or if he was trying to put a little more distance between him and Grandma.

"Not at liberty." Cheryl slapped her hands onto Steve's desk, bracing herself, she leaned forward.

I swear if Cheryl had the capability of breathing fire, she'd have done it right then and there. Steve would've been a pile of smoldering ashes. To think I was finally ready to admit I had a thing for the guy. My grandmothers adored Steve, but they loved me. If protecting me meant getting someone, even Steve, in trouble they'd do it. I felt bad for him. I saw the conflict on his face. He wanted to relieve Grandma's concerns but couldn't. Poor guy. He had no idea what he was getting into all those years ago when he agreed to play knight-in-shining armor.

"She's trying to implicate Faith in the murder and you can't help us." Tears filled Cheryl's voice.

Steve cringed.

Implicate me? Hazel was pointing the finger at me? Not for long. I'd dig up the proof to show Hazel the real murderer. "Grandma, the accusation won't go anywhere."

"You never know." Cheryl dropped into a seat in front of Steve's desk.

True. I'd been in a similar situation before, not that Grandma knew about it, but in the end justice prevailed and I believed it would this time also. Besides, Steve went with me to the store so I had a pretty good witness for my side.

"Grandma, Hazel is looking for someone to blame so she doesn't blame herself."

Both Grandma and Steve stared at me. I couldn't read Steve's expression for a change but Grandma looked worried and intrigued by my words. I could almost see the words floating in her head, "Does my granddaughter actually think Hazel killed her own daughter?"

I rushed into my explanation. "If Hazel kept fussing about the necklace, Belinda went to the store to calm her mother down."

"We've never worked that late," Cheryl said.

Good point. "Maybe Belinda decided to sneak in and get it. Make it look like Darlene was responsible and get her in trouble. Darlene had embarrassed her by calling her out in front of all those customers."

"It's possible." Cheryl tapped her chin, the anger and upset slowly draining from her.

Steve studied me. It unnerved me a little. I really wished I could read his thoughts right now.

"I don't know the reason Belinda showed up," I said. "It's all a guess. But what I'm sure of is Hazel feels responsible for her daughter's death and needs to shift it to someone else."

"It's not fair of her to blame you or the store."

I placed a hand on Grandma's arm. "I know, Grandma. And I don't like being accused of a crime, especially murder, but this time I'll forgive it. She's grieving. She's just lost her whole world and is trying to make some sort of sense of the senseless."

Grandma stood and hugged me. "You're such a good girl. I'm so proud of you."

I returned her hug.

"I'll get back to the store." Grandma winked at me and nudged me toward Steve. "Why don't you visit for a while? Maybe you and Steve can go out for a late lunch."

Relief flowed through me. All was right with the world. Grandma had returned to matchmaker and no longer considered Steve an adversary. I wasn't quite sure how Steve felt about the major personality shifts Grandma showed. He looked shocked, with a little bit of miff mixed in.

We did barge in and interrupt his work day. I didn't appreciate when anyone did that to me and I wasn't trying to prosecute criminals. We very well could have heard something we shouldn't have.

Once Grandma practically skipped out the door, I turned to Steve and crossed my heart. "I promise I'll never show up unannounced again with a raging Grandma."

"This time?" Steve asked.

Huh? I blinked a few times. Instead of responding, I just stared at Steve.

He leaned back in his chair, eyes narrowing. "You said this time you'll forgive it. I'm wondering what you meant."

Oh scrap! Had I said 'this time?'

Why in the world did Steve have to really listen to what I said and remember it? Most guys had selective hearing. Had Grandma picked up on it? If she did, what did she think I meant, that I had been accused of murder before or I'd forgive Hazel for accusing me this one time but wouldn't the next?

Sweat broke out on my forehead. "I mean I hate people talking smack about me. I really do. Who likes it? Especially being accused of murdering a person. Really, me? Killing a person? How insulting."

My rambling wasn't achieving the affect I wanted. Steve looked more suspicious. Reel it in, girl. Get to your point and quick.

First, I had to find one. Hazel. Grieving mother. Shifting blame. Got it.

I drew in a breath. "I know it's not nice but I'll forgive Hazel this time. Once." I held up my index finger to emphasize my point. "The next time she starts saying stuff, I'll do something about it."

The suspicion left, only to be replaced by concern. "What do you plan on doing?"

I shrugged, deciding to go with the absolute truth for this answer. "I have no idea. But I'll think of something."

Steve groaned. "Please don't. Let the police do their job. The investigation will prove who the murderer is. Stay out of it."

"You want me to keep quiet while I'm being accused of murder?"

"No one would ever believe that about you."

Little did he know, some people had at one time, and Adam was much less trustworthy than Hazel.

"Right." I crossed my arms and glared at him. "I have a name for you. Michael Kane."

Steve rubbed his eyes. "No one thought you killed Michael. Detective Roget just thought you were aiding and abetting Marilyn."

"So, there's no reason for me to be upset about the police thinking I'm conspiring with someone. As long as they don't believe I killed someone I should just let it go. No one else would mind the police thinking they're involved in a felony."

"Come on, Faith. You know the detective had good reason for thinking that."

I crossed my arms and glared at him, no longer having to fake indignation. "So the reason you wouldn't answer Grandma is because you believe Hazel. I have something to do with Belinda being there."

Steve shot to his feet. "Don't be ridiculous. I don't think you're involved in Belinda's murder."

"You don't. But how about others?"

"How in the world did we get into this argument?" Steve walked around the desk.

"Because you think Ted should blame me."

"Why do you do this?" Steve sat on the edge of the desk.

Me? What was I doing? He was the one who said Ted had every right to think I conspired with Marilyn in committing a crime Marilyn didn't even commit.

Ted had been wrong on so many levels. You'd think Steve would be angry on my behalf, not take Ted's side in the matter, especially since Steve didn't really like Ted.

"I'm not doing anything. You are. You said Ted had a good reason for thinking I was involved in the murder."

"I didn't turn this into a fight. You did." Steve drummed his fingers on the desktop. "I said Detective Roget didn't blame you for Kane's murder. The man only thought you might have been helping Marilyn because—"

"Because I'm that type of person."

"You're doing it again. Why do you want to insist I think the worst of you?" Steve stood and went back to his office chair, probably preferring some sort of physical barrier between me and him. "Can you honestly say you didn't do anything to make Roget think you might have been helping Marilyn out? Finding out who killed Kane was the man's job."

I didn't want Steve to think the worst of me. Nor did I want him thinking I thought he thought the worst of me. Was I trying to recreate an emotional distance between Steve and me? I had decided to give this relationship a try. But, I had to admit I was doing my best to prove to myself I couldn't trust Steve.

Steve's shoulders slumped forward.

My heart ached for him. He had always been my friend and helped me and my grandmothers. If I wanted space, he gave me space. If I needed some attention and adoration, he happily offered it. Steve allowed me to establish the boundaries in our relationship and backed up, and moved forward, every time the whim struck me and I moved the line.

The guy didn't deserve it. I didn't think I deserved him, but for some reason he was willing to give his all for me even when I acted like I wanted none of him. I never hated Adam so much as I did now. I couldn't allow him to continue controlling my life.

I walked behind his chair and placed my hands on Steve's shoulders. I kneaded the tense muscles. "I'm sorry. I don't know why I'm picking a fight with you. I just seem to be at war with everyone lately. Hazel. Darlene. Leslie Amtower. Our customers. No one is happy with what happened on Saturday and they blame us. I guess I just wanted something to rage against."

"I wish you'd pick someone else."

"I have some options in mind." Primarily Darlene.

"I was joking. Please don't." Steve caught my hands and tugged me around. "This will all work itself out. Don't go looking for trouble."

"So you think I'm looking for trouble." I sat on his lap.

Steve groaned and dropped his head onto my shoulder.

I cringed. There I went again. "Sorry. Bad habit. I'll work on breaking it."

"I'm not a bad guy, Faith." His words whispered along my neck.

A shiver heated my blood and I wished with all my being Steve had some bad boy in him and wanted to act on it. Right then and there. "I know. I had some bad experiences in the past and I guess I'm still working through them."

"I figured that."

Yeah, I guess I wasn't so good at hiding it like I thought. "I'm sorry I hurt you."

"I'm an understanding guy." Steve smiled at me, his hands resting on my waist.

"I'm one lucky girl." I planted a quick kiss on Steve's lips.

"We're both lucky."

Since I knew we wouldn't be that lucky right now, I needed to get out of there and back to work. Maybe we could work on our luck tonight. I slid off his lap. "See you tonight? I'll make us dinner."

"I hope so." Steve's gaze devoured me. "A lot of it will depend on how the case turns."

"Want me to help you?" I couldn't resist asking.

Steve, on the other hand, didn't find any amusement in my sassiness. "No."

"Still afraid I'm looking for trouble?" I kept my tone light, hoping Steve knew I wasn't getting riled up again. I was curious about his seriousness.

"Not looking so much as finding it, picking it up, and carrying it home." Steve grabbed hold of my hand. I felt him trembling. "Promise me you won't find a way into this mess."

I wanted to tell him off but the fear lurking in the depths of his brown eyes made me stop. I leaned into him, hugging him for all I was worth. Steve knew something. He had been holding back—for our own good.

It scared me.

THIRTEEN

I half-heartedly waved goodbye to Mrs. Alwright as I walked under the archway and proved I wasn't exiting the courthouse armed and dangerous. I hoped Cheryl planned on Steve and me having a long lunch so she headed back to Scrap This. Catching me moping my way back to work wouldn't go over very well. She'd probably think I was pouting about being told to mind my business about the murder, rather than worried about what Steve withheld from us.

Feet shuffled behind me. Really close behind me. I gazed over my right shoulder. Hazel scurried over to the wall and flattened her back against it. The black and gold leopard print outfit, with prowling cheetah embroidered across her chest, stood out from the white wall Hazel tried melding herself into.

Did she have an outfit to go with every theme of her life? Shaking my head, I continued on my meandering stroll back to the store. I heard Hazel plodding along behind me.

The scent of fried chicken wafted toward me, rumbling my stomach. I didn't bring anything from home for lunch. The chicken smelled good. I felt a little like I was "cheating" on Dianne by going somewhere else for lunch but my stomach wanted chicken and nothing else would do.

I looked both ways and jogged across the street toward Beulah's. Why Aaron decided to name his small diner where frying was the theme of his food Beulah's no one knew as Aaron never offered an explanation beyond "I just like it."

A horn honked. I cast another look over my shoulder.

Hazel squatted in the middle of the street, presumably so I didn't spot her. Quickly, I turned my gaze forward so she'd get out of the middle of the road.

I pulled open the door to Beulah's, debating for a minute if I should hold it open for Hazel. Why ruin her fun. The door clanged shut behind me.

Aaron wiped his hands on his red and white checkered apron. "What will it be?"

"The two-piece special." I didn't know why Aaron asked.

Every day there was one item on the menu, the special. Today, customers could order the two-piece or the four-piece fried chicken special which included green beans with bacon, French fries and a biscuit made using his mother's county fair winning recipe. If you were particular about getting dark or white meat, you needed to go with the four-piece meal so you'd get two of each type. Aaron didn't accept "special orders" on his specials.

"Just one?" Aaron tilted his head toward the window.

Hazel was almost plastered to the window in her quest to spy.

I needed to nip this in the bud, might as well bring a peace offering when I did it. "Give me two."

"She's latching on to you now that Belinda's gone?" Aaron plopped a heaping serving of mashed potatoes into two foam to-go containers.

"I think she's keeping tabs on me."

"Like I said, she latched on to you." Aaron placed the chicken into the container. "That girl of hers never got much of a break from her mama. I don't think Belinda could ever take a step without her mama demanding to know about it."

"They were close. Nothing wrong with a loving mother-daughter relationship."

"If that's what it was." Aaron placed the meals into a plastic bag and held the handles out to me. "Good luck with it and all. If I was you, I'd be carrying a pair of scissors with me to cut the cord Hazel wants to wrap around you. She needs to attach her life to someone since she done lost Belinda."

"She's got Darlene." I looped the handle onto my arm.

Aaron coughed out a laugh. "Darling, Eliza already has dibs on that girl."

"Hazel isn't following me around because I'm a possible replacement." I pulled out her lunch.

"Then I'd be more worried. Her man didn't just run because of the crazy between the two sisters. Hazel has enough crazy she can throw some your way and still have more than enough to aim at her sister."

I decided to take Aaron's advice and put an end to Hazel's undercover operation. I stepped out the door.

Hazel spun around and started down the street.

"Don't you want your lunch?" I called out.

Hazel froze in mid-motion.

I wondered how long she could balance herself on one foot. She wobbled after a few seconds. Since I didn't want to be responsible for her falling over and breaking a hip or something, I went over and steadied her.

"Hazel, I can see you. I know you're following me."

Hazel tugged away. "I have no idea what you're talking about."

"You started tailing me when I left the courthouse."

"Did not." Hazel crossed her arms over her massive chest. "I just wanted to get lunch."

"Then why didn't you go inside?"

Hazel bit her lip as her eyes scrunched up.

Yeah, that's what I thought.

"You were in there. I will not step foot in a place where you're at."

"Because..."

"You know something about my daughter's murder. Don't think I'm not on to you, missy." Hazel snatched the container from my hand and fled in the opposite direction of Scrap This.

I guess she wasn't too mad as she had no trouble taking a free lunch bought by me.

A car rolled to a stop.

"Faith, is everything all right?" Grandma Hope leaned toward the passenger side window.

"Yeah." I opened the door and climbed inside.

"Was that Hazel running away?"

I didn't want to lie to my grandmother but also didn't want to tell her the entire truth. One, I didn't want her worrying. Two, I didn't want Hope to take off after Hazel. Even the quiet ones got their dander up on occasion.

"She didn't want to talk to me."

Hope's eyes became slits. "You're not questioning her about Belinda's murder."

"Of course not. I saw her standing outside Beulah's and bought her a special."

Hope didn't comment. She started driving toward the store. Her silence said everything. She knew I had been up to something and it involved Hazel...and more aggravating I wasn't going to tell her.

When we got back to Scrap This, I scurried into the break room and devoured my lunch. I made sure to keep my mouth full so Hope and Cheryl refrained from asking me any questions. Every grandma knew a grandchild shouldn't talk with food in their mouth.

Sierra bounded into the break room. She gaped at my eating technique of shoving so much food into my mouth I rivaled a chipmunk.

"You're going to choke." Sierra walked over to the sink and got a glass of tap water. She placed it in front of me.

My heart warmed at the gesture. Maybe she was thawing toward me.

Sierra sat down across from me. "I have the perfect idea for a class."

I motioned with my hand to go on as I couldn't speak.

"A three-dimensional Halloween card that can be attached to trick-or-treat bags." She grinned.

I swallowed. "Halloween is in two weeks. It's kind of late."

"That's plenty of time. You know some of our regulars would love adding a crafty touch to their treats. If we can get a sample up by tomorrow and have the class this weekend or beginning of next week, a lot of scrappers would take it."

And by "we" Sierra meant "me" as she wasn't a stamper and had no interest in adding stamping to her scrapbooking repertoire.

Sierra offered an olive branch, the least I could do was hand one back. One afternoon of pulling supplies and creating some samples wasn't going to put us in a bind. What could it hurt?

"Okay. I'll get right on it."

"Great. I'll tell Hope and Cheryl you love the idea and will be running with it."

I tossed the remainder of my lunch. I had work to do and my hastily devoured food sat like a rock in my stomach. I went to the sink and scrubbed my hands good to make sure no chicken grease remained. There was no way I'd leave my fingerprints on the merchandise.

I grabbed a small basket to place the items I needed into. Maybe if I demonstrated a couple of techniques and gave them choices it would work. Classes where we taught a foundation technique, giving some ideas on how the basic idea could be switched up, always filled up fast.

After grabbing white cardstock, I chose an easy to color Halloween stamp. I picked one of a cartoon-like haunted house. The crafter had the option of using an X-acto knife to cut open the doors and windows and placing a sticker or other stamped image in it.

Next, I pulled out the alcohol-based markers I wanted to use. I loved these markers; the blending capabilities added a realistic touch to the coloring. It reminded me of how I loved coloring as a child.

I set everything up at one of the crop tables and got to work. The first time I stamped the image it came out a little fuzzy so I tried again. And again. Ugh. This was one of the problems I had with larger stamps, getting the pressure even. I stood and took great care in pressing down then lifting the stamp.

Perfect. I wanted to cheer; instead I sat down as we had a customer in the store. I didn't want them thinking it was unusual for me to stamp an image correctly. It wouldn't help convince people to take the class.

The bell jingled and jangled. I colored and colored. I was in the groove and having fun. There was nothing like coloring and scrapbooking to relax me.

A shadow loomed over me. "You probably know by now, but Detective Roget believes I killed Belinda," the person on top of my I-do-not-want-to-see list said.

Monday was getting worse. First the little argument with Leslie Amtower, then Hazel upsetting my grandmother and her poorly conducted stalking attempt, and now Darlene's visit. The only way it could possibly be even more of a trial was if Belinda decided to haunt the place.

I made a sound, a cross between how-interesting and well-duh.

Darlene nudged my arm. "Are you listening?"

The marker jerked across the cardstock. I stared down at the stamped image I had been carefully coloring for the last hour.

Darlene tsked. "I'm not so sure that works. If you wanted it to look like lightning, I'd have tried a gray mixed with silver. It would work better with the background color you're using."

The woman sure did live in a world of her own.

I sighed and studied the card front. This was a Halloween image so maybe I could make the dark slash of orange work for me.

"I'm thinking tonight after the store closes we can work on our plan."

Our plan? Since when did we have a plan? Or even agreed to work together. A lack of an answer wasn't an agreement.

"There is no we."

Darlene drew back and frowned. "Excuse me?"

Were those words that hard to understand, or was Darlene baffled by people not following her orders? Maybe Oliver White needed to give Darlene a class about word usage.

I don't know what type of people she usually hung out with, but it certainly wasn't anyone with a backbone.

"I'm not helping you." I slammed the stamp onto the sheet of paper, pretending I was tattooing Darlene. Something about the woman brought out my violent side. Not a fact I was proud of, and it gave me another good reason to stay away from her. The first being she already left me to deal with a firing squad on my own once. No way would I set myself up for a second time.

This time, she was on her own. She could sit in a small room pondering what everyone was telling her family, and explain herself to Detective Roget.

"What?" Darlene blinked a few times.

I stared at her with wide eyes. I didn't think I could get any clearer than that. "There's is no plan for us to work on. I'm not getting involved in your mess."

"My mess?" Darlene rested a hand against her heart. "How in the world did this become only my problem?"

"Umm...because the police think you did it. Not me."

"It happened at your store."

"Still not my business." I lifted up the stamp. Surprisingly, the image came out very nice. Maybe the trick was thinking about using the stamp to decorate Darlene.

"You helped Marilyn solve her husband's murder."

I did. But, I actually liked Marilyn and in a way had kind of gotten her onto the police's radar. Darlene had pushed, shoved, and kicked to get herself on the police's most likely suspect list.

"I'm not getting involved." I sorted through my markers. Same color scheme, or did I want to try a different one?

"I need help. I can't believe you'd turn your back on a customer."

"My job is to help customers learn how to scrapbook and find supplies they need for their pages, not solve murders. Besides, look how well it worked out for me last time."

I decided to work on the house and save the sky for after Darlene left.

"Seemed to work out well. Marilyn was freed and the real murderer went to jail. You have a knack for solving crimes." Darlene beamed at me like a proud mama when their baby first rolled over.

Compliments would get her nowhere. I trusted her as much as I did the Hooligans. Heck, I trusted the Hooligans more than I did her. I knew for certain they'd be up to no good and would create a disaster. Darlene couldn't be counted on for good or evil. There was something quite lovely about predictability even if it was for behaving badly.

"I lucked out, and as the saying goes luck does run out." No way would I waste any of my remaining luck on Darlene.

Darlene made a shooing motion with her hand, brushing away my words. "Stop being so modest. You have legal experience and are quite adept with using it. Everyone knows it wasn't luck but keen insight."

I snorted. Right. Tell that to all the people I suspected before I discovered the real truth.

"I won't leave until I get an answer. I see a nice spot over by the paper racks where I can sit."

"No." A short and sweet answer left little room for argument or negotiation.

"Why?"

"No is a complete sentence. I don't have to give you a reason."

"Yes you do."

"No I don't." I uncapped another marker and started shading the lighter blue into the sky.

Darlene huffed out a disgusted breath.

"I don't care if you don't like my answer."

"It's not about that. I can't believe your Halloween card has a blue sky. Halloween is a dark, mysterious time. I think blending purple into the medium blue you chose would create the proper mood."

Black would create my proper mood. "You make your own card and I'll make mine."

"Great idea." Darlene dropped her purse onto a vacant chair across from me. "I'll just go pull some of the supplies I'll need."

I refrained from beating my head on the crop table. I didn't want to end up with ink on my forehead or a bigger headache than I already had. A headache who returned to the table with three markers and a haunted house stamp.

Darlene plopped herself down in the chair and pulled a blank card from the stack in front of me. "I'll just use your black ink pad rather than getting another. No sense in wasting money."

Of course not.

Darlene placed the stamp image onto an acrylic block then pressed the stamp image carefully into the ink. With care, she lined up the stamp and pushed down. Slowly, she lifted the stamp and revealed a clean, precise image on her first attempt.

I was impressed, not sarcastically either. Though, she should've bought the stamp first. Fortunately from her broad smile, I could tell she liked the image and the way she twisted and turned the card let me know it got her creative juices going.

She uncapped a navy blue marker.

"For an unofficial cropping, stamping session, you need to purchase the products first."

Darlene frowned. "These are samples for the store which you requested. Teachers don't pay for their supplies..."

"Depending on the class, teachers either get a discount or the product for free." The free products were given when a company sent us free items to use to get an interest in their line. We didn't allow teachers free reign over items in the store, especially a stamp that retailed at a little over ten dollars.

"Well then I should get the teacher discount. You did ask me to create a card."

I did tell her to make her own, but it wasn't because I wanted another sample. I wanted her to leave me alone. Instead of getting my wish, I had her help which might cost me a favor unless I gave her the stamp. Since I got personal items at cost, it would be cheaper for me to pay for the stamp and gift it to Darlene.

Though the thought of giving Darlene a gift made me want to shudder. She was the type of woman who made a worse friend than she did an enemy.

I sighed dramatically so she'd get that I was annoyed. "Since this misunderstanding is my fault..."

Darlene made a noise of agreement.

"I'll let you have the stamp..."

"And the markers."

I frowned. These were the Copic markers. Expensive. "Don't you have the full set?"

"But these would be for teaching only, not personal use."

I tallied up the amount in my head. Still less expensive than owing Darlene a favor, and I had her occupied with something other than me helping her solve a crime. "And those three markers."

"Good. While we're working, I can tell you my plan on getting some evidence from Belinda's house."

I shook my head. "Don't tell me. I'm not good at keeping secrets."

Darlene rolled her eyes. "Of course you are. No one knows anything about your time out of Eden. Not one teeny, tiny hint of the scandal that forced you back home."

"What makes you think I have a scandal?" I dropped the blue marker then wiped my hands on my jeans, hoping Darlene didn't see the nervous gesture.

"You're a woman. You don't like to talk about yourself." Darlene capped the marker and placed it on the table.

I appreciated the care Darlene treated the supplies with. Some croppers didn't treat the store's shared supplies as well as their own, or maybe it was the way they treated the stuff they owned and why they decided not to buy the more expensive brands or items and just used ours.

"Regardless of how much you admire my ability to keep quiet," I said. "I'd rather not know your plans."

Ted had a way of sneaking up on me and figuring out when I got the urge to investigate. I didn't want to tell him what Darlene planned. While I wasn't fond of the woman, tattling on her didn't seem right. If she wanted to clear her name, which I couldn't blame her for trying, who was I to stop her.

The second the hand on the clock hit closing time, I raced toward the door. I had never wanted a work day to end so badly. The bell jingled and Annette slipped into the store with her small bundle of joy attached to her.

No! Not today.

I hadn't received a call from Steve saying he couldn't stop by so I figured we were a go for tonight. I really wanted to show him I wanted to move our relationship to the next level and make a nice dinner and not just throw something together.

Technically, we were closed and I could ask Annette to leave, but we needed all the customers we could get and she had ventured out with her two-month-old son. The woman had to be desperate for scrapbooking supplies if she felt it worth the effort to bundle up a baby, put him into a car seat, then take the baby out of the car and strap the baby to herself. The woman deserved consideration for all the work.

I locked the door behind Annette and closed the blinds, in case someone walked by. Last thing I needed was wails of showing favoritism to other customers.

"What can I help you find?"

"Nothing." Annette held tight to the straps around her shoulder. The baby slept contently against his mother. "I need to speak with you."

"Okay." I wanted to ask her if it could wait until morning but she was already here. Besides, I'd just obsess about it all night so might as well find out now so I could at least obsess about what she actually said rather than what I thought she wanted to say. More productive.

"I'd have come by earlier but needed to say this in private." She glanced around the store. "We are here alone. Right?"

I'd have been a little concerned she had nefarious plans except Annette had a child attached to her. One didn't attack a person when they had their beloved baby practically in their arms.

"Yes. My grandmothers headed out about an hour ago. It's been kind of slow so no need for the three of us to stay here."

"That's what I thought." Annette sighed. "I really shouldn't be telling you this. It's just not fair what they're going around saying. No one should be gossiped about."

My interest peaked. "They?"

"Leslie Amtower and Hazel. That Leslie woman is trying really hard to show the store, you in particular, conspired with Belinda to get her to win the contest. She's saying Belinda was told by someone she trusted it was okay to submit those layouts as hers. Hazel is backing up Ms. Amtower. Hazel says there is no way her daughter would've done anything underhanded. Someone in the know convinced Belinda it was okay."

"Why would I do that? Darlene shops at the store and has more of an association with it than Belinda. It makes no sense I'd tell Belinda to submit Darlene's layouts under her name."

Annette shrugged. "Sometimes people don't care if things make sense. Just that it makes a plausible story. The reason they gave is you don't like Darlene."

That was it? The major proof of my involvement was I didn't like Darlene. Most of the town didn't like Darlene, including Hazel and Belinda. "How did you come about this information?"

Annette blushed. "An attorney was talking a little too loud in the cafeteria where I work. I feel bad about this. In a way I'm gossiping but I don't think people should try and set someone up for a crime."

It was nice Annette believed me innocent of wrongdoing. "Thanks for letting me know. But, if this could get you into trouble, why are you telling me?"

Annette rubbed the baby's back and planted a soft kiss on the nearly bald head. "You and your grandmothers have been nice to me."

I needed to get home. I had some preparing to do. Make dinner. Slip into a cute dress. Make an intentional effort for Steve.

The baby stirred, snuggling closer to his mommy and letting out a sound of contentment. Annette cradled the baby and rocked him gently. The serene look in her eyes filled my heart with longing. It was so sweet. So filled with love, I envied her.

Maybe one day. Hopefulness bloomed in my heart. If I was thinking about babies, it meant I was thinking about a long-term relationship. Tonight could be the start of having a new life plan, one that included having a love in my life.

FOURTEEN

After Annette left, I scoped the store for anything left behind or placed where it didn't belong. I found a pack of stickers placed in a slot with patterned paper. Blue cardstock shoved into a space for red cardstock. I wrinkled my nose and delicately picked up a used diaper left in the corner of the store near the hallway.

I guess I should be happy it was only a wet diaper. We did have a bathroom with a changing table. No idea why the person decided using the floor was much better, or how Sierra didn't spot them.

Wait a minute. I tossed the diaper then went over to the stamps. Any stamps with an image of a person were arranged in battle field formation. A cheerful little girl on a swing looked like she was about to take out a woman walking a poodle. A boy on a bicycle was "driving over" a witch. Yep, just as I suspected, the Hooligans came in to visit their mother and decided a practical joke was in order.

I grinned when I spotted the stuffed green blob with eyes and a felt tongue sticking out from protruding felt teeth. Looks like one of the little monsters, left their little monster behind. If they wanted their creature, they'd have to come back and claim it. Maybe I'd return the wet diaper also.

I dropped the creature, which was kind of cute in an ugly dog cute kind of way, into the lost and found basket. The necklace and bracelet I placed in there yesterday glittered at me. I sat down at the computer and started typing a brief message before I turned everything off.

Found: One necklace and one bracelet. Please contact Faith Hunter about the items.

Leaning back, I studied the message. Too brief.

I picked up the necklace and examined it. The silver clasp was broken. The silver beaded chain was welded to a swirly heart with diamond like gems embedded in the heart. Dangling inside the heart was a larger stone. It looked like the necklace had been ripped off from someone's neck.

I sucked in a breath. What if this was the necklace Belinda came to retrieve? If those gems were real diamonds, I'd want it back as soon as possible. I turned the necklace over. The sterling heart wasn't large enough for any engraving.

I held it in my hand. Should I call Ted and tell him about my discovery? What if it hadn't been Belinda's? This necklace would become evidence and who knew when the owner would get it back.

I closed my eyes and pictured Belinda. The diva necklace had been prominently displayed. I couldn't "see" another piece of jewelry on her. Why would she hide it?

The diva necklace hadn't been broken when Darlene got a hold of it. If Belinda had worn both, why would one break and not the other. How would Darlene know which clasp to undo if Belinda had both on?

My cell phone rang. Steve's ring tone.

I snagged it and glanced at the clock. I needed to get out of here. I saved the message, logging off as I tucked the phone against my chin and shoulder.

"I'll be home in a few minutes. Anything in particular you'd like for dinner?"

"I can't make it," Steve said in a flat voice.

"Oh." I heard my disappointment in the one syllable. I hated guilt trips so I didn't want to give one. "Want me to bring you something by? A man can't live on microwavable dinners alone."

"No."

I waited for an elaboration. It took me a few minutes before it got through my thick skull one wasn't coming. "Okay. I hope you don't have to work too late. I'm going to stay in and watch a movie. You can come over when you get done."

"I can't."

"I don't mind if it's late." I added some flirtation into my voice. You'd think after all these months of him wanting to liven up our relationship I wouldn't have to work so hard.

"I'm sorry I'm disappointing you. But tonight is not a good idea."

"Maybe some other time."

"I've got to go."

I stared at the phone. Did I just get the brush-off? From Steve?

Fine. Who needed him to have a good evening anyway? I'd pick up some take-out and check out some movies from the library. This way, if I did allow my pout to get the better of me, I wouldn't have wasted money on rentals.

I finished closing and went to my car. Muttering to myself, I made my way to the library. I took the first parking spot and raced into the large building, scurrying between a mom and young child who were exiting. The mother huffed and let out a small giggle when I almost collided into one of the pillars in front of the library.

"Better hurry," a deep voice by the magazines said.

I glanced over.

Leonard's face was half-hidden behind a photography magazine.

"Are you sure you don't want to copy the article?" Oliver tried to loom over the man.

"I'm sure." Leonard smiled and settled back into the chair.

Holding back a grin, I headed for the movies. Oliver locked up tight at eight. He didn't believe in allowing patrons a few extra moments of browsing.

"I'm not staying open for you either," Oliver's voice followed me.

"I know. I know."

The library opened at nine in the morning and closed at eight at night on the weekdays. Precisely. I had fifteen minutes to find some movies and some books. I wanted to know a little more about the publishing side of the scrapbooking world and hoped there might be something useful in the stacks.

I grabbed two movies from the "New" section, then hurried back to the non-fiction books.

I knew where the scrapbooking books were located. I hoped anything dealing with scrapbooking was located there and not in business or publishing as I didn't know where I'd find them. The only browsing I did in the library were in the sections I preferred, I wasn't too eclectic in my reading tastes. I stuck to scrapbooking, crafts, romance, and mysteries.

It might be good to branch out into business. My grandmothers had already hinted they might take more of a "back seat" approach to running Scrap This and I needed to learn how to run the store. I might also brush up on managing employees as my techniques failed with Sierra.

Of course, thinking an employee's spouse was a murderer wasn't a topic likely covered in a business book.

I scanned the titles in the scrapbooking section. Technique books but nothing on the industry side of scrapbooking. I plucked a book about digital scrapbooking I had intended to buy off the shelf.

More money for scrappy goodies.

"The library closes in ten minutes." Oliver stood at the end of the row and tapped his watch. "You should bring your selections to the desk."

"Where would I find a book about the publishing industry? Particularly on putting together a magazine for a hobby."

Oliver tilted his head. "Is Scrap This going to be putting out its own idea book?"

An intriguing idea I'd pass on to my grandmothers. An eBook might be doable, or publishing customer layouts on the store website. Kind of have our own design team.

"No. I'm just thinking it might be good to figure out one of the other sides."

"The other side of what?" Oliver crossed his arms.

"Of the industry. We have the memory preservists, the artists, business owners who sell supplies, and the publishing side of scrapbooking."

"You're not interested in venturing into the publishing area but still want to learn about it."

I smiled. "Sure. It's always good to learn."

"This learning wouldn't have anything to do with Belinda's murder?" Oliver's eyes narrowed.

Heat scorched my cheeks. Caught. Why did he care anyway? I wasn't going to admit or deny anything. "Do you have anything about it?"

Oliver closed his eyes and tapped the side of his head with his index finger. He raised his finger, shook his head, then returned to tapping his forehead.

The tick tocking echoed in the room. Was Oliver deliberately withholding information so I couldn't get what I wanted? Stop being ridiculous. Why would Oliver care about what I wanted to read? As long as it didn't make him stay open later.

Oliver snapped his fingers. "I've thought of a few titles that might be useful."

"Great."

Oliver weaved through the stacks, pausing long enough to snag a book from the shelf, before moving on to the next section. We had gone through the 800's, 700's, and 600's at speed reserved for the 100-yard dash. When we reached the 300's, my cell phone sang about the acknowledgment of one's sexiness.

Oliver halted. Slowly, he turned and glared at me.

Juggling my phone, I hit the answer button. "Hi."

My greeting came out louder than intended as I still struggled with getting control over my gymnastic performing breath.

"We are done." Oliver stalked over to the checkout desk.

"What's going on?" Steve asked.

He must have heard Oliver's annoyed tone. "Talking loudly in the library. I came by to check out some chick-flicks. Since my date dumped me."

"Sorry." Steve sounded apologetic. "I just got caught up with something at work. I can't walk away from it and it had to be done tonight."

"I understand. Is it about the case? Belinda's murder."

Oliver slowly scanned the checkout codes on the books he selected for me.

"You know I can't answer that."

I motioned for Oliver to hurry up. He glared at my hand not holding the cell. Oops. Forgot about the movies. I placed them on the counter. I did know Steve couldn't answer my question but I couldn't not ask.

"Hey, if you're done..."

"I'm wiped out, Faith. I won't make good company tonight."

I heard the weariness in his voice. I wanted to push it, but would hate it if my wishes weren't respected.

"I'm going to stop and get some take-out. I'd be happy to grab you something too."

"I already ate. Thanks anyway."

I clicked off the call and dropped the cell into my purse. I snatched the books from the counter. "Thanks."

"The books are due in three weeks and the movies two days."

"I know."

"And the library closes at eight. Next time, come earlier if you have a large request of items needed." He shot a glare toward the magazines. "Have you made your final choices?"

"Still have one minute." Leonard fluttered the pages of the magazine.

I ignored Oliver and gave Leonard a jaunty wave goodbye as I left. Oliver really needed to read a book about customer service. I unlocked the car and got inside. Twisting, I placed the materials on the passenger seat. A bright orange cover caught my eye. I pulled it from the stack.

The Complete Idiot's Guide to Private Investigating. Thanks a lot Oliver. I tossed it on top of the other books then slowly backed out.

I followed every speed limit and sign to a tee. There was no way I wanted to get pulled over with that book in my car. Ted would never believe I had nothing to do with the selection.

FIFTEEN

Thunder boomed through the house. I gazed out the window on a dreary Tuesday morning into my backyard, watching the lightning dance across the sky, wishing it was my day off. The plan I had for yesterday evening fell through and my mood matched the weather. The books Oliver chose for me were about writing crime novels, and self-help books on judging people. Not very helpful at all.

Last night I looked online and couldn't find any magazine publishing information that would tell me why Leslie was targeting us.

Steve's attitude also worried me. It was *so* not like Steve, I didn't know how to feel. I wasn't sure if anger was the proper response. I couldn't see the harm in me bringing him dinner. It was like he wanted nothing to do with me and went with whatever lame excuse popped into his head. Had Karen turned his eye toward her?

Or was he worried about me picking another fight with him? Maybe the universe was telling me to go with my first inclination of not getting involved.

I had thirty minutes to get to work. I didn't want to go. Should I call in sick? I wasn't in the right frame of mind to deal with more demands of refunds and apologies.

No. Lying to my grandmothers wasn't the answer. Plus, I'd just sit around the house trying to answer the unanswerable question of why Leslie and Hazel thought we conspired with Belinda, or were in cahoots with Darlene, depending on which of the finger-pointers I happened to fixate on.

I snorted and turned from the window.

Yeah, like my grandmothers and I planned for Belinda to pull off a scheme, then a wrestling match with Darlene. In a way, it worked out for Belinda. She didn't have to teach the class and prove beyond a doubt she didn't know how to do her "own technique." Darlene trying to ruin Belinda's reputation had actually helped her save a little face.

I paused with a mug of water over my coffee machine. My mind whirled like the wind outside. No. No. No. Don't go there. Gossip was bad, even if it remained between me, myself, and I.

The thought wiggled and squirmed, demanding my full attention. What if Belinda and Darlene had planned it? It didn't really make sense. Then again, the entire relationship between the cousins didn't make sense. They were bitter enemies and also best friends forever. It could be Darlene burned all the bridges in the scrapbooking publishing world with her behavior at expos. All industries black-balled people, the crafting industry was no different. There might be a rule that a layout, no matter how incredible, unique, and trendsetting it was, would never be chosen with Darlene Johnson's name on it.

My theory got tangled up in knots when I added in the fight. If Darlene used Belinda to get her work out there, why get into a brawl at Scrap This? The only thing that made sense was to stop the class, though Belinda's confession made it impossible for Belinda to ever submit anything again either.

Maybe Darlene hadn't expected Belinda to admit to it, or for the fight to get out of hand. It did look like the necklace came off easily. Maybe Hazel participating in the throw down with Darlene hadn't been expected. Hazel's role was an ad-lib.

What had the cousins been up to?

The only one alive with the answer was Darlene—the one woman I planned on staying away from.

The lights flickered. Thunder shook the house again and rain poured down. I didn't want to leave today. I yearned for a day when I had a good excuse to hole up in the house and not venture out. The washing machine was full and I had to wait until I had at least an hour free. My grandmothers taught me to never have appliances running when no one was home. Without proper supervision, machines had a habit of breaking and creating a worse mess than if someone had been around to contain the flow of water.

Rain slapped the windows. I kept my longing gaze from the dining/craft room area. I had some new goodies I wanted to try out and the perfect pictures to go with the new washi tape.

My cell phone squawked at me. I needed to change the ringtone for when I woke up or I'd toss it out the window one day. Not a good choice when I paid a small fortune for the phone.

An unfamiliar number.

Frowning, I answered. "Hello."

"Today is the perfect day to go to Belinda's. With this storm, no one will be out and about." Darlene's voice grated against every nerve in my body.

I tightened my hold on the phone so I didn't chuck it across the room. "I don't care what you're doing today."

"You were serious when you said no."

"Yeah." The woman was either very obtuse or didn't think no's of any kind applied to her.

"I thought you were just mad at me."

She did pick up on something.

"Darlene, I'm not a private investigator now or ever. It's not what I want to become my life's work."

"And being an assistant manager of your grandmothers' scrapbook store is?" Darlene emphasized grandmothers.

I opened my mouth to fire off a retort. Instead, I clicked the lovely, wonderful button that ended the call. I refused to explain or defend myself to Darlene of all people. What I did with my life was my business. I liked working at my grandmothers' store. I loved living by them. I liked the safe world I created and didn't want to risk it for Darlene.

For Marilyn, sure. For my grandmothers if need be, no hesitation at all. For an annoying customer who liked to insult me and everyone else with the misfortune of meeting her—never.

I placed my coffee into a to-go mug and headed out the door into the storm. The wind whipped rain at me. This would be a slow day. I'd call Sierra when I got into work and let her choose if she wanted to come in or stay home. With three rambunctious boys and a husband, she didn't get much alone time for scrapbooking. She might like staying in rather than braving the weather.

I carefully made my way to the store. My cell phone buzzed from the cup holder. Once I parked beside my grandmothers' car, I retrieved the phone. I groaned. The number on the display was becoming too familiar to me.

Darlene. Again.

She might have to become familiar with the term "restraining order." Or maybe I'd tell Cheryl about Darlene bugging me. Let Cheryl and Darlene's mom, Eliza, go at it.

Ignoring the beep announcing a voicemail and the umbrella in the back seat, I scooted out of the car. I ran for the back door and got inside in record time. I shook the water off myself like a dog.

Grandma Hope peered into the storage room and frowned. "Did you forget your umbrella again?"

"It's in the car. It would take me as much time to open it as it would to get inside. Seemed better just to run in."

Hope sighed. "Go dry off in the employee lounge. I don't want you dripping all over the inventory. I don't think water spots on paper will ever be a trend."

"Yes, grandma." Sometimes it wasn't worth arguing, and the fact I left my drink in the car meant I needed to use the coffee maker in the lounge. No sense playing in the rain when a coffee pot was in the building. I liked making the easiest and well-thought out choice, contrary to some of my other decisions.

After getting my caffeine, I went straight to work. Since the store was empty, a fact I decided to attribute to the downpour, I took out my sketch pad from under the counter and brainstormed some other class ideas.

I circled the idea about Steve doing a class. I should call and make sure it was okay with him. I know I wouldn't like being volunteered for something. My grandmothers might do it to me on occasion, but they signed my paycheck.

What else? I needed something so inspiring that women would flock in to have their fee transferred rather than refunded. Christmas gift tags? Possible.

The phone rang. I snagged it from the receiver and tucked it between my chin and shoulder. "Scrap This, how can I help you?"

"You didn't return my call," Darlene said.

"I know." I hung up and dusted off my hands. Hopefully, I took care of the problem of Darlene this time.

The morning held a theme. The phone rang. I answered. Darlene spoke. I hung up. You'd think by the fifth time Darlene would receive the hammer-to-the-head hint I wouldn't speak with her. Not only was the routine old and annoying, but it kept interrupting my thought process and I still had no other ideas for new, unique classes.

The rain pounding the sidewalk hinted at what I wanted to do to Darlene, if I was that type of girl, which I wasn't.

Yet.

The bane of my existence went off again. I moaned and picked up the receiver. Closing my eyes, I began my spiel. "Scrap This, how can I help you?"

"Faith is that you?"

"Yes..." Suspicion raised its ugly head with the use of my first name and the lack of introduction from the caller.

"I hate to bother you at work, sweetie, but some person has been driving up and down the block a few times now. They seem really interested in your house. You aren't moving are you?"

The hopeful tone gave away the caller.

Mrs. Barlow wanted her daughter, son-in-law, and granddaughter to move to Eden and she had her eye on the townhouse I lived in. What she refused to accept was her daughter wanted nothing to do with the town of Eden, and my grandmothers would never sell the townhouse in hopes that if I ever left again I'd return.

"No, I'm not moving."

"I wonder why someone is keeping an eye on your place." She drew in a sharp gasp. "The murder. Are you trying to solve this one too?"

"No." I had an idea who decided to skulk around in a car instead of on foot. Hazel probably thought she'd be better at that method of spying. "Maybe someone lost their pet and is looking for them."

"Oh. That sounds practical." Now, she sounded disappointed.

I hated trampling on her parade. Mrs. Barlow didn't have much excitement in her life and she loved being in the thick of things. I should at least try and make someone happy.

"You know...someone might think I'm involved."

Like Darlene. I grinned. I wouldn't put it past her to stalk my house in hopes of finding me home and trying to talk me into helping her. The woman was relentless. Whether it was Darlene or Hazel, a talk from Ted might work better as neither woman listened to me.

"Do you think so?" Mrs. Barlow's voice got breathy.

"It is possible. The murder happened at the store, and I did help Marilyn. Someone might think I'm involved in finding the killer."

"Yes. Yes you did. And you did a wonderful job," she gushed.

"It might be good for you to keep an eye out. If the car shows up again, call Bobbi-Annie. Or ask to speak to Detective Roget. He's handling the case."

"I don't know if I should bother the detective. It might be nothing."

"Of course he'd want to know. Your information might be just what he needs to solve the case. Matter-of-fact, I wouldn't trust telling him over the phone. It's too important. With the weather, the phone lines get a little fuzzy. Ask him to stop by your house."

I grinned. Okay, it wasn't really nice to toy with Ted but he deserved it. He did drag me down to the police station.

Mrs. Barlow loved two things in life, family and drama of any sort. Real, television, or self-created. She'd love nothing more than having the town's homicide detective show up at her door. She'd definitely win the most-heart-attack-inducing-event at the weekly bingo game.

"Faith, there's some guy here to see you." Sierra tugged back the maroon curtain blocking off our storage area.

"Guy?"

I opened a box containing an older idea book we had planned on sending back. It was better to have a book considered "dated" than an empty spot on the book rack.

"Yeah." Sierra held a business card in front of her face. "Leonard Blue. He's a photographer with the paper. Has a couple of questions for you."

My heart pounded. Questions? For me? Was Karen now enlisting other members of the paper to help in her quest to turn me into front page news? Did she think I'd let my guard down around someone else?

She didn't know me very well. I grabbed a stack of the idea books for beginning scrapbookers.

"I'm coming."

I slipped past the curtain and headed for the book rack located near the door. I nodded at Leonard.

"Be with you in a moment."

Why would he show up with his camera? In the rain? Did Karen need a picture to go along with her exposé and thought a stormy background worked best?

"I'll just look around."

Leonard shuffled along the perimeter, checking out the patterns. He stopped in the pink section and squatted down, examining the bottom row of papers. The fuchsias, neon, and bubble gum shades of pink. Our least sought after colors, but ones that had a little bit of a following.

I placed the books into a slot then fiddled around with rearranging the placement of the rest. I really wanted to get an idea of the quest Karen sent Leonard on. So far nothing. Unless she wanted to know exactly what colors and textures of papers we had on hand.

The hairs on the back of my neck rose. I slowly turned. Sierra sent fireballs in my direction with her eyes. She then moved her angry eyes to Leonard and back to me.

So the person who's been snippy with me for the last few months was concerned about my behavior over the last few minutes.

"Sorry about the delay. How can I help you?" I gave Leonard a bright grin.

"I noticed you checking out my camera on Saturday." Leonard placed a hand underneath the lens and lifted the camera I wanted to have an affair with away from his chest. So beautiful. So powerful. So steady.

"I was wondering if Scrap This would be interested in having a photography class."

I beamed. "Actually, we are. We've been talking about it and bouncing ideas for instructors."

"I'd be willing. I can draw up a few ideas and drop them off." Leonard touched a sheet of glossy purple cardstock. "One of the ideas I had was on how to photograph layouts. Contests seem important to some of the ladies and they'd have a better chance with crisp and clear pictures."

"Some of our customers are getting into blogging and love to include photos of their layouts. I think it's a great idea. I'll pick out the paper our customers usually use so you can work with them and find the best lighting and setting. Unless you have cardstock and pattern paper lying around your house."

"No. I don't," Leonard said. "I left my card with your employee. Give me a call with the dates you have in mind."

After putting together a paper sampler for Leonard, I spent the rest of the afternoon crafting an email about the store being closed Saturday for Belinda's funeral service. We thought it was the most respectful thing to do and everyone wanted to attend and support Hazel.

I read the email word-by-word, running through all the possibilities of definitions for each word and how it was placed. I didn't want anyone reading too much, or too little, into this simple announcement.

Should I call it an announcement? Was it tacky to use the term announcement in the subject line? I mean we made announcements about sales, crops, and closings because of weather. A funeral should be more important than those.

I should call Oliver and run it by him. It was because of him I now over-examined and questioned every little thing.

I wondered if Oliver ever got journaling done in his scrapbook albums or if he analyzed words so carefully he never wrote any of the stories of his pictures. I'd have to check out some of his layouts the next time he came to a crop.

Usually though, I only spotted him peeking at Darlene's layouts and trying to encourage Wayne and Wyatt to document something other than arrests and hunting trips.

The phone mercifully rang and allowed me time away from my obsessing. "Scrap Th—"

"Thanks a lot, Faith." Ted broke into my greeting, a tinge of annoyance making his rough voice even harsher.

Ah, so Mrs. Barlow took my advice and made a phone call to the station.

Bobbi-Annie, who made the police station a well-tuned and run organization, had sent Ted straight over. Why send Jasper or one of the other officers when the town's homicide detective was available? No sense wasting the man's skills on traffic tickets, drunk and disorderly, and Hooligan wrangling detail when suspicious activity related to a murder was happening.

"You're welcome. For whatever it is I've done to help," I said as sweet as pecan pie topped with caramel sauce.

"You knew darn well I'd be stuck at your neighbor's house for hours while she read me a detailed list of possible criminal behavior."

I did, but I wasn't stupid enough to admit it to Ted.

"When Mrs. Barlow called about the car driving back and forth in front of my house, I figured you should know about it. I didn't think you wanted me running over to check it out. Or did you?"

"So, for once you heeded common sense."

"Shouldn't I have?" I placed the phone between my shoulder and chin and colored another image as a sample for the Halloween themed class.

Might as well multi-task. The image was a zombie-looking hand trying to grab hold of a person. I planned on decoupaging the colored image to the bottom of a bowl used for trick-or-treating candy.

"I'm glad you didn't rush over there. I just don't think you needed to hint to Mrs. Barlow I was the only one capable of handling it."

"I thought you'd like to know. And since you kind of think I'm sticking my nose into the case, I thought it was better I stayed out of it and recommended she call you."

"I don't kind of think. I know you are."

I let out an over dramatic shocked gasp. "I'm offended. What's so wrong about going to my own store and putting away supplies so we were ready for Monday morning?"

"It was a crime scene."

"I didn't see any tape by the backdoor. And no one said I shouldn't go inside."

"You went looking for trouble—"

Ugh! There was that stupid accusing phrase again. Why did both men who said they were interested in me think I looked for trouble? "I was looking for evidence—"

"So you admit it."

This conversation wasn't as fun as I envisioned it. I let another huff of breath. "I wanted to know why Belinda came to the store that night. She died at Scrap This. I need to know why."

"Someone killed her, Faith. That's all you need to know."

"No it's not. I want to know why. Why our store of all places?"

"Answering all those questions is my job. Let me do it."

"I'm trying. You're the one who called me all annoyed because Mrs. Barlow wanted you to come by and see her." I grinned. Got him.

The doorbell jingled and a customer strode into the store. She opened and closed her umbrella a few times, splaying water all over the display board I put in the crop area. I had wanted customers to see the two choices we had so far for classes. Now, I'd be redoing those samples.

I watched as the rain splatter caused some of the ink to trail down the card, giving it a nice eerie effect. "Customer is here, I have to go."

I hung up on Ted and stared at the card I painstakingly made. The splatter added a nice...dare I say Halloweeny...effect to the card.

"I'd like a refund..." The woman paused in mid-sentence and ventured closer to the board. "Is this a new class?"

"Yes," I said. "It's step one for making weather-related images, like you're looking out a window."

"Kind of creepy." The woman faced me, grinning. "Can I switch my fee from the disaster of a class on Saturday to this one?"

"Sure. And, I'll even offer a discount on supplies."

The woman beamed brighter.

It was the least I could do for the woman who inspired the class by ruining my project with her slight rudeness. Easily forgivable behavior since she gave me a great direction for a set of classes, how to use scrapbooking mistakes and accidents as a jumping point for enhancing pages and creating mood.

SIXTEEN

Home never looked quite so good. The porch lights bounced off the rain-slick roads. Heat blasting from the heater warmed my body. My heart was a different matter. It still felt cold from rejection. The rain tapered off toward the late afternoon and more customers had come into the store. Unfortunately, except for the customer with the umbrella, it had been to get refunds for the class. No one wanted to take my wonderful "how to turn mistakes into art" classes. I really thought I had come up with a brilliant idea.

At least we had Leonard willing to give a class. I needed to get dates and samples from him before I advertised it. I made a mental note of calling him in the morning.

I climbed out of my car and headed for the front door. The door was cracked open. Grandma decided I needed some home cooking tonight and with my mood knew I wasn't up for company. Sometimes it was great living close to family.

I pushed the door the rest of the way open and stepped inside. "Thanks, Grandma."

I froze.

My living room was torn apart. I wanted to race out of there but I didn't know if one of my grandmothers had come inside during the trashing of my home. Swallowing down the fear, I made my way further into my own home.

Stay calm. Stay alert.

I drew in steadying breaths and tiptoed toward the kitchen, listening out for any sound overhead. I took a step into the immaculate kitchen. Nothing was out of place, nor was there any dinner on the counter, so my grandmothers hadn't been to my house.

Yet. I needed to get out of there before my grandmothers did come over. If the person was still here, they heard me call out and might be sneaking up on me.

With my heart pounding, I spun around, prepared to karate-chop whoever might be behind me. Fortunately, the intruder wasn't there since my shaking limbs might not cooperate enough in showing how tough and capable I was at taking care of myself.

I ran out the door and headed straight for my grandmothers. I couldn't take a chance the person who wrecked my home wouldn't show up there next. I had no idea if this was a random burglary or related to Belinda's murder.

I banged on the door just once before charging into their house.

Grandma Hope placed a hand on her heart. "Goodness Faith, you gave this gal a scare."

"Where's Cheryl?" I grabbed my grandmother's purse from the hall closet near the front door. "We have to leave. Now."

"Honey, what's going on?" Hope hurried over to me.

"I'll explain in your car. Let's go. Cheryl!"

Cheryl came from the kitchen, wiping her hands on an apron. "What is all this ruckus about?"

"We have to go." I started hustling Hope out the door, keeping my eyes focused on my house.

"I'm cooking—"

"Leave it."

"I'm not burning my house down." Cheryl crossed her arms. "I want an explanation right now."

"Someone broke into my place."

Hope gasped. Shock filled Cheryl's face.

"I don't know if they're still there." I heard the wobble in my voice.

Cheryl raced into the kitchen then back into the living room. "Good girl. You didn't look. Let's head to the police station."

Hope ran outside, cell phone clutched in her hand. "I'll call Randall at home and let him know."

Randall?

Grandma was on first name terms with the chief of police and had his home phone number?

I didn't have time to ponder this piece of news. I needed to get my grandmothers some place safe before I returned and discovered how much damage had been done to my house.

And more importantly, why.

"No," Ted said as he headed out of the station to his squad car.

Jasper waited in another car, ready to peel off after Ted. The anger rolled right off Ted and enveloped me. Part of me said to stop pushing the man, the other said I'd know what was missing and could help direct his investigation.

I knew Ted was more furious at himself right now than with me. He had been in my neighborhood this afternoon, went over to my house and tested the doors and saw nothing unusual. He believed Mrs. Barlow's love of crime drama and knowledge of my nosiness had her conjuring up illegal activity.

"I can help," I said, placing my hand on the passenger side door handle.

"You're more of a help staying here and keeping an eye on your grandmothers. If you come with me, they'll convince the Chief they need to come also."

If my grandmothers knew I'd won this argument with Ted, they'd insist Chief Moore take them to the house to talk me out of being there. Before I'd know it, Steve would end up joining us along with whomever else my grandmothers felt capable of talking some sense into me.

I pushed anyway.

"I can tell you what's missing."

Ted paused by his car. He placed his hands on the hood and leaned over, his shoulders heaved up and down.

I took a step back, giving him the opportunity to get his temper under control. While I usually didn't mind egging him on, this was one time I would back away from our continual battle of which one of us was right.

"It's not safe," he said, between gritted teeth.

"I'll stay in the locked car until you two clear the house."

He looked at me, interest in his eyes. Not a surprise the man was interested in locking me up.

"I won't move until you say it's okay." I crossed my heart.

"How can I trust you?"

"Because I'm not stupid."

Ted let out a snort. "Debatable."

"Come on, I came here to the police station rather than go exploring and seeing if the culprit was still there."

"Culprit." Ted smiled, slightly.

"Culprit, criminal, jerk, possible murderer..."

"Wait a minute..." Ted held up his hands. "What makes you think the murderer has anything to do with this?"

I shrugged. "Belinda was killed at the store. Hazel and Leslie Amtower have been hinting around town I might have something to do with the investigation. And then there's the fact you're going to check out my place."

Ted's eyes narrowed. The red lights from the top of Jasper's cruiser flickered over Ted's face, making his expression even more menacing.

"And I don't know of any other reason someone would break into my house."

"Thieves don't need a reason, just an opportunity."

"In the rain? Doesn't seem like the best time for breaking and entering. You're likely to ruin everything you just stole."

Though, it was the best time not to get caught as people weren't out and about.

Darlene! I wouldn't put it past that woman to break into my home to either convince me to help her or see what I might have on her.

Ted noticed my expression and groaned. "Not that. Please don't come up with a suspect."

"Someone has to. I'm going. That's final." I ended my sentence by stomping my foot.

"Fine. But you must stay in the car until I say it's okay to come out."

"Agreed."

"And if anyone asks why I brought you, I'm saying you hid in the back of the cruiser. No way am I getting on your grandmothers' bad side. Those gals kind of scare me."

SEVENTEEN

Red lights flashed around us, creating an odd sort of creepy halo, as the cruiser hurried toward my house.

The town whizzed by us. I had left Eden to get away from the quiet, and returned to embrace it. Now, the quiet serene life I wanted kept getting snatched from me. My grandmothers would probably insist this came from my wanting to play sleuth. If someone thought I dug up dirt on them, it was natural they'd go where it was and clean it up.

I shivered and fiddled with the heater.

"I have a jacket in the trunk." Ted looked out the front window.

He hadn't taken his eyes off the road once. How did he know I was cold? Police officers probably had a sixth sense about those types of things, and were good at discretely keeping an eye on people in their cruiser, especially if they messed the with stuff on the dash.

"I'm fine."

"Just mentioning it. Remember, you stay in the car."

I rolled my eyes. Like I'd forget one simple rule so soon. I sighed and settled back into the seat. In no time, Ted turned down my street and pulled right up to my house.

The neighborhood looked quiet. Rain pitter-pattered softly. A light sheen coated the sidewalk and streets.

"Remember..."

"Stay put. I got it. I do understand English."

Ted got out of the cruiser. He met Jasper in my driveway and they had a little meeting. With his hand on his gun, Jasper headed toward the back. Ted slowly made his way to the front door.

My heart acted like a bronco, jumping and clashing against my ribcage. Please don't let the person be inside my home. I wanted them caught, but not have Jasper or Ted hurt.

Time inched by. The dark seemed to grow darker. The rain continued to leak from the sky. Instead of calming me, the sound had me rotating to observe different check points. Behind me. To the right. To the left. To the front. I felt like I was in a never-ending dance of the *Cupid Shuffle*.

I peered out the passenger side of the police cruiser. Jasper and Ted shone flashlights around the property. A couple of times, they paused and squatted down, staring intently at a few places in my yard.

They had gone into the house, and came back out so they had to know it was clear. Right? Why make me wait?

My heart pounded. My legs bounced up and down. Anxiety raced through me, growing with each minute. I was going to lose my mind if Ted didn't give me the all clear. I debated breaking my promise but I didn't want to ride back to the station in the back seat of the cruiser behind the Plexiglas shield. The front seat was more comfortable and required less of an explanation.

Mrs. Barlow peeked out her window. I swore she had a pair of binoculars pressed to her eyes. Was she venturing fully into amateur sleuthing, or more likely checking out Ted and Jasper? She had a thing for men in uniform. Bobbi-Annie had told her numerous times not to call feigning a heart attack so the cute paramedic could be sent over. Mrs. Barlow swore it wasn't the reason. The fact she always asked first if he was on duty before stating her medical emergency gave her away.

Ted started toward me.

About time. I flung open the door.

Ted stopped. "You said you'd stay put until I told you otherwise."

"Isn't that why you're coming over here?" I got out and slammed the door shut.

Ted sighed. I knew it meant I was right. Something Ted didn't like admitting.

"What have you found out so far?" I walked over to him.

"Telling you this is an ongoing investigation won't work will it?" He asked.

"Nope."

"How about it's not your business?"

I shook my head. "It's my house."

"That's what I figured." Ted sighed again.

Come on, was I really *that* exasperating? "Did they jump the back fence and go through the kitchen door?"

"Yeah." Ted slid a look at me. "What made you think that?"

I wasn't sure if he thought I withheld information from him, like receiving threats, or was once again delving into amateur sleuthing. "Mrs. Barlow would've called if someone forced their way in through the front door."

"Good observation. I'll have to see if she took down any more license plates this afternoon. Is that a new hobby of hers?"

I shrugged. I knew she kept notes on suspicious activities. If she was starting to jot down everything, I might need to use the back door if Steve and I had some late night dates at my or his house. There were some things my grandmothers, or the neighbors, didn't need to know about my relationship.

Ted took hold of my hand, halting me from stepping inside my house. "Are you sure you're up for this? Some areas are a mess."

"I saw the living room and kitchen. I can do it."

"The upstairs is a lot like the living room, except for the bathroom. Whoever broke in avoided that room."

I guess that was nice of him—or her—if my theory was right. I wouldn't put it past Darlene to create a huge mess to convince me I needed to help her because I was in danger.

Slowly, I walked around the living room. I righted the chair and the lamp. With my direction, Ted and Jasper put the couch and coffee table back into the proper place. The television was still in its place, along with the DVR, Blu-ray player, and movie collection. Whoever broke in hadn't come with the intention of taking anything, at least not anything worth selling.

"Nothing seems to be missing here."

"What about in your dining room?" Jasper asked.

"It'll take a while for you to look," Ted said. "They did a real number over there."

Heat crept along my cheeks. "It kind of looked that way when I left for work this morning."

"Wow. Your grandmothers let you get away with that?" Jasper's eyes widened.

I narrowed my gaze. "This is my house."

Jasper took a step back. "Just saying. I know if my grandma saw my place a wreck she'd be swatting me with a broom until I picked it up."

"It's my crafting area. What looks like chaos is actually creativity."

"I'll tell my grandma that the next time she pops over for a surprise inspection."

At least my grandmothers weren't that bad. They liked to interfere in my life but it was to get me a man. Though, Jasper's grandma might be on the same plan. What girl wanted to date a guy who lived in a pigsty?

I knew Karen wouldn't and that's the woman Jasper had his eye on.

Quickly, I sorted through the paper, stickers, die cuts, and glitter tubes on my table. Everything accounted for. It's possible something was taken as I had so many embellishments I couldn't remember what I owned. A few times, I've found duplicates of dimensional stickers and I only intended on buying one.

Where were the pictures? I had a stack of photos on the edge of the table. Who would break into a house and steal photographs of other people? Someone who thought those images might disprove their case.

I clenched my fists. "I'm going to—"

The rage in my voice caught Ted and Jasper's attention.

I slapped my mouth shut. The last time someone I knew uttered the word kill, she landed in jail accused of murdering her husband.

"Going to what?" Ted asked.

Of course, he couldn't let it go. "Going to sue her." It worked. A little bit. Better than saying I planned on ending her life. "Thinking she could swipe my pictures."

"Your pictures?" Ted asked.

"I had a pile of photos that I was going to scrap and they are gone."

"Who'd take your pictures?" Jasper knelt down by the trashcan in my craft room. His features contorted into many unattractive shapes while he fought back showing his opinion of my pink daisy-stickered trash receptacle.

"I'm interested to know also." Ted flipped open a notebook, poising a pen above the page.

"Really? That's not the impression I got earlier," I said.

"Faith, give me the name instead of an argument." Weariness came through in Ted's voice.

Guilt wiggled through me and I relented. The man had to have been working non-stop since Belinda's accidental death was changed to murder.

"Darlene."

"Darlene Johnson, the woman who got into a fight with Belinda." Ted said. "The woman you tried to help."

"Her. But I didn't try to help her. I got conned into helping her." I sorted through the items on the table. Stickers. Ribbon. Pattern paper. Cardstock.

"She'd want to take the pictures because..."

"To annoy me."

Ted and Jasper exchanged a glance I didn't like. I wasn't an irrational, hysterical woman. Wanting to annoy someone was a valid reason for taking someone's pictures.

It sure wasn't because Darlene ran out of photos to scrap or had a fondness for me and my grandmothers and wanted our images plastered in her home.

Unless she had turned stalkerish. I dismissed it. Darlene didn't have enough interest in another person to go through the trouble of stalking them. Whatever she did benefited her in some way. She was more likely to set up mirrors all over her house to catch her own eye than vie for someone else's attention.

Hazel on the other hand...

"Are these the pictures you're missing?" Jasper held up some photos.

I snatched them for his hand and flipped through them. Yep. My missing photos. Darn it. Now, I had to admit it to Ted.

He waited with a slight smile on his face. The guy was maddening. He knew it.

I dropped them onto the table.

"Well..." Ted grinned at me.

I sighed. "Yes. Those are the missing pictures."

"Not very nice to blame Darlene."

"I'm not saying she didn't do this..." I waved my arms around the mess. "Okay, maybe not technically this mess in my crafting area, but in the living room and other parts of my house, I'm certain it was her."

Ted tried valiantly not to roll his eyes. "Do you base that on the design style of the mess?"

Jasper snickered. If Ted hadn't been standing there, I'd have given Jasper a little kick in the derriere. Just for that, I'd let it slip Jasper wasn't keeping his apartment in a way that appealed to women. His grandmother would be over before the full sentence left my grandmother's lips. If there was one thing grandmothers did in this town, it was helping their counterparts get some great-grandchildren onto the family tree.

"No, I base it on the fact nothing of crafting importance was ruined. If there is one thing Darlene treats with great care, it's scrapbooking supplies and photographs."

So there, smart-aleck.

Ted's eye widened. I almost saw the wheels in his mind clicking. I actually made a point worth considering.

"The kitchen and bathroom were left alone. The electronics weren't stolen. Things are in disarray."

"Why overturn the couch?" Ted asked. "How was making a mess of your home going to help her find anything?"

"It'll delay me..."

Ted's eyes narrowed again.

Oh no. His face twisted into the you're-playing-PI look again.

"Go on."

I wasn't walking any further into the verbal trap I created. I pressed my lips together and shook my head.

"Let's go up and see if the damage there matches your theory."

Sounded like the best idea ever. I started up the stairs, reminding myself to keep my temper and watch what I said. I took a few deep breaths outside the door to my office. I glanced across the hallway to my closed bedroom door. I hoped Darlene at least had the decency to stay out of there. I had never had a man in there before, and did not want Ted and Jasper to be the first ones in there.

I didn't want the first man to be in there because he was investigating a crime instead of me.

"Let me know what's missing." Ted placed a hand on the small of my back and guided me inside the office.

Shock ripped through me. This wasn't what I had expected.

The devastation upstairs was different. Vicious. Books torn in half littered the floor, some mine, and the others were ones I checked out from the library. Mud was ground into the carpet so hard it smudged the print and distorted the size of the shoe. Pictures pulled from the walls were thrown onto the floor. The glass shattered and spider webs ran across all the faces showing the happy moments of my life with my grandmothers.

I blinked furiously to stop the threatening tears.

All of the desk drawers were pulled out, the contents scattered all over the floors. Pens. Markers. Beaded bookmarkers I collected and had hung on a peg board beside my desk now torn and on the carpet. A Raggedy Ann doll Grandma Hope had given me for my fourth birthday lay crumbled in a corner.

I picked her up, cradling her against my body. A stuffed bear Steve won for me at a carnival was nearly decapitated, the stuffing strewn about. Tears blurred my vision. I swiped them away.

"Let's do this later." Ted wrapped an arm around my shoulder and pivoted me toward the door.

"No. I want to do it now. Maybe something here will tell us who did this." I turned slowly in a circle and stopped when I returned to my starting point. "Whoever did this wants to hurt me."

"I think they were angry because they didn't find what they were looking for." Ted knelt down and picked up the bear. "My ex-wife runs a doll and stuffed critter hospital for our daughter and her friends. I'll take your friend to her and she'll fix it good as new."

Ted's understanding and concern touched my heart. As much as he annoyed me, and did he ever, he was a good, honorable man who took people's feelings into consideration.

I drew in a deep breath and released it. "Thank you. Let's see what we can uncover."

For twenty minutes we sorted through items. Ted had Jasper bring up a garbage bag and a box. Anything I wanted to have fixed or replaced went into the box, and the items beyond saving and had no sentimental value went into the garbage. It was easier going through everything having Ted's help.

"Do you think this ties into Belinda's murder?" Jasper asked, tying up the filled garbage bag. "Someone might think you have something to do with the murder..."

"And why would anyone think that?" I planted my hands on my hips and glared at Jasper. "I'm not a suspect. I had no reason to kill Belinda."

Jasper held up his hands and backed up a few inches. "I'm not saying you did. But someone sure doesn't think highly of you."

I drew in a deep breath, preparing to unleash some wrathful words but Ted cut me off.

"Jasper, be useful." Ted pointed to the door. "Take those downstairs."

"You want them at the curb or in the trunk of the squad car?" Jasper slung the bag onto his shoulder.

Ted paused and seemed to contemplate the question. "Take it back to the station and get some help sorting through and cataloging it."

Jasper groaned. "Come on, Detective. You can't be serious."

Ted leveled a very serious look on him. "This break-in could be tied into a murder case. It's easy to overlook something viewing it as part of the whole. Individually, something might stand out as being out of place."

I pressed my mouth closed so as not to heave out my opinion. Ted wouldn't appreciate me pointing out he sounded like he was doing a segment for children's television show on matching like items.

Jasper's lips twitched. He knew what I was thinking.

Ted's gaze flickered over to me then back to Jasper. I got serious. This wasn't a funny matter at all. Finding some amusement in this disaster helped keep my emotions under control. I didn't want to be blubbering with Ted and Jasper in the room. I'd rather wait until they left before I indulged in a mini-breakdown.

"You think there's a clue in there?" I pointed at the bag Jasper left with.

"It's possible. I'll have you come by tomorrow to look over everything. Maybe something was left, rather than taken, and will give us a clue on who did this."

I hoped so. I wanted this person found. It wouldn't bother me as much if they had stolen something. They tore through my house like they were looking for something.

My gaze became glued to the computer. The keyboard hung from its cord, dangling from the desk. The basket I kept extra memory cards and my flash drive in rested on its side. Empty. Sketches, doodles and my notes from Saturday night littered the desk.

"No!" I ran over to my desk. I pushed the papers away. They fluttered to the floor. I wanted my pictures safe. I yanked open my top desk drawer. Also empty.

I booted up my computer and searched my files. My folder marked pictures held two files: a form for our crops, and the other a customer survey. Everything else wiped out. I checked my documents folder. All the journaling I'd done and saved to print also erased.

Tears filled my eyes. Gone. All of the files on my computer had been wiped out and the memory cards taken. I know I didn't have much of a life to document according to some people, but it was still my life. Since I left home, I hadn't had many good memories to preserve, but the few I had I cherished.

The words I spoke to Leslie Amtower yesterday haunted me. Why did I tell her I had the real conversation? The safety net I had for my grandmothers was gone. Wait a minute! The thread. I'd find the thread and print it out.

Okay. Keep calm. I clicked on my browser and went to the message board. This shouldn't be hard. I remembered Darlene's user name so all I had to do was look it up and I'd get a list of what she posted on Saturday.

"What's going on?" Ted stood behind me, his hands on the back of the chair.

"I'm getting your proof of who broke into my home. I know who did it."

"You already told me. Darlene."

I shook my head. "She wouldn't have done this."

I knew Darlene was capable, and willing, to create havoc but not this level of destruction. Scrapbooking was her life. Her purpose. She loved the hobby as if it was an actual being. That was why she was so upset with Belinda. Belinda hadn't just pulled one over on readers of a magazine, she betrayed scrapbooking. Something Darlene held dear.

This was done by someone who hated me. Not just a person who found me annoying, aggravating, and not quite that likeable.

This was done by someone who thought I was out to destroy them so they wanted me to know they could, and did, destroy a part of me first.

The person fitting the bill was Leslie Amtower.

"I'm fairly certain it's Leslie Amtower. She is out to prove my grandmothers and I...mainly I...had something to do with the scam Belinda ran on *Making Legacies*."

"What scam?" Ted asked, his rugged voice a little confused.

"The layout. You heard about it. Belinda submitted layouts designed by Darlene as her own and became a Life Artist Diva because of them. This news has the potential of ruining the magazine."

"It's that big of a deal?"

"Yeah. It's a huge deal in the scrapbooking industry. Scraplifting is for your own personal fun, not for profiting off of."

"Scraplifting?"

"Copying someone's layout. Scrapbookers will use a design they see on the internet or in magazines as a blueprint for a page in their scrapbooks. Sometimes croppers will get blocked and not have an idea for a page so they copy one they like. Not using the same exact paper or embellishment but the placement of photos and the techniques used on the page."

"And that's okay?"

"For personal use, absolutely. To submit to contests or design teams, no way."

"Ms. Johnson stated Ms. Watson stole her pages not scraplifted."

"Yeah. Belinda seemed to have taken scraplifting to a whole new level and submitted to the *Making Legacies* contest the actual pages Darlene had made."

"Which Ms. Watson confirmed."

I nodded. "And for some reason the editor-in-chief of *Making Legacies* believes I was involved."

"Why would she think that? For the record, the question is not an accusation." Ted rushed through the last sentence.

"I don't know the why, just that she does. She's been going around town linking my name with this fiasco."

"Hmmm..." Ted's non-word comment and the unsurprised look on his face told me he already knew about this. "That's quite an interesting change in direction."

"I don't expect you to run out and arrest the woman."

"I appreciate you not making any demands." Ted's lips twisted into a half-sneer.

Sarcasm did not look good on the man. I turned my attention back to the computer. The thread proved someone was out to get me and the fact Leslie Amtower used a doctored account of what transpired instead of the whole thing.

Where was it? Maybe Darlene changed the thread title. I clicked through all the threads Darlene responded to on Saturday and Sunday. None of them was the infamous "livid" thread. My stomach felt like I was traveling at top speed on the down section of a mountain road.

I pounded on the keyboard, adding words I remembered from the thread into the search engine. Nothing. The witch got the thread pulled! I knew it was Leslie Amtower. There was no way to prove it to Ted. He wouldn't understand the clout an editor-in-chief of a popular scrapbooking magazine would have over the owners of the website.

Maybe Darlene kept...no. Asking Darlene for help was asking for a migraine. I'd owe her a favor and if there was one person in this life I never wanted to owe it was Darlene.

I just had to find different evidence. I threw myself back in the chair. The wheels rolled a few centimeters on the carpet. "It's gone."

"What's gone?"

How in the world did this man ever solve a case when he couldn't remember a conversation that took place a few minutes ago? "The thread I was going to print out for you proving Ms. Amtower blamed me for Belinda tricking her."

"Ms. Amtower posted on this thread."

I grimaced. "Not exactly."

Ted shook his head as if to clear it. "You're saying Ms. Amtower accused you on the internet of being in cahoots with Belinda to pull this layout scam over on her, yet she didn't exactly say it. If she didn't say those words, what did she actually type on there?"

I sunk down in the chair. Why did Ted have to make this so hard? "People were saying I was involved."

"These people were..." He motioned for me to supply the names.

This was going to help me. Not. "Little Lamb. JealousMuch." I included a few of the regular posters names I remembered.

"Then this should be easy. There shouldn't be too many people named Little Lamb. A couple of record searches and I'll be able to round them up." Ted snapped his notebook closed. "You wouldn't happen to know any shepherds in this area?"

I glared at him.

"I didn't think so."

"You are not amusing." I shoved the chair back a little bit further and stood.

"I'm here investigating a crime, not for entertainment purposes." He looked me up and down; a spark increased the green in his eyes. "Though..."

I shoved my hands in my jean pockets to stop from swatting him. "Mind your manners, Detective Roget."

"We should go to your bedroom."

"What?" I screeched. "I don't know what type of girl you think I am—"

He rolled his eyes. "I need you to tell me if anything is missing from the bedroom."

"Oh." Yeah, I guess he'd want to go there for that reason, and not for the reason his gaze hinted at. Or what I read into his gaze.

Which, I shouldn't be thinking about in the first place. I had a boyfriend. Or almost did anyway.

"Want me to open the door?"

"Shouldn't you dust it for prints or something?" I wrapped my arms around myself, suddenly feeling chilled.

"Jasper and I did it earlier." Ted pointed at the doorknob coated in black powder.

At least I knew what took them so long. Ted hadn't been making me sit in the car just to annoy me. "Go ahead."

Ted opened the door. I braced myself for what I was about to see.

Relief rushed through me. I forced out the breath clinging to my lungs. Everything looked orderly. For me, it gave more credence to the theory Leslie Amtower had been the one going through my belongings.

Another woman would know how much an invasion of privacy it was to search the bedroom. Someone going through my dresser drawers made me a little nauseous. This also said the break-in involved business and not personal.

The places searched were the living room, craft room, and my computer. The places I'd keep proof. Since my job was also my hobby, she looked in my craft area to see if I had kept the items there. Or maybe she thought I was putting together a layout about the brawl and including a print out of the thread into my scrapbook.

Some scrappers believed omitting the painful things in their life made a person dishonest and your memories a lie. I called it self-preservation. Why would I want to have a visual and written reminder of all the horrible times in my life? It was bad enough I couldn't wipe them out of my head.

"Does it appear anything is missing?" Ted drew me from my musings.

"No. Everything looks pretty much in place. Just the way I left it." I turned toward the closet and frowned.

It was opened an inch. I always closed it. I walked over to it, telling myself Ted or Jasper left it open. Everyone knew closets were the go-to hiding place for criminals and nosy people when the owner of the residence or the police arrived.

I finished opening the door. A few shirts were on the floor but for the most part everything was in place. A shoe kicked out of the way here and there. The criminal had definitely checked out the closet but hadn't damaged anything. They had saved their rage for the computer room. The edge of a quilt hung down from the shelf a foot over my head. I grabbed the end and tossed it back up. It dangled back down. I glanced over my shoulder. Ted was pretending he didn't notice me fighting with the quilt.

Since I didn't want my skeleton scattering all over the floor, even if Ted knew about it, I hauled out the step stool from the other side of the closet.

I stepped onto it and started tucking the quilt back onto the shelf. My eyes drifted over to the far corner. My breath hitched. A corner of my "skeleton" box peeked from a pile of sweatshirts thrown on top of it. Sweatshirts I hadn't put up there.

With heart pounding, I inched the box out. The top fell off. No! No! No! I grabbed the container and yanked it down. I and the box crashed to the ground.

Ted said something. My mind refused to process it.

My wedding picture was gone. Along with the folder containing the case the military tried making against me. The newspaper stories from the post newspaper. Notes I had found showing Adam's deception and intention of using me. My victimization. My vindication. All gone.

No! No! No! Fear and anger raced through me. The blood pounded in my head and grew cold in my veins.

No wonder they didn't continue their search in my bedroom. They started with the closet and found just what they needed to prove me a murderer—the box holding my past.

EIGHTEEN

"What's wrong?" Ted knelt down and placed an arm around me.

I shook my head and stared into the almost empty box.

He reached for the box. "I might be able to get prints off of it."

"No!" I threw myself across it.

The main damage to my life was gone but a few scattered pieces still remained. I didn't want to have everything out in the open. I should be able to keep a few things to myself.

"What in the world do you have in there?" Ted worked on prying me off the box...evidence. "Naughty lingerie? A skeleton? Evidence of a murder?"

I sniffled. "I have never owned naughty lingerie."

"Pity."

I shot him a glare intense enough to roast him alive.

Ted smiled and bumped his shoulder into mine. "Good for you. Keep the spunk going. Don't let a break-in make you believe your life is gone. I bet your grandmothers have some of the same pictures you did, or your other friends."

"You don't understand." I sat back on my heels, tears dripping down my face. "My life is gone. Or part of it anyway."

Ted made himself comfortable on the floor. "Okay, I'm listening."

Did I want to tell him? Could I not tell him? Whoever took those specific items did so for a reason, and it was likely to make me look like a murderer.

"Stuff I had kept from when I was in the military."

"Okay." Ted's brows drew down. "I'm sure you could write to some agency or organization in the armed forces and ask for your records. If it's other memorabilia, you could ask on some scrapbook boards or military alumni boards and see if anyone can help you find a way to replace them. You're resourceful. And 'no' has never stopped you before from getting what you need."

I liked how Ted kept stressing "you" instead of using the usual "we" Steve and my grandmother preferred. It made me feel more in control and powerful. I needed those feelings right now.

"It's not personnel file type of stuff, or ribbons and medals." My chest tightened. I choked on the words. Taking in a deep breath, I blurted out the truth before it strangled me. "My wedding picture. Articles about the murder."

"The murder in Germany Adam Westcott tried implicating you in."

I nodded. "Now you know why I don't want the rest of this leaving my house."

"Prints might be on the box." Ted rubbed his chin and stared at the box. "Okay, how about you let me take the empty box."

I shook it. "It's not empty."

He looked at me like I was a very drunk family member he actually liked who couldn't see the simple solution in front of them. "Take whatever is remaining in the box and put it in a different container."

Simplicity sometimes seemed difficult. Like when you're trying a new technique labeled for beginners and it takes an hour to understand the directions, much less complete the "done in fifteen minutes" page.

I waved my arms around. "Now I have to find a box in all this mess."

"You could just let me..."

"Be quiet." I snapped.

I pushed to my feet and scouted around the house. Ted followed behind me, keeping his opinions about my behavior to himself.

I had a lot of different types of scrapbook storage items in the dining room. I'd borrow something to use for now and get a box from the store tomorrow.

I scanned all the storage systems. I had a nice array...collection...of them. Every time I found the perfect organization system, something cuter came along and I needed the new ones. Right now, my weakness was cute tote bags I could personalize with clever sayings, or Captain Obvious style statements like paper, stamps, flowers, etc.

I pulled out a large pink and white tote from under the table with Crop It embroidered across it in turquoise. "This will work for now."

I carefully took out the photos, papers, and embellishments I had placed into packets. I put them on top of the dining room table. Hopefully, it encouraged me to get busy scrapping. Maybe tonight once Ted left. I needed something pleasant in my mind or else I'd never get to sleep.

"I'll be back down with the box," I said.

Ted nodded as he examined the afghan that had belonged to my grandpa. A lump built itself in my throat. He was looking for damage, probably knew someone who could fix it.

Quickly, I re-housed the items from my "skeleton" box into my crop box and returned downstairs. "Here you go." I thrust the container at him.

Ted nodded. "I'll get this back to you."

Nervousness wound through me. I twisted my fingers together. "What are you going to say if someone asks about it?"

"What I always say to nosy people, I'm conducting a police investigation and can't answer any question that might hamper the case."

"I'm sure Chief Moore will accept that answer."

"The Chief isn't worried I'm harassing citizens by deeming items evidence and carrying it out of their homes."

I swallowed hard and brought up the name I was really worried about. "What about Steve? He's a prosecutor."

Ted rested the edge of the box on his hip. "One, Davis can't prosecute this case. Two, if you're going to date the guy you should tell him."

I shook my head. "I don't know if he'd understand. I don't want—" I couldn't explain anymore as tears wobbled my voice.

"Then why are you seeing him?"

"Good night, Detective." I held open the front door.

"Message received, Miss Hunter." Ted nodded once and stepped out into the rain.

A pair of headlights pulled onto the street. I stopped and watched. Was the chief bringing my grandmothers home, or had they called Steve to check up on me?

Ted kept vigil in front of my door, keeping an eye on the car. It slowed but crept past mine and my grandmothers' driveways and pulled into Steve's. The dim light from the porch lamp let me recognize Steve.

He glanced over at my house.

"Doesn't look like trouble." Ted nodded a greeting at Steve as he walked to his cruiser.

I waved.

Steve opened his door and went inside, without one hint of acknowledgement toward me.

Tears whispered along my lashes. What was that about?

I backed into my house, closed the door and locked it. I leaned against it for a moment, fighting back tears even though I knew no one saw me. I wanted so much to unleash the sob building in my chest and heart.

No. I wouldn't let a man crush me again.

If Steve somehow found out already about my past and thought me unworthy, then so be it. I didn't grovel. Anymore. I begged and pleaded for a man once and ignored signs that should've made me run.

Not a mistake I'd make a second time.

Wiping my tears with the bottom of my shirt, I wandered back into my living room area. I paused, sniffing the air. A weird scent lingered. A cross between stale donuts and some woodsy scent crossed with lavender. Ted did woodsy but not with a flower mixed into it.

Not that I spent a lot of time smelling Ted or anyone else. It also took Darlene off my suspect list. Whenever we had a crop, she always marked in the comment sections of our survey we need less sugar in the snacks we served, including a rundown of the nutrition facts on the sheet. Or if homemade, a question if we had inspected the kitchen to ensure proper food handling and preparing techniques. Yep, Darlene made a crop fun.

The weird mix clung to the room, or something in it. I sniffed around until I came to the culprit. My grandfather's afghan. Why did my grandfather's blanket smell like—nope, not going there. I didn't need to gather up a bunch of theories of why this one item in my home took on such a strong smell of the criminal. I'd rather be dense on the topic.

Gingerly, I picked it up and carried it to the washer. I opened the top then dropped it on top of the dryer. Darn it. It was full. I had to do a load of laundry now. What a great way to end this truly, horrible, miserable, no good day.

An image flickered in my mind. I grabbed the bottle of detergent. The memory tickled my mind again, insistent. I closed my eyes and concentrated. I was in the office. Grandma Cheryl busted in. I shoved a flash drive into my jeans pocket.

The flash drive! Did I leave it in my pocket? I dropped the bottle to the ground, it bounced off my toe. Ouch! I waded through my dirty clothes until I found the jeans I wore Sunday. I shoved my hands into all the pockets. Yes!

I pulled it out and did a happy dance. More like a happy hop as my toe throbbed. What was a little injury when I found the evidence someone didn't want me to have. Take that bad guy. Thought you could thwart me.

My celebration was short lived when I remembered what they had on me. Maybe, they'd be up for a trade. After I made a copy of everything and hid it in a place they'd never think of looking, like

Darlene's house. Everyone knew we didn't like each other. There was no way they'd think we'd work together to protect the other one.

Yep, they'd think Darlene would turn on me faster than the numbers on the national debt clock.

I retrieved my cell and went to the recent calls section. I highlighted Darlene's number and hit send.

She answered on the second ring. "You're in."

"I'm in."

"Good. Tomorrow morning strategy session at the store."

"Someone will overhear us."

"Where wouldn't someone overhear us that wouldn't look suspicious? It's not like we visit each other's homes."

True.

"We need someplace that easily explains why we are there together and where we can meet soon," Darlene said. "The 'you're guilty' finger is keeping a steady bead on me right now. I'm not going to jail. I'll do whatever is necessary to stay out."

Like destroying items in my home and taking my ugly to display to the world. Oh shut up, I told myself. I already decided it wasn't Darlene so I shouldn't travel back down that road of suspicion.

We needed a meeting place where Darlene and I would naturally show up at the same time. There went three-fourths of the buildings in town. The grocery store, we only had two and residents frequented both. It held the same risk as Scrap This...too many ears. The hospital. No, her mother and my grandmothers would drive us both crazy. We'd be in Ted's office fighting over which one of us did kill Belinda just to escape the worry and lectures.

"I'm waiting..." Impatience tightened Darlene's voice.

"I'm thinking..." I responded, mimicking her tone.

Ted's office. The police station. Not bad, except we didn't want Ted or Bobbi-Annie figuring out what we were up to. We might as well just take an ad out in the paper. The newspaper. Now there was a good possibility. Except for nosy chasing-after-Steve Karen

England. She'd be on the phone to Steve to tell him all about my new buddy. Not that he really cared what I did anymore.

A heaviness filled my being. No moping over a guy. Besides, who said it was about me. The man had a tough job and had been working all hours. Even though he wasn't on Belinda's case, the county had a lot of other crimes he needed to prosecute.

It seemed everyone in town wanted in on taking out legal action against someone. The perfect idea hit me. I grinned. "The courthouse."

"Courthouse?"

"Yep. If anyone sees us there, they're going to think we're going to war against each other."

"Brilliant. The person who's trying to set up one of us will think their plan worked and we're working to prove each other guilty."

"Exactly."

I'd feel a little bad using Darlene except I knew she was also joining forces in this sleuthing gig to save her own hide.

NINETEEN

I parallel parked in front of the courthouse. Hitching the strap of my purse onto my shoulder, I exited my car. Showtime. I lifted my chin toward the sky and marched forward, getting into the act from the get go.

"Oh Faith..." A voice sing-songed.

I nearly tripped over my own feet.

Karen England. Not someone I wanted around when I was creating the diversion of a lifetime. It was going to be hard enough for me and Darlene to pull this off without an observant reporter watching us. If anyone could figure out we were up to no good, it was Karen...and Steve. I hoped he was in court this morning and Mrs. Alwright didn't notify him of my presence.

My shoulders slumped forward as I turned around. No sense getting on Karen's bad side when I needed her kind of liking me and not wanting to cause trouble. Right now, she figured being my friend was a way to win Steve's heart so I might as well use it for my benefit.

"Good morning, Karen."

"You're sure in a hurry. You forgot something." Karen placed a hand on the parking meter by my car. "I'd hate for you to get a ticket. I know these beauties always get checked."

Of course they did, the meter people, not just gals in this town, didn't have to go far. Most people were either running late or so much in a tizzy they routinely forgot to feed the meters in front of the courthouse. Easy source of income for Eden.

"Thanks." I opened my large bag and dug around for a quarter as I walked back to my car. I turned up a book of stamps with only two stamps, a couple of cough drops, three hundred pens, or something along that number, but no quarter.

"I got one." I heard a muffled plink.

"Thanks," I said, trying not to sound begrudging.

This was such an odd start for a day, thanking Karen for being helpful to me. I started worrying about the meeting with Darlene. I had a bad feeling it wasn't going to go as planned.

"Visiting Steve this morning?" Karen kept her eyes opened wide, portraying a friendly innocence not matching the glint of steel in her blue eyes.

The question I had to answer first was did I want to tell her the truth, a slightly off-centered truth, or a bold faced lie. Decisions. Decisions. Decisions. Thinking fast on my feet, after drinking only one cup of coffee, wasn't a strong suit of mine.

Piquing her interest with a version of the truth might work best in my favor. I went with a mix, and left Steve out of it. He'd thank me for it later.

If he ever found out.

"No. Though, I wouldn't mind seeing him of course." I had to make sure she knew Steve kind of belonged to me.

"Of course." Karen's smile became thinner and less happy looking.

"I have a tiny bit of business here at the courthouse. Stop people from speaking out of turn."

"Do you now?" The smile turned into a sneer. "Anything involving a murder?"

I locked my knees to stop myself for taking a step back. Fear wiggled through me. Was Karen sent all that information about me? What better way to hurt me, and stay off the radar, then for the burglar to send the illegally obtained info to the newspaper. Karen wouldn't care how it came into the anonymous informant's hands, just that it was now in her's. She wanted a big story. And she'd have it, and very possibly get Steve as a bonus.

"I'm sure you've heard what Hazel has been saying," I said as nonchalantly as I could muster with my heart trying to escape from my body.

"It's not what Hazel's saying I'd be worried about." Karen waved her hand, showing it was no concern of hers. "No one is surprised Hazel went off the deep end. Her life was wrapped around her daughter. Still is. I'd be more concerned about the editor-in-chief from Utah. She has a lot of clout, money, and resources to make your life miserable."

"Thanks for the advice. I'll do my best to stay off her radar."

"Try harder, Faith, because she's about to roast you alive."

I hurried into the courthouse. Karen's words swirled around me. Leslie Amtower had resources. Enough to hire someone to help her search my house. It explained the mix of donut and flower smell. I patted the pocket of my jacket where I kept the flash drive. Another one was in the coin section of my wallet. I wasn't stupid enough to give Darlene the only one I had.

I squared my shoulders and gave myself a little shake, ridding myself of the ominous feelings Karen's words stirred in me. I needed to look confident, perturbed, and determined...not like I had something to hide.

Mrs. Alwright looked away from her computer screen. Her eyes grew wide and she shot a horrified glance toward the hallway lined with chairs used as a waiting room for those not wanting to stand in line with friends or family paying taxes, filing documents, or having to give rides for a court appearance.

I glanced down the hall.

Darlene sat on one of the chairs, tapping her foot and glancing at her watch. She looked up and caught me staring at her. She made a point of looking at her wrist.

I was late. I got it. But before I went over there, I had to put on another little performance. I needed to get this case over with. All my working around the truth was going to lead to a lot of explaining on judgment day...or sooner if my grandmothers found out. I wasn't sure which I feared more.

"Good morning, Faith." Mrs. Alwright offered a toothy smile. "Let me just check Steve's schedule. I do believe he'll be out of court in ten minutes. I'm sure he wouldn't mind if you waited for him in his office."

"I didn't come here to see Steve." I leaned forward, talking in a loud, conspiratorial whisper.

"Did you buy a new car and need to register it? The line is short right now, it'll pick up soon. I'd hurry in there."

I bit back a smile. Darlene laid the groundwork real good. Mrs. Alwright wanted to make sure I didn't spot my nemesis. "I'm not here to register anything or pay a ticket. I'm going to get the paperwork to file a restraining order..."

Mrs. Alwright's eyes bulged out. Guilt reared its not so pretty head. I wanted to create a little explanation for my and Darlene's talk, not give someone a heart attack.

"Honey, things like that get ugly. Do you really need to do that? It's so extreme. Word will be all over town." Mrs. Alwright emerged from behind the desk and gathered my hands into hers. Concern reflected in her hazel gaze.

Now I felt worse. She meant to help me, not knowing I had no intention of filing anything. I kept up with the charade. "She keeps calling me. Just because I work for my grandmothers doesn't mean I can take phone calls all the time. I get it. She didn't do it. I don't know why she's telling me, constantly, instead of Karen. Karen is the investigative reporter not me. Why would I even care?"

I halted myself. Boy, when I got going, I sure got going. I wanted to give reasons, not work myself into such a frenzy that I actually went and took out a restraining order on Darlene.

"This week has been so tragic already. There is no sense bringing more pain into the community. People taking sides..."

Not really a concern for me because I was pretty sure who most people would line up behind. Hint: it wasn't Darlene.

"Gossip isn't such a good thing for a community either," I said.

Mrs. Alwright frowned. "I thought you said you were bothered by calls."

I did, didn't I. Drat. Okay, I needed an add-on for my explanation.

"Other people are talking also. I've had a few people say I'm involved."

"No sense taking it out on Darlene." Mrs. Alwright linked her arm through mine and led me toward Darlene. "Why don't you girls just talk this thing out? I'm sure this is all a misunderstanding."

Thank you, Mrs. Alwright!

Darlene huffed and swiveled, giving me her back. "Of course you're on Faith's side. You work for one of her boyfriends."

One of? So we were going there. Fine. I'd play. "You're just jealous."

"Of a hussy. I don't think so." Darlene snapped her fingers in the air.

Those were fighting words, pretend insult or not. "So a woman who has a man interested in her is a hussy? I'm sure your mom would like to know that's what you call her behind her back."

Darlene shot to her feet. "Excuse me! Ex...cu...se me."

"What? Hard of hearing, Darlene? Your mother has a boyfriend—"

"Young ladies, enough from both of you." Mrs. Alwright pressed a hand onto mine and Darlene's shoulders, forcing us to take a seat. "If you keep this up, I'll call both of your families. Besides, do you really want to be giving Karen something to write about?"

Darlene and I craned our necks.

Karen had taken up residence on the far side of the entrance area, a better position for staying within earshot without us being able to see her. Until she played a giraffe and stretched her body and neck out like she was reaching for the top of a tree for an early morning snack.

"No," I said.

Darlene remained silent, glaring at me.

Geez, she started it. I nudged her ankle with my toe.

"No," Darlene said none too happy.

I forgot for a moment Darlene was the type who liked giving it but thought she was above receiving it back. Since I had to work with her, I needed to eat some very unappetizing humble pie.

"I'm sorry. I never should've brought your mom into our argument."

"No, you shouldn't have." Darlene crossed her arms.

Mrs. Alwright perched her reading glasses on the end of her nose and gazed down at Darlene, the disappointed Sunday school teacher scowl.

"I apologize also. I shouldn't have called you a horrible name. It's not your fault two of Eden's most handsome, available men are interested in you."

"Much better. You girls talk about this civilly." Mrs. Alwright stuck out her index finger and moved it back and forth, calling us both out. "I'm going to see what Miss Pancake is up too."

Mrs. Alwright was one of the people in Eden who refused to call Karen by her 'made up last name' as some of the older people in our town called it. They didn't care if it was a legal name change or not. She was born Karen Pancake and would stay Karen Pancake.

The secretary straightened her spine and marched over to her desk, muttering under her breath. "She better not think she's visiting Steve."

Darlene placed her purse on her lap and opened it. She stuck her hands inside and withdrew a pen and a small notepad. "So, competition is what has you staking a firm claim into Steve."

Color me impressed. She found what she wanted without having to look.

"He's not a piece of property the first girl to sink her nails into gets." I stuck my hand into my coat pocket and pulled out the flash drive. "Keep this safe."

Darlene stared at the device like it was a poisonous apple.

"It's not a bomb. Nor does it hold journaling confessing a murder."

"What's on it?" Darlene clutched her pen and pink and green paisley notebook. "We came here so I could tell you the plan."

"I have a plan also. This..." I held the drive in front of her nose. "...is part of it. Someone broke into my house last night and erased all my files."

Darlene examined her nails. Bored.

"Including all my photos."

Darlene gasped and clutched her chest.

"He or she also broke the glass on all the framed pictures and took every single memory card I had."

"All your photos are gone?" Darlene took hold of my hands.

I nodded.

"Animal!" Darlene clenched my hands harder. "Don't fret. I'll help you find the person responsible and get back your memories."

There was something sweet and comforting about Darlene's outrage. She was truly mad over this person taking away and wiping out my family history.

"I appreciate it." I swallowed down some tears.

Darlene patted my hand. "I know. So, what's on this?" Darlene plucked the flash drive from my fingers.

"The identity of who broke into my house and if I'm right..." I paused for dramatic effect. "Belinda's murderer."

"Why didn't they take it?"

"It was in a place a criminal wouldn't think of checking, a washing machine."

Darlene nodded. "Very good hiding place for valuables. So, do you need my help in deciphering what you found?"

"No. I need your help in letting me know if there was any more to the conversation before the thread got deleted."

"The thread?" Darlene tilted her head and then her eyes widened. "Oh, *the* thread. I guess I know why you didn't want to help me earlier."

Actually, I wouldn't have wanted to help her even without the thread. A thought I politely kept in my head.

"I got carried away. I was so angry about what Belinda did. She knew I wouldn't want her submitting under her name. Someone had to encourage her..."

"Naturally, you thought it was me."

Darlene smiled a little bashfully. "Considering how no one would ever mistake us for friends or even acquaintances it wasn't a far stretch."

I crossed my arms. "Didn't I grant you a little favor during our last contest? I'm not out to get you."

"I let my emotions get the best of me. Those women started coming after me..." Her hands splayed open, Darlene rested them under her throat. "...like I was lying about Belinda. Not that it's important now. I hate the fact the last words I had with my cousin were cross ones."

"I'm sure Belinda forgave you."

Darlene lowered her hands to her lap and stared at them. "I'll never know for sure."

With her usual brusque and condescending manner, it was easy to overlook Darlene's grief. Her cousin was murdered after they had a very public brawl and people now believed she did it. It was bad enough for people to think you killed a stranger, but a family member was a different kind of heartbreak.

Compassion welled up in me. I draped an arm over Darlene's shoulders. "We'll find out who did this and clear your name. I promise."

"Really?" Steve's angry voice drifted toward us.

We both jumped in our chairs. Darlene's purse tumbled to the floor.

"I believe that's called interfering in a police investigation, which I know you've both been warned about." Steve's angry tone floated around us.

And I'm sure down the hall. I kept my gaze to the front.

"Look at the time." Darlene scrambled to her feet. "Mrs. Alwright was correct. We needed to have this little chat. I don't need the court after all."

"Me neither." I shot to my feet and attempted my getaway.

Steve snagged an arm of mine and one of Darlene's. "Not so fast, ladies. My office. Now."

Darlene shot me a do-something look.

I stared at her with "what" in my gaze. Scream. Cry. Faint. Kiss him. How in the world did she expect me to get us out of this? I'd only prolong the inevitable. Steve would get his lecture in sooner or later. I preferred sooner, before the later happened in front of my grandmothers—or even worse, Detective Roget.

Besides, there might be something in Steve's office useful to our investigation. I heaved out a defeated sigh. "I thought you were in court."

"I'm sure you did." Steve released our arms and made an "after you" gallant gesture.

"There goes the plan," Darlene muttered under her breath. Steve trailed behind us.

Mrs. Alwright ducked down and fiddled with the cords under her desk. She ratted me out. Probably thought Darlene and I were too quiet. Or else Karen did. Mrs. Alwright wanted Steve and me together. Karen wanted her and Steve as the couple.

"Quit the pessimism. I can work with this." I lowered my head, feigning shame.

"You better," Darlene said.

I would. If nothing else, I'd find out exactly what Karen knew and told Steve. And why he'd been avoiding me the last few nights. After all, he was the one who wanted our relationship moving forward and once I said yes, he started running backwards.

I chased after answers, not a man who changed his mind based on rumors—or the truth.

TWENTY

Steve clicked the tip of the ballpoint pen. In and out. In and out. The noise scratched along my nerves. It felt like a torture device. He waited for us to crack. Kind of silly since he overheard us. He already knew what we were up to, why the need for our admission.

I wished he'd get the lecture over. I had places to go, snooping to do, and other people to avoid.

I squirmed in the chair. Darlene crossed her legs and clutched her purse to her chest.

"Are you two aware interfering in a police investigation is a crime?" Steve placed the pen down and steepled his fingers, tapping his index fingers as he glowered at us.

I rolled my eyes, finding no reason to answer an obvious, and a rhetorical, question. Of course I knew. He knew I knew.

"Since when is two women offering each other support interfering?" Darlene asked.

"When it's based on them deciding the police can't do their jobs and are going to investigate a murder on their own."

I fixed my innocent-damsel eyes on Steve. "I didn't say that. Neither did Darlene." Or at least not to my recollection. "Did someone say we did?"

Darlene snorted then lifted her nose in the mock aristocratic way she had from watching and re-watching *Downton Abbey*.

"You did." Steve centered a hard look on me. "I clearly heard you promise to find out who did this and clear Ms. Johnson's name."

Oh! I did say that. Now I needed a good reason for saying it.

Darlene bumped my elbow while she dug around in her purse. She pulled out a handkerchief and dabbed at her eyes.

"Great. Now, I'm going to have to admit this in front of Darlene." I heaved out a long sigh adding a little moan on the end. "I said it to make her feel better. She told me how distraught she was over the argument her and Belinda had in Scrap This. What she said during the fight were the last words they spoke to each other. I wanted her to know that someone knew she wasn't that horrible of a woman, to kill her own family member."

"You don't believe me!" Darlene wailed. She squashed the handkerchief against her face.

Okay, she was going a little over the top. Steve wasn't going to believe this display. If she didn't want to help, she should at least not hamper my work.

"I never thought you did it, I just don't want to hunt down a killer. I'm not fond of jails." I tapped Steve's desk. "That's for the record, so don't forget to write it down. I was talking about finding out who was spreading vicious rumors about her being a murderer. No one's been charged—"

"This is so embarrassing." Darlene broke in, whispering out of the side of her mouth.

"You should be ashamed. Believing I'm accusing you of murder."

"Not that," Darlene said between clenched teeth. She glanced down at her lap then shot me a wide-eye look. "I think that I need to leave."

Steve looked from Darlene to me, a frown etching itself onto his face. If he wasn't careful, the scowl would stick there. "This conversation isn't over."

"We're not dense. We get it. We're not police. We shouldn't be investigating crimes. Fine. I won't. But, I will help Faith find her photographs someone swiped. I don't think the police really care about those."

Concern grew on Steve's face. "Someone took your photos."

About time I got some sign he still cared about me. I nodded while pouting. "Also deleted all the ones I had on my computer."

"Why?" Steve tugged a sheet of paper toward him and scanned over it.

Was that the police report from last night? What had Ted written on it? If he wrote down what had been stolen from the box, I'd... Well, I wasn't sure what I'd do yet but I'd think of something. Maybe start with calling his brother and then his mother.

Darlene opened her purse and glanced inside. She groaned. "I'll never get over this trauma."

"I have no intention of mentioning to anyone what I overheard you and Faith discussing." The shift of Steve's tone when he said "discussing" told me it wasn't his first choice of word.

Darlene shot an exasperated look at me. "He really does not get it."

I rolled my eyes. "He's a man, of course he doesn't."

Steve's eyebrows rose. "Now it's my turn to ponder if I should be offended."

I let out a small laugh. "It's not being offended you're going to have to worry about. Darlene needs to leave. It's an emergency."

"Someone sent you the news telepathically." He looked over the top of the sheet of paper.

"No. Women kind of know."

Steve's quizzical expression reminded me of a puppy being told "no" when they tried chewing on a tempting leather shoe.

"Trust me. You. Don't. Want. To. Know."

Darlene clutched a cylinder shape in her hand.

His face reddened then whitened. He finally got it. "You can go."

Darlene gingerly got to her feet. When she opened the door, she fired off a wink at me.

Well played. I avoided fixing my admiring gaze on her as she skedaddled out of the room lest Steve pick up on the fact he'd been had.

I stood.

"I have something I still need to discuss with you." Steve placed the paper on his desk.

"Who says I want to hear it?"

"Please, Faith." Steve pointed at the chair.

"I thought you weren't talking to me."

Steve placed an elbow on the desk then dropped his face into his hand. He rubbed at his temples. "It's not what you think."

"Doesn't matter what I think, or what the truth is. You made some lame excuse the other night then didn't even acknowledge me yesterday. It's rude and hurtful. You had to have known something happened with Ted showing up."

"Why would I think Ted showing up meant someone broke into your house?" Jealousy weaved around his words. "You guys seem to spend a lot of time together."

It made me a little glad but more annoyed. Not that it mattered. I could take Steve or leave him.

Who was I kidding? Now that I decided I wanted Steve, I wanted him to want me. I wasn't good at pretending to myself his aloofness didn't bother me. Silence enveloped the room. Not the warm, companionable silence we usually shared, but the awkward kind when a couple ran out of stuff to say.

"I didn't want anyone accusing you of something terrible," Steve finally said.

"Like insinuating I was playing two men against each other." I spun toward the door.

"Someone in this office leaked confidential information that might be the basis for a crime."

I froze. "They think it was you. That you told me something?"

"I'm not the suspect, and I'm also not in the clear. I didn't want you dragged into it. This office is looking for a person to blame. Jobs will be lost. If not charges filed."

"It can't be that bad."

Steve collapsed into his chair. "It is."

I sat in Steve's lap and drew him into a hug.

"If someone comes in..."

I saw the reluctance in his eyes and in the half-hearted attempt he made in pushing me away. I tightened my hold. For once, I wanted to make him feel better. Show him I cared about him as much as he cared about me.

Steve would do anything for me. Stand by me. He showed it when Ted and I went toe-to-toe when Marilyn was arrested. Steve didn't like me getting involved. His feelings were all about my safety rather than 'keeping me in my place'.

He gave me the benefit of the doubt. Always. Even—and especially—when I didn't deserve it or acted like I wanted it. I knew what I had to do. It was time. Tell Steve about Adam. Fear churned my stomach.

"I'm sorry for giving you a rough time." I repositioned myself so we looked into each other's eyes. We needed the air cleared between us for us to move forward.

Steve locked his hands around my waist. "How are you giving me a rough time?"

"Arguing with you the other day and all the days before. I just don't want you to tread carefully around me so I don't blow up."

"I want to tread carefully, as you say, because I care about you and it pains me when I hurt your feelings. I don't like it when my words, or actions, make you feel bad about yourself. I've never wanted to be that type of person."

"You never are." I hugged him tight, pressing my cheek into his chest. The cologne tingled my nose and the rest of my body. "I'm sorry I made you feel that way."

"You're not making me feel that way." Steve stressed the word "making." "It's something I want to always be aware of. I want you to feel safe with me. Trust that I believe in you and know you're nothing less than amazing."

I heard the pain in Steve's voice. I knew that pain. It came from experience. From fighting the demons others created inside of you because of their treatment. A tightness began in my chest and spread across my whole body. Someone had hurt Steve, made this honorable, decent man question himself and his worth.

"I feel the same way about you," I said.

"You should probably get going before your grandmothers send out a search party." Steve's voice was a little rough around the edges.

"Mrs. Alwright wouldn't tell anyone on me." I grinned at him. "She helped me see the light when I wanted to take a restraining order out on Darlene."

All traces of playfulness left his eyes. Steve went to stand with me still in his lap.

"It's time for you to go."

Oh no! Mrs. Alwright. She was the suspected leak. She walked in and out of everyone's office, had access to all places. Knew where everyone went. No one thought anything of speaking in front of her because she was a fixture of the courthouse, like the Lady of Justice Statue guarding the entrance to the courtroom.

"Will she be fired?"

Remorse clouded his dark brown eyes. "Firing is the least of her worries."

"She'd never mean any harm. Mrs. Alwright likes being help-ful. She hates seeing people going after each other, even through the court—"

"It's not her place. She's not a counselor. Consequences to oth-ers overrule good intentions at times."

I drew in a sharp breath and gripped the edge of Steve's desk. His eyes said it all. I wasn't the only one who was talked out of filing a restraining order against someone. But unlike Darlene and I's being a ruse, the other person had a valid concern.

And was now dead.

I stumbled to my car. Mrs. Alwright wanted to help. How could she have predicted such a horrific event? I covered my eyes, blocking out the sun and the world. My thoughts spun out of control.

Question after question. Fact after fact. Belinda had seemed so happy and carefree Saturday. Not like a woman who was afraid of someone. Then again, how did a woman fearing for their life act? No one knew how scared I started becoming of Adam. Everyone saw the hero. The good guy. The officer and the gentlemen. Not the Hyde lurking behind Jekyll.

Belinda had been a little hesitant at the class but I chalked it up to her having borrowed the class idea from Darlene. Had she been afraid of someone in the class? Someone she expected to take the class? When the fight started, Belinda had pulled back and half-hidden behind her mother. Did Hazel know who her daughter feared?

If Hazel's behavior indicated anything, I was the person Belinda feared. I was darn certain I had never threatened Belinda or acted in a hostile manner toward her. Now, if Darlene had wound up dead, I could understand the finger pointing at me.

My mind drifted toward Leslie Amtower. Had Belinda worried about the possibility of the editor-in-chief of *Making Legacies* finding out and feared the woman's reaction? Or did she want to stop the woman from finding out, kind of expecting the blow-up with Darlene, and wanted to keep the woman away by using a restraining order.

Or hoped a restraining order would keep Darlene away. I had to find out. I reached for the handle of my car and groaned. Tucked up under my windshield was a ticket. Could this day get worse? Scratch that. I didn't want to know.

I yanked the ticket from underneath and noticed the license plate number. Not mine. And the date was from two weeks ago. Pen scratches on the reverse side poked through the paper. I flipped it over.

Seven. Church. Movie night. Be there.

No one ever attended the movies Pastor Evans showed. The first time the young, hip and trendy pastoral couple had movie night at the church the whole town showed up...then left. We'd assumed it would be one of the usual church movie fares, *Fire Proof, Facing the Giants, Flywheel, Courageous,* instead it was movies Mrs. Evans made of her husband's sermons.

I'd be there all right. If Belinda had a stalker, her cousin would know. Unless the person Belinda feared was Darlene herself. Steve wouldn't tell me. And Mrs. Alwright had enough trouble closing in around her.

Before any meeting, I had to do some investigating. Before I involved myself further into the mess with Darlene, I needed to know if Darlene was innocent once and for all. There was no way I wanted to help a murderer.

I pulled out my cell phone and dialed the store. "Hi Grandma. I'm going to be even later. I have a couple more errands."

"Why don't you just take the day off, honey," Hope said. "You had such a rough night."

I took the excuse offered and ran with it. "You're right. I'm going pick up some new reading material. Not much in the mood for mysteries right now. I should also explain to Oliver about the damaged books."

Hope clucked her tongue in sympathy. "I understand. If Oliver gives you a hard time, let me know. I'll have a chat with his aunt. And sweetie, I have some samples for a new Christmas line I could drop off tonight."

While tempting, I declined the offer. "I have to sort through all my supplies and reorganize. The person made a mess."

"I just can't believe it happened. To think I was home and didn't hear or see anything."

For which I was very thankful. "It probably happened earlier in the day. The person jumped the fence. It's just things."

"Sounds like vindictiveness to me. Deleting your photos. Don't worry about those, sweetie. Between me, Cheryl and Steve, I'm sure we can replace those."

"You're right. I should have thought about that."

Someone tapped on my window. I startled. A uniformed parking authority officer pointed at the meter then made a go-away gesture. "Have to go, Grandma."

"You better not be driving and talking to me on your cell, young lady."

"No. Never." I ended the call. I eased away from the curb and headed for the library. This time, I'd use a public computer for researching. If the culprit got back into my house, they wouldn't be able to figure out what I was up to this time.

TWENTY-ONE

Chipped paint from the large columns flanking the library doors decorated the sidewalk. I shuffled my feet on the mat outside the doors in case I picked up a few paint samples.

A huge sign was taped to the front window of the library. "Turn cell phones off before stepping through this door."

One little phone call and the man went crazy about it. I complied with the request. Earning a library degree sure did make Oliver White one grumpy man. I tugged open the door and stepped inside.

Oliver pointed at me. "Cell phone."

"I know how to read."

He crossed his gangly arms over his thin chest and scowled. "Hear it all the time."

"It's off. If it rings, call my grandmothers."

"Don't think I won't young lady." He wagged his finger at me.

I stormed over to the counter. Oliver took a step back. I braced my hands on the gray surface.

"You are five years older than me. Five." I held out my hand and displayed the number I meant with my fingers. "Don't talk to me like I'm a child."

"Well...umm..." He swallowed a few times. "I wasn't. I talk to everyone like that."

"And there's your problem. Try treating adults like adults and they might not work so hard at annoying you, like keeping cell phones on and calling each other."

Of course, adults setting up special obnoxious ring tones just for library use weren't very adult like. I headed for one of the computers.

"Sign in." Oliver held up a clipboard.

"There's no one else using them." The five computers donated by the Gates Foundation were on the starter screen.

"Rules are rules. Everyone must follow them."

I stomped over and scribbled my name down and the time. "Happy?" I thrust the clipboard back at him.

Oliver smiled. "Yes. Thank you so very much. I hope you enjoyed the books I choose for you."

The books. My shoulders slumped forward. "Yeah, about the books..."

"Let me guess, you dropped them in a puddle." Oliver shook his head. "Why do people refuse to take care of other people's items?"

"I didn't drop them. Someone broke into my house and destroyed them."

Oliver tapped on the keyboard. "Of course. Some criminal forced their way into your house to destroy library books. Must say at least you have an original excuse."

The printer hummed. Oliver leaned over and snagged the page from the printer. "Here you go. The cost to replace those books is one hundred and sixty dollars."

Was he serious? He expected me to pay for those books? I had a good wage and since my grandmothers didn't charge me rent, I held my own financially, but not enough to feel an almost two hundred dollar unexpected expense.

"I was a victim of a crime."

"Bring me a copy of the police report and I'll see what the board members say." Oliver leaned against the counter, like every ounce of energy drained out of him. "The fact of the matter is those books need to be replaced. Someone will have to pay for them. Our funding has gone down."

"Maybe they don't all have to be replaced."

I'm sure Ted would rather the library didn't have a book encouraging citizens to become private detectives.

Oliver's eyes narrowed.

I shouldn't have said that. Now Oliver thought I was making up a story to keep the books. If I wasn't careful, he'd call the police on me for stealing the library's property.

"It might be a couple of months."

"That'll be fine. The books are due back in three weeks. Then there's a month's grace period before your account will be placed on hold until the bill is paid."

I walked over to the computers. I'd just have to curtail my scrapbook spending for a few months. I'd rather pay than have the police report passed around the members of the library board.

I picked the computer furthest from the door and Oliver's eyes. I glanced over my shoulder. Oliver inspected books he plucked out from the return book bin.

I was either getting paranoid or a little narcissistic. Everyone in town wasn't interested in what I was doing or even cared. I typed Leslie Amtower and *Making Legacies* into the search engine. The first item was the link to the magazine. No dirt I needed there. The next few listings were places selling the magazine.

Using the mouse, I hit the arrow on the bottom and went to the second page of results. I scrolled down the list. Look at that, a complaint thread about another Life Artist Diva on a scrapbooking message board. Now I was getting somewhere. I clicked.

Ms. Amtower didn't do a very good job at picking her divas this year. There was a controversy surrounding another one of the choices for this year's life artist panel. The rules had stated the photographs used in the projects had to have been taken by the life artist and it seems the new reigning queen had a little help. Unless she had the arm span of Elastigirl. Two of the queen's layouts showed her getting a mammogram, and another straddling a live alligator.

I doubted, along with a large numbers of members of this message board community, she took those pictures herself. I found a lot of smoke, so I went on the hunt for the fire.

An hour later, I had enough flames to create a backfire and stop the plans Leslie Amtower had to destroy Scrap This. I pulled out my cell phone. There were two places in town where Leslie Amtower could be staying. It's time I arranged a meeting with the woman and found out for certain what she was up to.

Oliver cleared his throat. The man had a sixth sense when it came to phones. I dumped the history on the computer. Better safe than sorry. I had enough sorry in my life right now, and some of it was running loose around town.

The old Victorian house converted into a bed-and-breakfast was located at the tip of Eden. A few more feet and you'd be in the next county and state. The house had been spruced up by the owners with an interesting color palette. Unfortunately we didn't have a thriving historical society and so the vintage house now sported yellow and blue paint, Mountaineer colors.

I understood supporting the "local" college team but not by defacing a house. It was easy for travelers to find and did bring in some tourists. Fans loved staying in the house filled to the rafters with WVU memorabilia.

I had to park on the street as the driveway was full. Four cars crowded the tiny space. I hated walking into the temporary territory of the enemy. When one wanted to interrogate a suspect, and wasn't a police officer, they had to accept the meeting place the might-be guilty insisted on.

Leslie sat on the bright yellow porch swing. She stood when my foot hit the first step. She clutched the ends of a cream shawl and shrugged it back onto her shoulders. Tendrils of her blonde hair escaped from its high ponytail. "The game room is free to use."

"Why don't we go up to your room?"

"So you can leave something incriminating behind and have one of your boyfriends come look for it? Just because I'm not a resident, don't think I haven't heard about your affairs with the homicide detective and the assistant prosecutor."

So, my dating two men, which I wasn't doing, had been upgraded by someone to actual affairs. I hoped this piece of gossip slipped right pass my grandmothers' ears and the members of our church. Maybe I should offer to put together the next newsletter to make sure I'm not in the "pray for" section.

The door closed behind Leslie with a resounding bang. I guess I knew how she felt about this meeting. I opened the door and headed for the game room.

Two pair of eyes peeked from around the corner. Jill and Ed hid behind the wall separating the foyer from the main part of the house. Their eyes widened. Whispers exchanged fast and furious between them. I clasped my hands together and sent them a beseeching look. Please, please don't tell my grandmothers.

They zipped their lips. It would cost me, but whatever price I'd gladly pay. I strolled into the game room. My breath hitched in my throat. Sweat coated my hands. What was she doing here?

Karen smiled and gestured at a seat across from her and Leslie. The plan had switched. I was becoming the subject of interrogation. Not for long.

I took my place, then made a production of arranging notes and a pen in front of me. "Interesting friends you've made, Leslie."

"Same could be said for you," Karen said. "You and Darlene sure are chummy."

I shrugged. "You know the saying. Keep your friends close and enemies closer. What's your excuse?"

"I don't need an excuse, Faith." Karen smiled, a sly I-got-you smile that crept along my skin and burrowed into my nerves. "My job in this town is reporting news. The woman who found the body of Belinda Watson and is now demanding a meeting with the editor of *Making Legacies*, is news."

It looked like I should've worried about more than the church news. Most people folded it into a fan or a tool to swat misbehaving children. The town newspaper was read from cover to cover. It took every ounce of will power not to squirm on the wooden dining chair.

Leslie tipped her chin up and raised her brows, "I got you" the look said. Well, I wasn't the only one caught.

"Considering she's trying to slander Scrap This, my grandmothers, and me, I have every reason to want the air cleared between us."

"I don't have anything against your grandmothers."

Interesting. She omitted my name.

Karen jotted down the comment.

"What do you have against me?" I asked.

"Slandering my name all over message boards. Conspiring with Belinda and running this ruse on my magazine. You're out to destroy *Making Legacies*."

"I didn't post anything about the incident at Scrap This. Why would I? It would hurt our store as much as your magazine."

Karen tapped the end of her pen against her plum colored lips. "Faith has a point, Leslie. Why would she want people thinking she not only scammed you but her customers? If she knew Belinda was a fraud and had her teaching, it would destroy a portion of their business."

"Maybe it's because she's thinking about starting her own scrapbook magazine." Leslie shot a triumphant look.

Karen's pen paused above her paper.

"And why would you think that?" Had she been in the library when I asked Oliver? Or had he told her? It would've been more proof she broke into my house but none of the books I checked out were about magazine publishing.

"So, you're not going to deny it." Leslie settled back in her chair. "Hazel knew you put Belinda up to it."

"I have no intentions of starting a magazine." I crossed my arms. "It just seems strange you'd jump to that conclusion. Doesn't it seem like an odd thought to pop into someone's head?"

Karen shrugged.

Thanks for the help.

Leslie squirmed. "It doesn't matter where or whom I heard it from."

"Of course it does." I slapped my palms on the table. "You're accusing me of being involved in Belinda's death."

"The police are going to agree with Faith." Karen finally went to bat for me. "Why would you think she set out to destroy your magazine because she wants to run one herself? And how would she do it without capital?"

"Some people's decisions make no sense," Leslie said, her cheeks turning bright pink.

I think the woman realized she listened to the wrong person. I went in for the slam dunk, or home run, whatever it was called. "Like thinking scrapbookers wouldn't figure out a woman couldn't take a picture of herself getting a mammogram or riding an alligator?"

"Are you kidding me?" Karen's pen slipped from her fingers.

Leslie sputtered and turned at least four hues of red, the last one the most unbecoming with her blue eyes and blonde hair.

"Nope." I slid a print out of the rules of the Diva contest and the thread I discovered toward Karen.

Leslie snatched them up and tore them into confetti.

"I can print them out again," I said.

"How dare you!"

"You started this. You accused me of deceiving you when you've been deceiving everyone in the scrapbook world. Just wait until they find out."

Karen scribbled away on her paper.

"Stop writing!" Leslie grabbed at Karen's paper.

"Touch it, lady, and you're going down." The anger and determination in Karen's voice put a quick and sudden stop to Leslie's grabby hands.

"You just wait, Faith Hunter. You won't get away with this."

"You're threatening me." I rose. Bracing my hands on the table, I leaned toward Leslie. I dropped a flash drive into Karen's open purse. "Are you and your smelly goon going to break into my house again? For your information, I made a couple of copies of the information and have been leaving them with people."

"What are you rambling about?" Leslie sputtered.

"You thought erasing my hard drive and stealing all my memory cards would make the truth disappear. What's on a message board, never just stays on a message board. It ain't Vegas."

"She's accusing me of a crime." Leslie nudged Karen. "You heard her. That's slander."

"Not when it's the truth. You and the smelly goon trashed my house and stole my memories." I pointed a shaking finger at Leslie. "You won't get away with it."

"Faith, take it easy," Karen spoke softly, resting a hand on my arm. "I brought a friend with me. A picture is worth a thousand words."

I spotted Leonard the photographer holding his camera toward his face. Karen shook her head and made a cut motion in the air. Leonard lowered the camera.

"I won't stand here any longer and be accused of crimes. You'll hear from my lawyer." Leslie spun on her heels and rushed out of the game room.

My harsh breathing was the only sound in the room.

"I'm sure you know a good lawyer or two." Karen smiled and gathered up her stuff. "Don't worry about her."

"I'm not," I lied.

"If what you said pans out, her lawyer will advise her to keep her mouth shut."

"It will."

"Photos were stolen from your house." Karen's tone was ambiguous. I wasn't sure if she asked a question or made a statement.

"Annoying but nothing irreplaceable," I lied again. "My grandmothers have duplicates of most of the pictures I took."

I decided to return a kindness and not mention Steve.

"Kind of creepy to take someone's family portraits and stuff."

"They wanted to make sure I didn't have a copy of a message board thread. They missed one."

"You should tell Detective Roget what happened here."

I snorted out a laugh. "That's a brilliant idea."

"He'll find out." Karen pointed at the ceiling. Above us were the bedrooms. "Better coming from you."

"You're right." Darn it all. What was this week coming to? Agreeing with Karen, and working with Darlene. "Can I ask you a question?"

"Sure." Karen hitched the strap of her purse onto her shoulder.

"Why did you stop Leonard from taking a photo?"

"Because I like her even less than I like you."

TWENTY-TWO

Tugging my coat tighter around my body, I exited the warmth of my car into the cold night. The temperature had dropped twenty degrees since this morning. I'd rather have been inside my nice warm house scrapbooking with Sierra. She asked about having a cropping session tonight. I wanted to work on mending the fence between us. Instead, I told her I had plans. Vague plans. Plans so vague she now thought I was mad at her.

I hated hurting her. This whole clandestine meeting stuff was getting real old. Darlene better spill out her plan or I'd be in jail for assault and battery. I'd even make the phone call to Ted.

Even wearing a t-shirt, hoodie, and a winter coat the wind snuck inside. Its cold fingers chilled my spine and head. I should've listened to my grandmothers and wore a hat, or even better, stayed home. They thought I was going on a date with Steve. At least with them, my non-answers pointed me in the direction of a man instead of looking for trouble.

Or at least so far. If they saw Steve come home, I'd be in for it.

A large vehicle hummed in the parking lot of the church. Its lights were off so all I saw was a dark outline of the vehicle, but the visor light allowed me to see the beady eyes peering over the steering wheel. Hazel.

I contemplated waving but decided toying with the grieving mother wasn't a wise move. She wasn't hurting anyone sitting there so I'd let her be. Plus, calling the cops put a little knot in the plans of having a secret summit with Darlene. Kind of hard to have a clandestine meeting when the cops are sent to the location. And knowing my luck, Ted would be the one showing up.

I'd rather take my chances with Hazel.

I opened the door leading into the sanctuary. Darkness met me. Feeling my way along the wall, I scooted down the aisle. If Pastor Evans started the movie from the balcony instead of his office using his remote access, one could actually see, instead of Marco Polo-ing it without the benefit of a caller toward a seat.

Pastor Evans might not have expected anyone to come. The reason he didn't sit in the balcony any longer was to avoid hurt feelings and spending another Sunday giving a sermon about supporting ministries.

I banged my knee into a pew and sucked back the curse wanting loose.

"You could just use your cell phone," Darlene's voice weaved through the darkness.

"Oh shut up." I yanked out my phone and walked to the front.

"Aren't we in a pleasant mood?"

"I vetoed a crop date, made up an excuse to my grandmothers, and had to walk through the cold. Now, I have to sit through whatever lame movie Pastor Evans picked."

"We don't have to stay and watch the movie."

"Good. Let's get this over before someone comes in."

"No one ever comes."

"We did."

"I don't need your help," Darlene's voice rose. "If you want to be snippy, go home."

"In your dreams." I whispered harshly. "If it wasn't for me, you'd have nothing to go on."

"Fine. You find out who killed Belinda, since you're the one with all the knowledge. No reason to involve me."

"I don't want you involved. You wouldn't leave me alone."

"What is your problem?" Darlene shifted. The light from the movie flickered over her face. "What did Steve say to you after I left?"

Did I now doubt Darlene's innocence because of what I learned from Steve? Or was I feeling guilty about using people to get to the truth? I lied to my friend. I lied to my grandmothers. I've been lying—withholding information—from Steve and Ted. In the back of my mind, I wondered if Darlene was lying to me.

Time to ferret out the truth. "Belinda was scared about someone. Why didn't you tell me that?"

"What are you talking about?"

"Belinda had gone to the courthouse to get a restraining order."

Darlene shook her head rapidly. "I would've known. Belinda would've told me."

"You didn't know." I kept my words neutral, not a statement nor a question.

"It's a misunderstanding. Belinda wanted to be a mystery writer. She wasn't the best with design principles, but her journaling skills were fantastic. It's why we were working on my mom's cruise album together and I let her have those pages. She'd be able to tell the stories like we were currently living the experience rather than just reading it."

Darlene's words grew softer. Grief laced her words. My heart ached for the woman. She lost her cousin and the police seemed no closer to finding the murderer. Their best suspect was her.

"I am sorry for your loss."

"One thing I know about my family is we don't keep things quiet."

"Belinda did about submitting your layouts," I said.

Darlene opened her pocket book and pulled out a set of keys. "Tomorrow we're going to Belinda's house. We'll find out who's right about the restraining order. Either she was scared about someone and kept it a secret or she progressed on her novel."

"I don't think that's such a good idea." So far, we hadn't really done anything to interfere in the police investigation, but searching a house didn't just have us crossing the line, it had us picking up the line and waving it in Ted's face.

"It's our only chance at finding out the why so we can find out who killed Belinda."

"If we get caught?"

"We won't."

Cold swept into the sanctuary. I turned, assuming Darlene had a matching deer in headlights look plastered on her face.

Ted strolled down the aisle, a small Maglite lighting his way.

Darlene sidled up to me. "If it wasn't me Belinda wanted a restraining order against, it was her mother. And Hazel is laying the groundwork for it being either me, you, or both of us who killed Belinda."

I gaped at Darlene. "Hazel," I hissed. Maybe I should be a little more concerned about Hazel popping up every time I turned around. Of course, if she suspected Darlene, she might be hanging around to protect me.

No. It was more likely she thought I was a murderer.

"Who else is in her life?" Darlene faced forward. "Me, her mother, and her aunt Eliza. My mother has a solid alibi. She's on the same bowling team as the head prosecutor and the Evans'."

"Meet me at the store." I yanked my coat on and stood. It was getting a little too crowded in here.

"My house. Too many people care about what you're doing."

"You ladies didn't come to watch the movie." Ted settled into the pew behind us.

"Of course, I'm just cold. It's freezing in here." I sat back down. Did Hazel rat us out? I could ask Ted, but that also fell into the arena of not a good idea.

I folded my arms against my chest. Pastor Evans flashed onto the screen. His voice boomed as he recited the Christmas Story. A banshee scream had the three audience members doing a little hop into the air. The Hooligans, one by one, launched themselves from the balcony.

The faux angel wings did little to stop the plummet. Sierra's angry scream drowned out the pastor. Hank, Wyatt, and Wayne rushed forward to catch the falling angels.

Last year's Christmas play gone haywire. We warned the pastor not to cast the Hooligans in a role that told them they could fly. I texted Sierra. *Bring your men! Christmas play showing tonight.* They'd love this movie.

Darlene elbowed me. "No texting in church."

Bring snacks. Yeah, like texting in church was the real worry of the night. Why Ted showed up while we were here was a bigger concern. Followed by how we'd get out of this. I doubted Ted would believe Darlene and I just happened to show up tonight and decided to sit next to each other. Especially since there was a plethora of pews to choose.

The Christmas play was now at the moment of the shouting match between Pastor Evans and Sierra. The pastor had accidentally referred to Harold, Henry, and Howard out loud by their town nickname. The boys heard none of it as they had now turned their roles of "falling" angels to avenging angels and stabbing at the parishioners with their cardboard swords.

Another thing Pastor Evans was advised against doing. Play swords and rowdy boys were always a bad mix.

"Start it over! Start it over!"

I, and the two other people in the sanctuary, heard the Hooligans before the door was yanked open. Sneakered feet thundered down the aisle and I braced myself for having a child, or three, jump on me. The Hooligans believed in full out body contact greetings.

"I'd move over if I was you," I whispered to Darlene.

For once in her life, she complied without argument. She probably guessed where the Hooligans planned their attack.

Panic welled up inside of me. The door to the church didn't open again. Hank and Sierra dropped the Hooligans off and made their escape. I looked over my shoulder, willing and begging for Sierra and Hank or just one of them, to come inside. I didn't want responsibility for the three rambunctious boys. When I told Sierra to bring her men, I meant with her. Not to leave them with me. Ugh! What had I gotten myself into?

The boys stopped at the end of the pew where Ted sat. I grinned. I could work with this.

"Guys, this is Detective Ted. He works in homicide."

"You mean dead people." Glee filled Harold's voice.

"Dead people other people made dead." Henry knelt beside me, facing Ted.

"Do you have a gun?" Howard went to poke the detective in the side.

Ted shifted away. If it wasn't so dark, I'm sure I would've seen a glare in Ted's green eyes.

"Didn't your mother teach you not to talk to strangers?" he asked.

"Yeah. But we don't listen too good." Harold made himself comfortable beside Ted.

"Anyway, you're a cop. A good guy." Henry climbed over the pew and dropped onto Ted.

A grunt was forced out of the man.

"Dad says we should make friends with the law." Howard went to the pew behind Ted and stood on it. He reached forward and wrapped his little arms around Ted.

Ted made a strangling sound. Howard decided to hang from Ted's neck.

Darlene dabbed her eye with a tissue. "You are such a wonderful man to take such interest in the Hool...Hank and Sierra's sons. Imagine bringing them to church with you."

"I didn't..." Words gargled out of Ted.

"Cool! Will you take us home in your squad car?" Henry asked.

"With the lights on?" Howard continued to play the role of a necklace.

"Better without," Harold said. "Mom might think red flashing lights are a bad thing."

"I'd love to photograph this moment." Darlene heaved out a sigh.

A brilliant plan popped into my head. "My camera's in the car. I'll go get it."

I exited the pew from the opposite end where Ted sat. I wasn't taking a chance he'd grab onto me or send a Hooligan to tackle me as a game of cops and robbers.

I hurried outside and made a beeline to Hazel's car. She was holding a flashing and rivet to some kind of reading material. Too bad *The Complete Idiot's Guide to Private Investigating* got destroyed by the breaking and entering culprit; I'd have mentioned it was at the library and encouraged Hazel to spend some time reading it. I do believe she was going about it all wrong.

I knocked on Hazel's window. She startled. She really needed a new hobby. Spying wasn't good for her nerves.

"Darlene, Detective Roget, and the Hooligans are in there. I think there's some plotting going on." I skipped over to my car and got inside.

Hazel plodded toward the church, head lowered like a bull charging.

Quickly, I pulled forward and onto the main road. Ted would have his hands full between stopping Darlene and Hazel from going at it, and the Hooligans from...well, I'm not sure what those three little boys could concoct in their devious mind, but I knew it would be a doozy.

TWENTY-THREE

Thursday morning, Scrap This buzzed with energy. It annoyed me. The *beep* and *boops* of the cash register grated on my nerves as Marilyn rang up a large purchase of cardstock. The hushed conversation of customers pricked at my skin. Sierra hummed along to the music that piped in from the stereo in the employee lounge. I gritted my teeth to keep from asking her to stop singing.

I dropped the cardboard box I held onto the floor. It landed with a resounding thud. I knelt in front of the paper racks, yanked open the box, and ripped off the plastic protecting the pattern paper. The first sheet crinkled over my manhandling.

Two nights in a row I averaged four hours of sleep. I had no idea how I'd put up with Darlene tonight. I shoved a stack of pattern paper into the correct slot.

"Customers will demand a discount if the corners are bent." Marilyn joined me on the floor. "I wish you'd let us help you."

"One woman is capable of doing this job." I grabbed the next design.

Marilyn gently took it from my hands. "That's not what I'm talking about, Faith. Stop trying to pretend the break-in didn't scare you."

"I'm not scared."

"Okay. Whatever." Shaking her head sadly, Marilyn stood.

I caught hold of her wrist. "It bothers me. I know why they took what they did. I just can't figure out what they were afraid I'd figure out."

"We could help." Marilyn pointed at herself then Sierra.

"I don't want to drag anyone else into this."

"I'm asking, you're not dragging me. Besides, you helped me." Marilyn smiled.

I grinned up at her. "I do recall there was a little dragging going on then."

She held her right index finger and thumb a few centimeters away from each other. "Tiny bit."

I glanced around the store. "Once it's cleared out some."

"And your grandmothers head out for lunch."

"Exactly."

"I'll take care of restocking." Marilyn shooed up toward the counter. "Why don't you go look at the new lines coming out? There's some real beautiful stuff on page twenty-five. I think you'll really love it."

Sounded good. Nothing lifted my spirits like shopping and scrapbooking. For the next hour, Sierra and I oohed and aahed, yes-and-no'ed items. There was one paper that had a very sexy-looking Santa Claus on it. I lifted the catalog, twisting and turning it.

"I don't know," I said. We'd have some customers rushing in to buy, and others coming in to pray for our troubled souls.

"A few sheets would be good," Sierra said. "I'd like to request the firefighter and pilot."

I wanted the cowboy paper and the matching washi tape.

I heard my grandmothers walking from the back office toward the shopping area. Good. Soon, I'd see what Sierra and Marilyn thought about the thread I saved from total annihilation.

"It's nice," I said. "More than nice, but I don't know of a layout it'd work with."

Hope and Cheryl hovered behind us.

"I'd put it in a frame and hang it on my bedroom wall," Cheryl said. "I'd love looking at it every morning and night."

"No embellishments needed for that paper," Hope said. "That's what I call a yummy sheet of paper."

Heat licked my cheeks. I slapped the catalog onto the counter face down. "Grandmas!"

Giggling, they linked arms and skipped out of the store. I wondered what it would be like to have a best-friend-forever like Hope and Cheryl found in each other.

Sierra turned the book back over and jotted down the item number. "I double-dog dare you to put a framed copy in each of their bedrooms."

"So, what's going on?" Marilyn rushed over to the counter.

The only two customers, a mother and daughter combination, were in the back of the store browsing through our choices of Halloween themed products.

"I think I know the key to who broke into my house and is trying to implicate me in Belinda's death..."

Marilyn and Sierra drew in sharp breaths.

The customers spun toward us.

I grabbed the catalog and held it up. "Thinking about adding this Santa to our Christmas collection. Yes or no?"

The women headed over. Their eyes grew wide.

The gray-haired older woman fanned her cheeks. "Darling, get me a ream. I know who's going on the front of my Christmas cards for the red-hat society."

"Mother! What will father say?"

"To send one to his aunt and give her a merry, merry Christmas."

The thirty-something-year-old woman blushed and rushed back to the safety of the spooky and creepy Halloween items. "I'm never taking you shopping again."

"And I thought I raised me a liberal girl." The mom tapped the picture of the nearly naked pilot. "I'd like him also."

It had nothing to do with being prudish. There were just some things a gal didn't want to know her mother, or grandmothers, gushed over. Hot men were one of them. It felt a little weird to be thinking wicked thoughts about the man you're grandmothers were ogling.

Once the women became immersed back in the Halloween area, I explained my theory to Sierra and Marilyn.

"You're talking about the thread I called you about." Sierra reached for the flash drive I held.

Sniped about. I kept the correction in my head and nodded. Sierra opened the document. Marilyn stood behind her and read over her shoulder.

"This looks like what I read. I can check. I used Hank's email to send me a copy of it."

The three of us put our heads together and compared. After twenty minutes of checking and double-checking we came to the same conclusion. Duplicate.

"This Little Lamb persona has it in for you," Marilyn said. "I don't like it. I'm worried. You should stay with me and the kids."

I shook my head. "I think it's just keyboard bravery."

Marilyn opened her mouth.

"And if it's not, there's no way I'm putting your teens in danger by staying at your house."

"You can stay with me." Sierra grinned, but I saw the lick of fear in her eyes. "My boys are more a danger than anyone else. The poor sap will confess to all and anything to get out of their clutches."

"I'll be fine. If I'm that worried about my safety, I'm sure Steve will camp out in my living room."

"I'd have him protecting me in the bedroom." Marilyn waggled her eyebrows at me.

I did the best thing, ignored the comment and returned the conversation to its intended content. "Whoever Little Lamb is, they're local."

"I don't have a clue about who it could be." Sierra tapped her lip with her nail.

"Me neither." Marilyn patted my hand. "Sorry. Some big help I am."

"This was good. I now know this was the original conversation, and I'm not crazy that Little Lamb has something against me."

"The two people at the top of that list are Darlene and Karen," Marilyn said.

I would've added Leslie except I hadn't known until after the fact about the internet trash-fest. I scrolled and pointed at the posting times.

"Darlene posted under her own name. Unless she posted from a laptop and a desktop, there's no way she could've logged in and out so fast."

"That leaves Karen."

"Why would she be prowling around a scrapbooking board?" I asked.

"Cause she doesn't like you, and likes Steve."

The customers approached the register. Marilyn went to ring up the women.

Sierra squinted at the screen. "I know the answer is here but I can't see it. Ugh." She pushed away from the computer.

"Not everyone is talented at finding a hidden meaning."

Oliver. I grinned.

The bell jingled as our customers left.

"What?" Sierra looked worried.

"I think I need to show this to our resident email analyzer." I dug my cell phone from my purse. There were some calls I'd rather not make on the company line.

"What?"

"Oliver White. He has this uncanny ability of taking everything in a very literal manner." I explained about the email I sent and what he told Annette.

"Perfect." Marilyn clapped. "I hope he can figure this out."

"Shh..." I silenced them when Oliver picked up. "Hi Oliver, this is Faith—"

"Mr. White," he responded.

"Okay, hello Mr. White..."

Sierra and Marilyn rolled their eyes.

"I was wondering if you could interpret something for me. You're the best word guy around."

"And what would this document be? Family historical record? Old documents someone else found?" There was a hint of interest in his voice.

"Not exactly. It's a conversation I got off a message board. Stuff said about the store."

"If this stuff is slanderous or libel in nature, I would make an appointment with an attorney who specializes in those types of cases."

"I'm not sure it is. It's kind of vague. You're the only person I know who can read words as they are actually written." I hoped it came across the way I intended.

"Many people do say that. It's an inherited skill."

Sierra jabbed me, indicating she wanted me to hurry and get a commitment.

I'm trying. I mouthed. "Could you come over and take a look at it?"

Clicks sounded in the background. "I can come by tomorrow."

"Tomorrow?"

Sierra and Marilyn shook their heads.

"Yes. I have a board meeting tonight, followed by a date which I will not change for you."

A date? Oliver dated? Who knew, and who was I to interfere with a blooming romance. "Tomorrow it is. I appreciate it."

"I can schedule you in for lunch."

"That works. I'll pick up two of Home Brewed's specials and have them at the store."

"It's a date, Faith. I have it marked on my calendar." Oliver ended the call with a chipper "See you tomorrow."

I hoped Oliver didn't consider it a real date. I'd never hear the end of it from my grandmothers. Well, I'd find out tonight. If Oliver thought he and I were having a romantic luncheon, he'd tell his aunt, who'd tell my grandmothers. Maybe Oliver wouldn't want to be considered a guy who got around.

Who was I kidding? Oliver would love to be the "hottest" bachelor in town.

I passed the rest of the afternoon and early evening glancing at the clock and playing HWOI—How Would Oliver Interpret.

JealousMuch sounded like a random internet person who liked being in the middle of the drama. The bits and pieces they threw came from what Darlene posted that night, and possibly what Darlene posted in the past. Some of those women had long memories and spreadsheets so detailed it'd make the CIA jealous.

Little Lamb was different. Vicious. The poster said everything in a calculated way. Not accusing, yet laying the groundwork for others to think the absolute worst about a person. Like with me. Everyone in Eden knew the truth about Michael's murder. As did every scrapbooker interested in our store, it made no sense to accuse me of that crime.

My eyes kept returning to the phrase "Maybe that too." Was Little Lamb insinuating I was involved in Belinda submitting those fraudulent layouts or something more sinister? Like her murder. I sucked in a breath.

Marilyn spun toward me.

I shoved a finger into my mouth and held up a piece of paper.

She made a production of shuddering. Anyone who worked with paper knew how much a cut hurt.

I clicked out of the document, wishing I could just as easily get rid of the thought swirling in my head.

What if they were laying the groundwork for accusing me of Belinda's murder? A murder they knew took place before anyone else did. There were only two people in Eden who hated me enough to ruin my life. Karen and Darlene. And one of them had all the evidence of me having been accused before.

TWENTY-FOUR

What had I gotten myself into? I plucked at a thread hanging from the black shirt Darlene insisted I wore. The one the exact shade of black as the leggings she also instructed I wear.

Darlene frowned. "Stop that. My mother spent a lot time working on our outfits."

Groaning, I hit the back of my head multiple times on the headrest. "Your mother knows."

"Of course she does." Darlene continued looking straight ahead, hands in the two and ten position, and the speedometer precisely at thirty-five miles per hour.

At this speed, I could throw myself out the passenger side door and only suffer some minor cuts and bruises.

Thirty minutes ago, when I opened the door to Darlene's knocking, my instinct screamed "don't do it." I ignored it. Darlene handed me the outfit and said I needed to change into the proper sleuthing apparel, my brain said "Danger! Do not proceed." I ignored it also. My heart clenched when I grabbed the handle of the car and tugged it opened. I was getting used to ignoring these signs.

I was one of those too-stupid-to-live women in books my grandmothers and I complained about.

Darlene switched on the blinker and the *click-cluck* sounded through the car. If I was going to make a break for it, the time was when she slowed down for the turn. I gripped the handle.

Then let go of it. Apparently, I had enough sense not to jump out of a moving vehicle. I sighed.

"Oh come on, it's not that bad." Darlene finally looked at me. "You look great. Thinner. Black does wonders for your figure."

I wished I was the ninja the outfit portrayed me as. I'd take her out with one chop to the side of her neck.

Darlene parallel parked between a Jeep and a small sedan across the street from Belinda's house.

A loud, rowdy group of people clustered around the house Darlene parked in front of. Music blared and thumped the car.

How would this help us in not being spotted? Usually, when people decided to sneak into a house, they parked far enough away that their vehicle wouldn't be spotted and recognized.

"I think we should find something on the next block." Somewhere with less people milling about.

Darlene turned off the engine. "Let's go."

"We don't want to be caught. Remember? How is this inconspicuous? People here know your car."

"Precisely. It's not unusual for me to visit Belinda. Besides, how can we blend in with the surroundings if we're carrying evidence down the block?"

I hated the fact Darlene made a good point. Slinking down the street in the middle of the night with a bag of stuff wouldn't work in our favor. Halloween was still a week away.

"You'd better have a good plan if we get caught," I said. "And it better not be ditching me again."

"I don't plan on getting caught." Darlene flipped down the visor and peered intently into the small mirror.

My stomach tightened and I stared straight ahead, fighting the urge to look behind me and see what troubled Darlene. Knowing my luck, it was Ted, or worse, my grandmothers.

They'd warned me to stay out of this mess and couldn't fathom why I'd help Darlene. They understood allowing a friend to talk me into investigating a murder to clear their name, quite different when it was the person who got on my last nerve. I knew even pulling out it was the "Christian thing" to help a neighbor in need wouldn't sway them away from anger.

Frowning, Darlene ran a finger over and under her mouth. She snapped the visor up. "All ready. Let's go."

"Really, a lipstick check?"

"One must always look their best." Darlene sent a critical appraisal my way. "I wouldn't expect you to understand that."

"We're breaking and entering, not meeting the man of our dreams." I thrust open the passenger side door.

Stay in the car. The voice of reason screeched at me. This was going to go bad. I felt it in my bones and stomach. A headache sprouted and a tiny voice in my head kept repeating frenemy over and over.

I wasn't quite sure if the voice meant Darlene or myself.

"One never knows when the man of their dreams will show himself." Darlene adjusted the drape of her matching black tunic.

I shuddered and slunk out of the car, heading toward Belinda's house. I did not want the man of my dreams—not that I really had one—showing up when I was participating in a misdemeanor at the best, or a felony at the worst.

I glanced around and tiptoed over to the side of the house, figuring we'd go through the back door. I patted my pocket. I sure hoped a gift card worked. I didn't bring a credit card just in case I accidently dropped it.

Darlene clopped straight up to the front door in her designer high-heeled boots, instead of quietly making her way to the back of the house like I planned. Did she not watch any crime shows?

"Psst..." I hissed. I jerked my thumb down the small strip of land between Belinda's house and her neighbors. "The back."

Darlene stuck her hand into her the pocket of her figure defining black coat and pulled out a set of keys. The strap of her purse slipped and she yanked it back up. "I don't have a key for the back door. I have one for the front."

I stomped over to Darlene. My sneakers squished across the damp grass. "Thanks for telling me."

Darlene shrugged and smiled. "It seemed mean to ruin your fun. Sneaking around suits you."

I opened my mouth then shut it. I wanted to ask what she meant, but really didn't want to know the inner workings of Darlene's mind.

A tingling sensation danced over my head and nerves, feeling like little spiders were running all over me. I rubbed my hands over my arms.

Maybe I wasn't doing such a good thing proving Darlene innocent. There was something extremely calculating and manipulative about the woman.

I debated quitting right then and there, but unfortunately my curiosity got the better of me. And I was already there.

Darlene opened the door and motioned for me to enter.

I stepped inside. Darlene hit a switch and the area was bathed in soft lavender light. My eyebrows shot up. Turning, I stared at Darlene.

"Belinda liked color."

No kidding.

The living room looked like a box of sixty-four crayons exploded. Oranges, pinks, reds, blues, and greens of all different hues filled the room. The red couch had a white, pink, and purple cushion. Green accent pillows stood like soldiers. The table lamps were a combination of sea blues and greens. The area rug was a mix of orange and dark brown shades, quite tasteful considering the other items in the room.

"Our cover is we came to get a fondue set," Darlene said.

"We did some breaking and entering to take your cousin's fondue set."

Darlene looked at me like I was stupid. Which at this moment, I agreed with. Something was really off with my reasoning skills to have agreed to this plan. What in the world did we expect to find—the murder weapon with fingerprints all over it, or a note from the killer confessing their crime?

I needed to spend more time on scrapbooking than sleuthing. Poor Grandma Cheryl would be getting an earful from Hope for buying me the Agatha Christie collection for my birthday.

"I have a key so we entered lawfully." Darlene dropped the aforementioned item back into her coat pocket. "No breaking. Just entering."

I'm sure Ted would have a different opinion of our entry. Darlene was right though. She had a key. She used it. If Ted didn't want anyone coming in, he should've stationed a guard at the house.

Taking in a deep breath, I kept repeating all the good reasons we weren't committing a crime in my head. The dining room and kitchen were also vivid splashes of color. My poor eyes hurt along with my brain. How in the world did Belinda create in this area? I couldn't imagine being able to concentrate or tell one color from the next with the sensory overload surrounding me.

"I'm going to check Belinda's office and craft room. You can see if anything seems amiss in her bedroom."

"How would I know what's amiss? How about I check the computer files and you search her bedroom. You know her better." I crossed my arms. "Or we could stick together and I'll tell you my observations."

I wanted to make sure she wasn't putting things into the room. That large purse made me suspicious. So far, everything she needed she carried in her pockets. I wanted to know what the purse held.

"Because it will take too long. Use your cell phone and take pictures, we can stop for a bite on the way back to Scrap This and talk about them then."

I narrowed my eyes. "I don't think so. We're partners so we stick together."

Darlene's expression matched mine. "You don't trust me."

"Nope."

Darlene drew back. A smile brightened her face all of a sudden. "I like that. Brutal honesty. Well we're at an impasse here. We need to cover as much ground as possible, and you're afraid I'm up to no good."

"I know you're up to no good. I'm just not sure if your no good is going to come back and smack me or someone else."

"For goodness sake, why would I get you in trouble?"

"You don't like me."

"I need you. If a person is going to turn on their partner, they at least wait until they have no use for them."

Gee, that comforted me.

"So how about we get at it before the police arrive." Darlene headed up the stairs.

"I thought you said we wouldn't get caught."

"I figured we'd be half way done by now. Sooner or later the McGregors across the street will start a fight."

"How do you know?" I dashed up the stairs and into the room Darlene pointed at.

"Because it's Thursday night poker. A fight always breaks out during Thursday night poker."

"Then maybe we should've picked another day."

"Friday, I conduct an online chat with other life artists."

Well, one couldn't miss that.

"Wednesday is Bunco. I do believe your grandmothers and my mother have started attending."

"Your mother knows what we're up to."

"But your grandmothers don't. Thursday is my mother's cooking class with Chef Lorenzo. She never misses a class of his. If she wasn't busy, my mother would've invited herself and them to come over and help."

Then I'm glad we picked today. "Okay. I'll look in here."

"Remember anything amiss let me know." Darlene headed down the hall.

Like I'd know. I eased into the room, feeling a little uncomfortable being in a dead woman's bedroom. I knew Belinda, but hadn't been friends with her. It was strange entering into her private retreat space.

I stepped into the room and blinked. I felt disoriented with the mix of colors and patterns. Pink and green plaid comforter. White and red polka dotted curtains. I settled my gaze on the cherry wood hardwood floor. Finally, some peace and calm for my eyes. I drew in a deep breath.

A stale odor filled my nose and trickled into my senses and memory. Wait. Old donuts and a sweet flower fragrance. Like in my house.

Fear trailed up and down my spine. There was no way Belinda was involved in what happened at my house. Whoever had been at my place had also been here looking for something.

I dropped onto my hands and knees and lifted up the bed skirt. Dust bunnies and a pair of old moccasins greeted me. I crawled over to the bedside table. An iPod docking station doubling as a digital clock took up most of the surface, a small lamp took up the rest.

Draped over the knob of the bedside lamp was a gold necklace, four hearts formed a four-leaf clover. I opened up the lone drawer. Inside were two paperback mystery novels, a collection of beaded bookmarks, and a full bottle of a sleeping aid. A chain snaked out from under one of the books.

Carefully, I withdrew it. In my hand was Belinda's beloved diva necklace. If Belinda had the necklace, why had she gone to the store to search for it? Unless this wasn't the necklace she wanted back. The heart necklace. Did Belinda give up this necklace in order to save one more precious to her?

Had the other necklace been a milestone gift from her mother, or maybe her absentee father? I'd need to take a closer look at it. I placed the diva necklace back into the drawer and closed it. Darlene didn't need to know about the find. If anyone deserved the memento, it was Hazel.

The party across the street had grown rowdier. I tugged open the closet door. Belinda hung her clothes by theme and color. Scrapbooking themed shirts and pants. Next came her cute animal collection. She followed it up with cruise wear and almost shoved into the corner was her holiday attire.

My hand brushed against a silk fabric. Interesting. Everything else was made from cotton or polyester. I pushed the holiday wear into the cruise clothing and shoved the whole passel of them into the animal section.

Hidden in the dark recess of her closet were simple and trendy dresses, blouses and pants. A few still had price tags hanging off of them. I burrowed further into the closet and blushed. Belinda liked her nightwear racy.

I do believe Belinda had herself a man.

I snapped a couple of pictures with my cell phone then foraged my way out of the closet. "Darlene, there's something in here you need to see."

Lights bounced past the slats covering the bedroom window. Red rotating lights.

This was not good. Not good at all.

I ran out of the room. "The cops."

Darlene poked her head out of the office. "I'm sure it's about the noisy party across the street. Not everything is about you."

About me? The woman who screeched about any possibility of a loop hole in the small contests the store ran, the woman who insisted she get dibs for the "choice location" at crops even when she showed up late, the woman who only wanted to solve her cousin's murder to clear *her* name, insinuated I was self-centered?

I clenched my hands. I was not a violent person. At all. Darlene made me reconsider the stance. I went back into the bedroom and lifted a corner of the blinds. The red light bounced off the walls. A cruiser was parked in Belinda's driveway. The driver's door opened.

Why did I ever listen to Darlene? *Because you allow guilt rather than common sense and self-preservation to rule your brain.*

"They're here." I called out.

"Just keep calm. I have this under control." Darlene flicked her hair over her shoulder and adjusted the strap of her purse. She flounced down the stairs.

And because I had no sense of self-preservation, I followed after her. This wasn't going to go well. If Darlene handled this situation in the same manner she did any disappointment or disagreement while shopping or cropping at Scrap This, we'd both wind up in jail.

Would I be better off calling my grandmothers or Steve? Marilyn owed me. I got her out of jail, seemed fair for her to do the same for me.

The door banged open.

"What are you two doing here?" With gun drawn, Detective Ted Roget stepped into the house.

I wanted the floor to open up and swallow me whole. Of all the police officers to explain this to, it would be Ted.

"Picking up something I need for a party," Darlene said.

"Really, a party?" Ted's eyes narrowed and he looked Darlene and I up and down, very slowly and suspiciously. He holstered the gun. "Interesting choice of outfits. All black."

Darlene straightened her posture and stared back at Ted. I wanted to squeeze my eyes closed, and cover my mouth and ears. I couldn't quite pull off the see-hear-speak-no-evil stance by myself.

"It's a costume party." Darlene emphasized the word costume and threw a look at Ted that spoke of his lack of intelligence.

I blocked a moan from escaping. Of all people, why was Darlene challenging Ted? Okay, I did have my share of words with the man but we kind-of-sort-of got along, and I had been in the right in those situations. There was no way Darlene and I could pass this off as a good choice.

Costume party or not.

"You expect me to believe you're having a costume party with only two guests?" Ted eyed us suspiciously. "In Ms. Watson's home?"

Darlene licked her lips, squared her shoulders, and thrust out a hip. I knew this position. She was readying to start one of her verbal beat-downs.

I wanted to launch a sidekick at Darlene, but that would really give us away. The neck of the black long sleeved shirt I wore seemed to tighten the longer Ted stared, and Darlene prepared.

I eyed the door. Could I make a break for it?

Ted focused those angry eyes on me and shook his head once. I needed to work on my poker face.

"Of course not." Darlene huffed at him. "There are four people attending. My mother, my aunt Hazel, Faith and I."

"How unknowing of me." Ted rested his hands near his gun and handcuffs. He really had a thing for placing his hands at those locations of his belt. "That's quite an unusual guest list."

"We like to keep it to a foursome and with Belinda gone..." Darlene trailed off and drew in a deep breath.

"You decided to include Faith."

"Of course I did. My mother said it was the polite thing to do considering the little scandal I created at the store." Darlene rolled her eyes as she emphasized the word scandal.

"I'm sure Faith appreciated the invite." Ted's eyebrows shot up and he stared at me, almost willing me to say something.

I pressed my lips together and nodded.

"Neither of you thought it was a horrible idea to come into the house of a murder victim."

"That would be a bad idea," Darlene said. "But I was coming into the house of my cousin."

Ted rolled his eyes. "Well, forgive me. I didn't know there was a difference."

"I forgive you." Darlene bestowed a smile on him and hefted her purse strap back onto her shoulder. "Now, if you don't mind, I'll just get my fondue set and we'll be on our way."

"I don't think so." Ted maneuvered around us and stood in front of the kitchen entryway.

"Come on, Darlene." I grabbed hold of her arm and tugged. "We're going to be late. We'll just grab some frozen appetizers."

"Frozen!" Darlene squealed and placed a hand against her heart. "I do not serve frozen food. How dare you accuse me of such a thing!"

I drew back and held up my hands. "Didn't know it'd be an insult."

Ted stepped between us. "Ladies, ladies. Let's remain civil."

"Of course you'd take Faith's side." Darlene pivoted sharply, directing herself toward the kitchen. She charged forward.

Ted grabbed hold of her arm.

"Darlene, don't..." I started to warn her to listen to Ted, and then tried changing it when the large bag slipped down her shoulder. Too late.

Darlene yanked away from Ted. The bag slipped, tipped over, and items rained from her purse onto the floor. Lipsticks, pens, a glue gun, glue sticks, Chap Stick in different flavors, beads, scrapbook gems, paperclips, eyeliners. I watched in amazement at the variety of make-up and scrapbook supplies housed in her bag scattered across the floor.

What didn't the woman carry in her purse? If she had wanted to hurt, maim or kill a person, all she needed to do was whack them in the head with the oversized quilted bag.

Ted released Darlene's arm and gaped at the items rolling around on the floor. Well, at least someone else besides me would claim the title of most annoying woman in Eden.

"Now see what you made me do." Darlene released a huff of air. She slowly lowered herself to the ground and rounded up a few of her items, placing them back into her purse.

I dropped down and shoveled things into the cavernous bag.

"Is it really necessary to carry so much?" Ted asked as he joined us in the quest of returning Darlene's items back into their rightful place.

"I will not dignify that question with a response."

I kept to myself that what she said was a response.

Sighing, Darlene laid flat on the floor, and with her arm outstretched, wiggled her way to the couch. "You would think with this rug that my lipstick wouldn't find its way all the way under the couch."

One would also think that when going on a "search and seizure" mission, they'd take only the essentials. Bringing an empty bag made sense so you could fill it up, but a full one was not very bright.

Darlene stood and dusted off her pants. I scanned the area, looking for any more of Darlene's runaway items. Nothing.

Ted also rose and shot a glare at Darlene and a why-do-you-torment-me glance at me. I stopped myself from responding with even a shrug. I had no idea why I was being blamed for this mess. I was the tagalong, not the brains behind this ill-fated mission.

"Do you have everything?" Ted asked, the weariness evident in his voice.

Darlene opened her purse, stuck her hand, and part of her head, inside the bag and rooted around. "Everything is accounted for."

"Now, I must ask the both of you to leave."

"But my fondue set." Darlene clutched the purse to her bosom. "I can't go home without it. My mother has all the ingredients ready. What is a party without food?"

"I'm sure you can stop and buy one."

Darlene shook her head. "No. They don't make that set anymore. We must use the Halloween fondue set at Halloween. It goes with my decor."

"You'll just have to make do," Ted said.

I could see his patience growing thinner and thinner.

Darlene paled. She grabbed a folder from a long, high table located right behind the couch and fanned herself.

"Use the Thanksgiving fondue set for Halloween. No. No. No. That won't work. The color scheme is all wrong. The burnt orange plates, bronze pot and the sticks with the turkey, pilgrim, cornucopia, and pumpkin clash with the black and bright orange decorations I have out."

Darlene looked totally "aghast" about the situation.

"It's orange." Ted took hold of an arm of mine and Darlene and steered us toward the door.

"Oh no, it's not." Darlene grounded to a halt. Outrage splashed across her face. "Thanksgiving orange is not the same as Halloween orange. Thanksgiving orange is more muted, softer, a peaceful rather thankful color." She moved her hands through the air as if they were boats floating on calm seas.

Ted rolled his eyes.

Darlene narrowed hers. "Halloween is bold. In your face. Vivid." She displayed the color by flicking her fingers out and waving her hands in a big circle over her head.

"It's orange," Ted said.

"Colors are not one-dimensional." Darlene's left eye twitched.

"I can vouch the man does not understand shades. He thinks neon..." I stressed the hue, "green is perfectly suited as the background for a layout."

Darlene gasped and shook her head. "Background. That will not do. A mat and embellishments are fine, but not for the background."

I crossed the top half of my body over Ted's so I could speak to Darlene. "I know right? I'm thinking we need a class on hues at the store. Green is not just, well, green."

Darlene nodded. "That's a fabulous idea. Gear it toward men. Use simple terms or men speak."

"Men speak?" Ted opened the front door.

Darlene pointed at the cruiser. "Siren red instead of Christmas red. Pittsburg Steeler yellow as opposed to WVU yellow."

"Those colors are a little different," Ted said.

I stared at Ted for a little while, the wheels in my head spinning. I think Darlene was onto something. Something seemed to click in Ted's brain and I caught a little bit of a "that's what women mean about hues and shades," vibe of understanding.

Ted gave me a gentle prod out the door. "Call me when you schedule that class. I'd be interested in it. If for no other reason than my ex-wife's eyes will stop bulging out when I buy clothes for our daughter."

"Faith could always go along with you." Darlene said. "She's always color-coordinated."

Ted checked out my all black outfit one more time. "I can see that. That might be a good idea."

"Are you sure I can't run in and get my fondue set." Darlene looked at him with wide, trying-to-be-innocent eyes.

"I'm sure." Ted crossed his arms over his muscular chest.

"Could you get it for me?" Darlene pressed the issue. "There wasn't anything saying we couldn't come in, like crime tape or a note. So it has to mean none of the stuff is evidence. Right?"

Ted released a long suffering sigh. He pointed at her car. "Go wait in there. If I can find it easily…"

"My keys." Darlene shifted the folder from one hand to the other and pointed at the table behind the couch.

"I'll get them." Ted made the international sign for hand-it-over. "The folder."

Darlene blushed and smiled sheepishly. "Sorry. Forgot I had it."

She gave it to Ted. He exchanged the folder for the keys.

"What about the fondue set?" Darlene batted her lashes. "It'll be in the lower cabinet on the right hand side. You'll see a large, red stand mixer on the counter. It'll be in a box with a picture of an orange fondue pot, four plates, four sticks on the top. It'll say Halloween fondue set on it. In a cursive font."

"Thank you for that, I'm sure I couldn't figure it out without all those details." Ted pivoted and walked back into the house, muttering under his breath.

"Before he changes his mind and decides to arrest us, let's go wait in the car."

I grabbed her arm and tugged her toward the car. Fortunately, this time she was compliant.

"Don't be silly, Faith." Darlene brushed my hand off her arm. "It's not like he knows we did anything wrong."

Knows? I tripped and would've landed smack on my face if Darlene hadn't linked her arm through mine and jerked me back to my feet.

"You worry way too much, Faith. There's no way Detective Roget knows I brought all that stuff to purposely dump on the floor so we could check out the area."

It was kind of ingenious in a way. I know I would've never thought to bring props to play a game of 'pick-up-sticks' as a ruse for searching for evidence.

She dropped the keys Ted gave her into my lap and pulled out a set from her coat pocket. "Those are Belinda's keys. If she didn't have them on her when she died…"

"Someone went with her."

Darlene nodded. Her hands fisted around the steering wheel. "Someone she trusted enough to give a key to her home. I doubt she expected not to return."

"Her man."

Darlene stared at me wide-eyed. "Belinda wasn't dating anyone. Hazel would've said something."

"Then she had her eye on someone. I found some new additions to her wardrobe." I showed her the pictures and explained about the odor in my house and in Belinda's room.

Darlene took my phone and frowned at the images. "Why would she keep it from us? Belinda wasn't a secret keeper."

"She didn't tell you she entered the contest."

Darlene handed the phone back. "So all that's left is pinpointing which man in Eden killed my cousin."

"And why."

Darlene shoved the key into the ignition and twisted it violently. "I really don't give a damn why."

TWENTY-FIVE

I gathered up the notes I made when I got home. I had three key pieces to place in the puzzle, the mystery man, the necklace I found in the store, and how I tied into the matter. And I had a feeling it all hedged on the identity of Little Lamb. Once I knew who wrote the vaguely accusing sentences, I could figure out why they worded it as they did and brought my name up.

Dropping the notes into my bag, I patted the pockets of my pea coat. Cell phone. Check. Flash drive with information I needed Oliver to read. Check. Keys. Keys?

I patted my pockets again. I knew I forgot something. Leaning the top part of my body into the house, I reached toward the key holder hung beside my front door.

Someone knocked into me from behind. A startled cry escaped as I fell forward. My purse slipped from my shoulder and landed underneath me. The items in my purse dug into my stomach. A body pressed into my back.

Fear rendered me immobile for a moment. The person who broke into my house was back. In broad daylight. This time they intended to harm me.

Not without a fight. Screaming, I kicked and bucked until I shook the person from me.

A woman wailed.

I turned over and stared at Hazel.

"You punched me. I'm bleeding." Hazel cupped a hand around her nose. Her curls were matted and in disarray. She wore a mismatched set of a tunic with anchors and a pair of pants with rein-deers embroidered on them. "Why did you do that?"

My heart broke at her haggard appearance. My mind remind-ed me the woman had just knocked me down, and her body held a familiar stale smell.

"You attacked me." I scrambled to my feet. "Stay right there. I'm calling the police."

"No." Hazel blanched. "I tripped. I didn't mean to scare you. I wanted to talk to you. Make you understand."

"Faith!" Grandma Cheryl bellowed running toward us.

A pound sounded from across the yards. Grandma Hope was getting Steve.

"Please. I don't need any more trouble." Hazel clutched my arms. Tears glittered in her eyes. "I didn't hurt her. I didn't."

The perfume had more of a fruit than a flower scent.

"I wouldn't. I wouldn't do anything to my daughter." The pitch of her voice grew louder and higher, bordering on hysterical. Her grip tightened and her thin nails bent against my skin.

"Let go of my granddaughter." Cheryl broke the hold Hazel had on me.

"I didn't do it. Please, explain it to him. I didn't." Hazel trem-bled, tears running down her face in a torrent.

A car screeched to a halt in the middle of the street. Eliza, in a pair of dirty scrubs, jumped out of the car. "You had me so scared. You promised to stay home. Rest."

"They have to tell him. Make him believe." Hazel's gaze ping-ponged from me to my grandmother then to her sister. "He'll listen to Faith. I can't have people saying, thinking, that I...I."

"Steve must be at work." Hope dashed over to us. "I'm going to call Randall."

Choking on her words, Hazel fell into her sister's arms and sobbed. "My baby. She was my baby. I'd never hurt my baby."

Hope's kind heart took over. She shoved the cell into her jacket pocket. "Let's get her inside. Neighbors are thinking this is a show." She helped Eliza usher her sister into my house.

Grandma Cheryl looked frustrated. I knew she worried Hope's forgiving and helpful heart might get broken one day, especially since their granddaughter decided hunting down murderers sounded like a fun hobby.

"It'll be alright, Grandma." I dropped an arm around her shoulders. Together we went into the living room and watched Hope work her magic.

Hope settled Hazel and Eliza onto the couch. Tugging the coffee table closer, she lifted Hazel's feet and placed them on the wood surface. "Now I'll go make you a nice cup of tea."

"I don't think tea is what she needs," Cheryl grumbled and dropped into the recliner across from the couch.

"It isn't." Eliza rocked her sister back and forth. "What Hazel needs is either her daughter back, or the police not to think she killed her."

"That's preposterous." Cheryl tugged the afghan from the chair and handed it to me. "No one thinks Hazel killed Belinda."

I draped the afghan around Hazel. The restraining order. Belinda told Mrs. Alwright that she wanted to file an order against her mother. Hazel was intense. No doubt about it. Hazel hardly ever left her daughter's side. I was surprised they didn't still live in the same house.

Belinda moved out six months ago. Was that when Belinda met her man? Did he help...or make...Belinda break away from her clinging mom? Hazel had hovered over and around Belinda from the day she was born—until the day she died.

Hazel still cooked for her daughter, scheduled her classes, arranged the book signing and her other appearances, signed her up for crops, and made not only her daughter's clothes but matching outfits for herself.

Were the keys Darlene found ones Hazel had for her daughter's home? Did Belinda take them away?

On Saturday, I noticed how Hazel even styled and colored her hair like her daughter's. It was almost like she wanted to be Belinda. I drew back. I knew just because someone was accused of something didn't mean they did it. I also knew, just because someone said they were innocent didn't mean they didn't kill a man.

Cheryl frowned.

Hope placed a cup of tea on the coffee table. She tilted her head. "Is something wrong?"

I shook my head, wanting to deny the truth and also shake my jumbled thoughts into some semblance of order.

"Customers will be arriving soon. I'll go to the store and open up. Let you guys talk with Eliza and Hazel."

What was wrong with me? I rung up an order and handed the bag to the customer. Thinking Hazel killed Belinda. The woman was falling apart without her daughter. She had no life without Belinda.

"Can I have my items?" The customer held the plastic bag open.

"Sorry." I dropped in her packages of stickers, three-dimensional die cuts and bottle caps. "Have a nice day."

The woman huffed and marched out the door.

Marilyn looked up from the pile of paper she was tearing for a potential class.

Not my best display of customer service abilities. My mind was focused on the basket. I needed to look at the necklace again. Study it. It would be hard to do at the register.

"Marilyn, I need to check an ordering form in the office. I think I inverted the numbers for two items. We don't need one hundred reams of sexy fireman paper." I snatched the necklace and headed toward the back.

"Speak for yourself," Marilyn called after me.

Instead of going into the office, I went into the break room. If my grandmothers caught me sitting at the desk in the office, they'd know I was up to something. The only times I went in there was to get one of them or leave a note.

I stretched the necklace across the table and leaned forward. The silver hearts twined together to form what looked like a "B" or even a sloppy "D" where the hearts crossed over each other. Belinda. This had to be what she came to find, the necklace given to her either by her mother or her secret lover.

I turned the chain over and examined the back, my nose almost pressed into the silver. Why was she hiding the relationship?

Shame. The reason bounced in my head. The same reason I hid my marriage and got it annulled. I didn't want to answer "divorced" when I filled out paperwork, nor lie and write "single." Getting the annulment allowed me to say single truthfully.

Had Belinda been ashamed of her boyfriend? Or him of her? Did Belinda want to keep the relationship from Hazel? Afraid her mother's over-the-top behavior would end the romance and leave Belinda single forever.

The gems sparkled. The design was beautiful and intricate, different. I'd never seen a piece like it before. It had been designed for Belinda. The man wasn't ashamed of his woman.

There weren't that many available men in Belinda's age range in Eden. If she was dating someone older or younger, it might be the reason she kept it quiet. Though keeping a relationship quiet in Eden seemed impossible. Or at least for me. I wasn't even really in a relationship and had my name coupled with Steve and Ted.

I pondered who could tell me for certain about the restraining order and who Belinda's boyfriend was. I was sure she'd confide in him. This man either knew why Hazel killed Belinda, or was the killer himself. Why hadn't he made himself known since her death?

If this man hadn't set off our radars, it was because we knew him well or he drifted so far inside our community that we didn't pay any attention. I could only think of nine unattached men in our community who Belinda would have wanted to keep a secret, or wanted to be kept a secret.

Four names I scratched off without hesitation. Steve. Ted. Chief Randall Moore. Seventy-five-year old Clive. Number five, six and seven were possible but doubtful: Jasper, Wyatt and Wayne. Which left Oliver White and Leonard Blue as the choices for boyfriend, killer—or both.

Before I set out proving either of these men a murderer, I'd make sure the necklace wasn't a gift from her mother. If Darlene didn't answer, I'd go over to Eddy's Jewelry Boutique. She's the only one I knew capable of handcrafting such an intricate piece.

I walked into Home Brewed and waved at Dianne. She returned the greeting while grinding some beans. I loved the smell of Home Brewed. Roasted coffee beans. Fresh bread. A wonderful mix of spices crying out for me to choose them as the flavor my coffee needed. Today, I think I'd go with pumpkin.

A woman, and her perfume, strolled in right after me. I inched away, hoping I didn't leave smelling like her. I wasn't a gardenia kind of girl. I smothered a cough and glanced around, my gaze pausing on Darlene. Leonard stood by the table, hands pressed onto the back of an empty chair. He was making a valiant attempt at drawing Darlene into a conversation. She was having none of it.

Frustration built in the man's face. Was he trying to get information from Darlene, or ask her out? Either way, he was behaving highly inappropriately. The woman just lost her cousin.

I placed my standard order.

With Leonard still trying to win Darlene's attention, asking to join her seemed counterproductive. I wanted to eavesdrop, but knowing Darlene, she'd use me as a way of making Leonard leave. I did not want the man knowing anything about the necklace or my suspicions.

Frowning, Dianne had a keen eye on me. Great. My grandmothers called her and said I was up to something. I made the least suspicious choice, the table across the room. Gardenia woman headed for the last vacant table behind Darlene.

As I finished removing my lunch from the tray, a hacking filled the room. Diners near me cringed, faces twisting in disgust.

Darlene coughed and waved her hand in the air. Leonard shoved his hands into his pockets and strode out the door. Subtle was not a word in Darlene's vocabulary.

Closing my eyes, I sunk my teeth into the crunchy pita and reveled in the basil, tomatoes and toasty, melty, mozzarella cheese goodness.

Darlene coughed again. Loudly. Obnoxiously. Like she had a hairball to dislodge from her throat.

Customers rolled their eyes. A young man in late teens tugged a pair of headphones from his pocket and shoved them into his ears.

"Excuse me!" Darlene snapped her fingers. "Owner. Over here."

This wasn't going to go well. I slunk down in the seat. I needed to stop agreeing to these meetings.

Dianne marched over and halted beside Darlene. "Is something wrong?"

"The perfume on that woman is so strong I can taste it on my sandwich." Darlene wrinkled her nose.

The woman in question turned cherry red.

Dianne looked ready to explode. Her gaze fell on me. I widened my eyes. She used her chin as a pointing device to indicate the woman Darlene insulted and then me. Dianne clasped her hands together.

She wanted me to switch seats. I made a point of exaggerating a sigh and reluctantly gathering up my items. Dianne leaned down and whispered to the perfume woman. The woman nodded and allowed Dianne to move her.

"I owe you." Dianne gave me a relieved smile as we passed.

Not if she knew the insult and musical chairs had been Darlene's plan. I went to sit at the vacant table.

Darlene gestured wildly at the table. Now what was she up to? Before my derrière touched the seat, a woman with three kids rushed over, knocking me away with a swing of her toddler's sneakered feet.

Darlene pushed a chair back with her foot.

"Not very subtle." I sat down.

"But consistent with my personality," Darlene responded.

She had me there.

"Why did you want to meet?"

"Do you recognize this?" I placed the necklace lost at Scrap This on the table.

Darlene picked it up and placed it on the palm of her hand. She traced the hearts. "Is that a B?"

"Looks like it to me." I scooted closer to the table. "I think that's what Belinda came looking for."

"Not the diva necklace." Darlene gently turned it over.

"I figured it either came from the boyfriend or her mother."

"Not Hazel." Keeping hold of the silver necklace, Darlene hooked her index finger under a gold chain around her neck. She pulled out a matching necklace to the one I found hanging from the lamp's switch. Four gold hearts placed together to look like a four-leaf clover. "My mom and her sister bought two each when they got pregnant. Each of us has one. Our moms gifted them to us when we were sixteen."

"I saw one at Belinda's house."

Darlene paled and tears filled her eyes. "It wasn't on her."

I shook my head and kept quiet.

Darlene dabbed at her face with a napkin. "We all swore we'd never take them off. She wanted to replace us."

"I'm sure that's not it."

"It makes sense. Submitting my layouts as her own wasn't something the Belinda I knew would've done. Keeping a boyfriend a secret wasn't something the Belinda I grew up with would've done. Taking off the necklace we've all worn for twenty years wasn't something the Belinda who loved her family would've done."

"I'm sorry." I didn't know what else to say.

Darlene held the necklace out toward me, one end of the broken chain danced across the table top. The sun caught hold of it and glittered.

A hand reached out and snatched the necklace.

Darlene gasped. I gaped at Oliver for a moment before I reacted.

He spun away, the necklace in his grasp. I grabbed his arm and pulled him backwards, hard. He crashed into the table. Our food and drinks scattered.

Dianne rushed toward us.

"Give it back." I grabbed for his flailing hand.

Darlene slammed a chair into Oliver. "Shut up and sit down."

Oliver sat, the necklace held hostage in his fist.

"I want it." Darlene spoke barely above a whisper.

I inched back. I knew when a woman was about to send out a shotgun blast and wanted none of the scattershot.

Oliver swallowed and shook his head.

Darlene's face reddened, her breathing grew harsh and loud.

I scooted back a few more paces. "It's evidence. You really should give it back to us."

"Then why do you have it." Oliver shot a glare at me.

Darlene slapped her hand onto the table, she rotated her wrist and her palm faced up. She motioned for Oliver to hand over the necklace.

He shook his head, frightened gaze on Darlene. "It's mine. Well, yours—"

"It's a B," Darlene said with her teeth clenched.

"No! It's not what you think." Oliver's shoulders slumped. He opened his hand and allowed the necklace to puddle onto the table.

Darlene snatched it from the table. "I think it's evidence and belongs to Detective Roget."

"Please—"

Darlene held her hand away from Oliver's face, as if she planned on slapping him. "I have nothing to say to you."

Without a background glance, Darlene stormed out of Home Brewed.

"I think she hates me." Oliver dropped his head into his hands.

"I think that's the least of your worries."

Dianne hustled over to the table, a mop in her hand. "Is everything alright?"

I didn't blame Dianne for waiting until Darlene left. The woman was on the war path.

"Faith?" Dianne frowned, holding the mop like a weapon. One wrong, or right word, she'd knock out Oliver.

I needed to say something but wasn't sure what. Was I okay? Oliver was Belinda's secret boyfriend, her possible murderer.

"It's not what you think. I promise." Oliver muttered.

"How do I know?"

Dianne hovered nearby with the mop.

"This is all a misunderstanding. I shouldn't have ever trusted her."

"Who?"

Oliver tilted his head a few times in Dianne's direction.

I rolled my eyes. Right, after the scene he caused no one else was paying attention to our conversation. I motioned for Dianne to go away. Huffing and puffing, she did as I asked, and headed straight for the phone.

"Start talking. If you're scared of Darlene, just wait until my grandmothers charge through those doors."

"I came here to come clean with you today."

"Come clean?"

"Yes. Our lunch date."

Date? Oh scrap. I forgot I planned on meeting Oliver to show him the message board chat. I needed to stop tipping off the suspects that I was on to them. "Don't worry about explaining to me, Darlene is headed over to the police station. Shouldn't you try escaping or something?"

"You should try reading more literary fiction instead of those crime novels." Oliver crossed his arms and looked down his nose at me. "All those books are warping your senses."

I wondered if Ted would accept a books-made-me-do-it defense. Probably not. Oliver shouldn't look so smug; the cops were soon to be after him, not me.

"There's no reason for me to run out of here. There is nothing illegal about purchasing a necklace," Oliver said.

"No. But the police might be interested in the fact you've been keeping your relationship with Belinda a secret. Maybe your other woman got a little jealous and decided to get rid of the competition."

From Darlene's reaction, I'd wager Belinda set her competitive spirit onto winning Oliver...which meant Darlene went back on the suspect list.

Oliver's eyes widened. "I wasn't in a relationship with her. Heavens no. It was a mutual beneficial friendship. But it ended a few months before I entered into my current arrangement with Darlene."

I did not want to know that. "Did Darlene know about you and Belinda? And did Belinda know your friendship benefit plan was over?"

Oliver sighed. "You make this sound so unseemly."

I wasn't making it, it was. "Interesting design of the letter. Could be a B or a D. Depending which cousin you were friends with at the time. Just how many women are you friends with?" I air quoted friends.

Oliver turned crimson. "It's not what you think."

I narrowed my eyes, leaning forward across the table. "That's your go-to excuse for everything."

"It's the truth. When I said date yesterday, I meant a previous engagement. Private meeting."

"Date usually means two people who are interested romantically in each other and are going out together. To get to know each other better."

Oliver swallowed. "Usually."

"I thought you were the word guy."

"I had to clear what I could tell you with someone."

"Clear what to tell me? Why would you need to check with someone? It's not like you knew..." He knew what the thread said. I stared at him.

He nodded, gazing down at the table. "I'm Little Lamb."

I sucked in a breath.

Little Lamb had supported Darlene and threw me under the proverbial bus.

"The necklace wasn't for Belinda. You weren't playing them against each other."

"No. I wanted her opinion on the necklace. I brought it to the signing to see if the jeweler duplicated the design Belinda drew up for me. It wasn't what I had described to Belinda. Belinda said she'd take care of it. I left it with her."

"The clasp was broken when I found it."

"I was worried about leaving it with her. She told me she'd keep it safe and make sure it didn't get stolen. Maybe she put it on."

And her jealous boyfriend saw her wearing it. He dragged Belinda back to the store to make her leave the necklace where she claimed she got it. Belinda tried to make him see the truth and he lost his temper, pushing her.

Oliver must have read some of the thoughts in my mind. "You think the necklace had something to do with her murder."

"Someone told Hazel about the lost necklace and she told Belinda. If it wasn't important to her why did Belinda want it back that night?"

"Hazel was there when I gave it to Belinda. She knew it was for Darlene. I don't know why she'd want Belinda to go and get it."

Unless Belinda never specified which necklace was lost. Did Hazel call Darlene and taunt her about the "gift" to Belinda from Oliver?

Belinda had called someone about the necklace in Hazel's presence. Hazel thought it was me. Had Belinda instead called her cousin to meet her there? But why the store?

A horrible thought entered my mind. I shivered. Did Belinda plan on killing her rival for Oliver's affections and tried staging it to look like I killed her?

If so, was I now helping the real murderer, even if it was self-defense, clear her name?

* * *

Stunned, I walked back to Scrap This. This was a turn in the case I had never expected, or a relationship I'd have ever imagined. Oliver White and Darlene Johnson. And Belinda Watson.

I placed my purse under the counter and scanned, without taking in, the class plan Leonard dropped off.

Hope slapped her hands onto the counter. Her lips were thin and tight, almost collapsed into her face.

I jumped. Marilyn jumped. Cheryl looked downright pleased.

Dianne did get ahold of my grandmothers.

Marilyn scurried to the opposite side of the store, taking an undue interest in straightening the stickers.

"You, young lady, are not allowed out of this store for the rest of the month. Your work hours are from open to close. Am I clear?"

A smug smile stretched Cheryl's mouth. For once Hope was the bad guy and it threw me off balance.

"A month. Isn't that kind of drastic?"

"No. Throwing you in jail for obstructing justice would be drastic." Ted now stood beside Hope, feet planted apart and a smug look on his face.

He went to my grandmothers? I gaped at all of them. My grandmothers joined forces with Detective Roget.

"What did I do?" I had to ask, even though I knew the answer. Playing dumb was my only chance at having a saving grace.

"Withheld evidence."

Darlene hadn't been joking, she took the necklace to Ted. Ugh! I knew better than to trust her.

"I found an item lost in the store. How was I to know it was evidence?"

"Do you normally keep items you find?"

Hope crossed her arms and tapped her foot. "No. We usually send out an email."

I grimaced. "I meant to. I forgot."

"You forgot," Ted said, shaking his head.

"She forgot," Hope said, sliding a look over at Cheryl.

"I think I might forget to pay her this week since she's spent so much time gallivanting around," Cheryl said.

Heat flamed my cheeks. Sierra stared at us as did a customer who walked inside. Leonard hastily filled out a teacher's card, pretending he didn't notice my humiliation. At least he made an attempt.

I messed up. Big time. It didn't mean I deserved a public dressing down like a mouthy ten-year-old. "I'm sorry. My mind has been scattered this week. I meant to send out the email but let it slip my mind. It didn't seem important. Until today. There's been so much going on around here. The murder. The break-in. My house being trashed."

Hope's face softened.

"Hope and I understood, even though we didn't think it wise, when you helped Marilyn. This time I won't stand for it." Cheryl still had a little steel in her spine.

"Your job is here at this store. Not out investigating," Hope said.

I was readying to smart off when the terror in grandma's eyes registered in my thick skull.

She lost her son. Her best friend lost her daughter. Earlier today, she watched another friend grieve for the loss of their beloved child. Hope was terrified her granddaughter might die too.

"I got caught up in it. I couldn't let people think what others said about me was true. I had to find out who broke into my house and get to the truth."

"That's my job." Ted caught my gaze and held it. He knew the truth hinted at in my words. While he understood my need for finding my past, his look said he worried more about my future.

It was time to step aside and let the man do his job. Besides, I wanted nothing to do with this creepy situation between the cousins. I was out of it. "If I was you, I'd go have a nice conversation with Oliver White about the necklace. Belinda's murder might have had to do with a family squabble over a man."

TWENTY-SIX

I set the alarm on the store then hurried outside. The cold drifted down the back of my neck. The night was clear. The stars glittered against the sky, the light twinkling against the dumpster. I shivered and wished I had brought along a winter coat instead of my thinner jacket. Well, it wasn't like I planned on joining Hope and Cheryl at the football game. My grandmothers were headed over to the game like every Friday during football season. I, on the other hand, bowed out like I did every Friday. Sitting on a cold metal bleacher, watching a game I knew nothing about, wasn't my idea of fun.

I had promised my grandmothers I'd sit at home, scrapbook, and snack out on junk food. Maybe have a chick-flick playing in the background or some grooving music. I swore I wanted nothing to do with Darlene or this case. No way was I going to get in the middle of whatever dysfunctional family drama the cousins got themselves into and ended with one of them murdered.

A pair of headlights swept across the lot and headed toward me. The car inched forward. Panic built in my chest and flowed away when I recognized Darlene's car. Shouldn't she be in jail or something? I patted the door. No need to panic. One twist of the door knob and the alarm would sound, causing Nancy to call the police.

Darlene parked. I kept my gaze glued to her. I shoved my hand into my purse and rooted around for my cell phone. After I made a call, I could clobber her with it. I wished I had some glitter, it worked wonders on Saturday.

An arm wrapped around my neck and slammed me into a rock hard body. A round, cold object pressed into my forehead. What the—

"Don't move." Hot breath that smelled like old coffee, stale donuts and mint hit me in the face.

What was going on? I grabbed onto the arm holding me hostage and pushed at it. My other hand trapped inside my purse.

The arm squeezed tighter. "I said don't move."

Darlene stepped out of the car with her hands up in the air. "You don't have to hurt her."

"I wouldn't have, but you just had to become partners. You've left me no choice." The man removed his arm from around my neck and shoved me toward the door. "Get inside. Both of you."

I stumbled forward, my purse tipping to the ground scattering all my possessions. I caught my balance before I slammed into the brick wall.

Darlene hustled over to my side. I moved away from her. I trusted her as much as I did the man with the gun. I peeked at the man.

Leonard motioned at the lock with his gun. His face was contorted into a mask of pure hatred.

"Faith has nothing to do with this."

"That's a lie." Leonard pointed the gun at me then the door. "Open it now."

I stared at him, trying to figure out his and Darlene's role in the mess. I was pretty certain of his, the wanting to kill us kind of gave it away. Belinda and Leonard also? Did he see Oliver give her the heart necklace and get jealous?

"I mean it. Open the door." He reached for the keys I clutched in my hand.

"No." The fight returned to my body. I twisted away, holding them pressed against my stomach. There was no way I'd let this man kill me in my grandmothers' store. If he wanted to shoot me, he could do it now.

Leonard shoved me between the shoulder blades.

I pitched forward. My head thunked into the brick wall. Specks of light danced before my eyes. I braced my hand on the wall as my knees buckled. The keys clattered to the asphalt. The security lights flashed on. Good. Hopefully the police arrived before Leonard's patience ran out.

"Don't hurt her." Darlene snagged me around the waist and hauled me to my feet.

"Get her to open the door." Leonard licked his lips and scanned the parking lot. Sweat dripped down his forehead and nose.

He was scared. That gave us somewhat of an advantage. He did have the gun. If we remained calm, we both had a chance of getting out of this alive.

Think, girl, think. The storage room. We stored items in there before we put them on the shelf. Maybe I should open the door. I closed my eyes and concentrated, doing a quick inventory in my mind. Boxes of cardstock. No good. It was too heavy to lift and throw. Glitter. Unless we wanted a trail for the police to follow, it wouldn't help us much in getting away. Advance Tape Gliders, sometimes referred to as guns, was another useless scrapbooking product to stop a killer. It wasn't like we could stick his hand, and the rest of him, to the wall until the police showed up. The adhesive was permanent but not that permanent.

Darn it, nothing useful in there to get away from this guy. Then the other option was getting the gun away from him.

I squinted at Darlene. She stared at him. I frowned. She was either going into a panic causing her eye to twitch, or she was batting them at him. Darlene was a little strange but there was no way she'd be coming on to the man wanting to kill her.

"Praying won't help you." Leonard grabbed my arm and shook it. "Open the door."

"No." I pulled away from him, planting my feet firmly. Steeling my nerves, I drew all the reserve of courage I could and looked Leonard in the eyes. "If you're going to shoot me, do it now."

Anger leapt in his gaze. He took a step closer to me.

"Don't make the crazy man mad." Darlene whispered into my ear.

I crossed my arms, hoping to disguise my trembling. "Us being alive makes him mad."

"I don't care that you're alive." He leaned forward, speaking into my face. His hot breath washed over me. "I care that you couldn't leave it alone. First, you had to prove it wasn't an accident."

I don't think I'd ever be able to stand the smell of spearmint again. "The police did that."

He raised the gun like a club. "I've had enough...."

I raised my arms to shield my head. Tightness built in my chest, pushing up a sob.

Darlene yanked me toward her. Hard. "It won't look like an accident!"

We tumbled to the ground. I landed in Darlene's lap. Quickly, I scrambled off her, putting as much distance between me and Leonard and me and Darlene as possible. It was better for us to separate. At least one of us then had a fighting chance.

"You want me to shoot you now too?" Leonard spun his anger toward Darlene.

I scooted a few more inches away. Why couldn't I have minded my own business like my grandmothers, Steve, and Ted told me?

"Of course not." Darlene huffed. "What a ridiculous question?"

I got to my feet. It was easier escaping when you stood.

"Listen—"

"You listen." Darlene jabbed a finger in Leonard's direction. "I'm trying to help you. Think about your choices."

"She's right. You won't get away with this." It wasn't the most brilliant thing to say but the only statement that popped into my mind.

"Of course he won't get away with it if he shoots us. The police are never going to think a shooting is an accidental death," Darlene said. "Same thing with beating someone with a gun. You need to make it less obvious."

"Who says I want it to look like an accident?" Leonard sneered. "Maybe I want them to know it was murder."

"Well, I don't own a gun and Faith doesn't own one. Plus, you're a lot taller than either of us, if your brilliant scheme is to blame one of us for the other's murder, pick something else."

Leonard looked at her with a new found respect.

Great, he found himself a new woman. One who wanted to help him get away with murder. Mine. And her cousin's.

He loosened his grip on the gun. "So what is your suggestion?"

Could I get it away from him? Darlene made it obvious it was every woman for herself. I inched toward him. Darlene stopped me with a well-aimed glare.

"Take us to my house," Darlene said.

"Your house." Leonard held the gun firmly. "Sounds like a trap to me."

"I live alone. My Aunt Hazel has been acting like I killed her daughter so she won't talk to me. My mother isn't talking to her sister because her sister thinks I'm a murderer. And since I refused to cut Aunt Hazel out of my life...her daughter did just die...my mother isn't talking to me. And it's not like I have any friends who'd stop by for a visit."

"She has a point." I muttered.

Stupid alarm company. They probably thought I set off the motion detector when I left. Either that or the police officers were handling a brawl at the school. Where was the busybody detective when I needed him? Or Hazel for that matter? Now she decided to stop stalking me.

"We'll go all right. But we'll take our little party to Faith's."

"You are not very good at this." Darlene planted her hands on her hips. "Her grandmothers live next door to her. You broke into her house. My aunt ran over there today behaving all crazy. You don't think someone is keeping an eye on her place?"

"My grandmothers are nosy." I tried helping Darlene. I don't know what she had planned but there was no way I wanted this killer near my grandmothers.

"If you behave they won't come over." Leonard used the gun to raise my chin. "You'll be a good girl."

I tried keeping the fear at bay but it was breaking through the walls I kept building.

"Fine. We'll go to Faith's. Her grandmothers, and their shotguns, will be over. Soon after they arrive, so will the assistant prosecuting attorney and the town's homicide detective. You might as well shoot yourself in the head right now and save the detective the trouble."

"No one needs to die," I said. "I shouldn't tell you this. I really do want you to go to jail, but Detective Roget is certain I'm amateur sleuthing. He wants to catch me in the act. Chances are he has my house under surveillance."

Darlene raised her hand in the air as if serving Leonard a delectable treat on a silver platter. "I know it makes no sense that we'd help you, but Faith doesn't want to die at her grandmothers' store. I'd prefer to die in my own home than on the cold asphalt or a poorly decorated scrapbook store."

"Poorly decorated," I screeched.

Darlene patted my hand. "I know the truth hurts. You won't have to concern yourself with that much longer."

"You two are making my head hurt." He glanced at the store.

"No one will believe Faith invited me here for us to crop together. That's the reason you left a message on my car. It said meet me at Scrap This and was signed with Faith's name."

Leonard shifted from foot to foot.

"Here are the problems with that plan. I don't have my totes with me. The assistant prosecutor is in love with Faith. There is no way he'd believe Faith had me come over here to kill me and then kill herself. That was the idea?"

Leonard nodded sheepishly.

"Yeah, that won't work," I said. "Steve and Detective Roget know how much I love my grandmothers and this store. The whole reason I got involved was because it happened by our back door. They wouldn't believe for a second I'd commit a crime here. But, they would believe I went to Darlene's to confront her and let her know I knew she killed Belinda. So of course, she'd kill me and then would kill herself because she'd rather be dead than wear an orange jumpsuit."

"Why would they believe that?" Leonard looked into her eyes.

"Because it's a Darlene thing to do," I said.

Leonard zeroed in on me.

"There's really no other explanation. It's how Darlene is. Didn't Belinda ever..."

"Both of you into the car. We'll go to Darlene's house." He pointed the gun at my head. "You drive. Darlene in the backseat with me."

"I'm the more careful driver," Darlene said.

"I know better than to trust you. You've proven you're the mastermind." Leonard waved the gun at me. "Open the trunk."

Was he going to put Darlene in there?

"Now."

I opened the door and spotted Darlene's cell phone in the plastic map holder attached to the door. I snagged it when I pressed the button to open the trunk, quickly placing it on the driver's seat.

"Happy?"

"You put this in the trunk." Leonard leaned over and keeping the gun pointed at Darlene, grabbed something from under the dumpster. He unwrapped a sweatshirt embroidered with palm trees from around the object.

Darlene stared at the hammer.

"Go on. Take it." Leonard held it out toward her.

Belinda's. From the class kit. I kept the knowledge to myself.

"So my fingerprints are on the murder weapon." Darlene tried taking a step back.

Leonard grabbed her arm. "I'll shoot you now and put you in the trunk."

I gestured for Darlene to take it. I couldn't get us out of this mess here, but I could once we got into the car. I prayed she trusted me.

Darlene snatched, what I presumed, was the murder weapon and gently placed it into the trunk.

"Now both of you in the car."

I sat before Leonard spotted our hopeful saving grace. The cell pressed into the back of my thigh. I ignored the discomfort.

Leonard buckled Darlene in. "If you try anything, I'll kill her and say you did it. You've given me plenty of stuff to use against you."

The silence in the car was pricking at my nerves. The fear made its way from my frozen toes, to my trembling knees, and finally reached my stomach. I needed it to stop before it got to my chest and made me hyperventilate. I needed my wits to pull off my hastily devised plan. First, I needed to distract Leonard and get some needed air into my lungs. Talking.

"Why did you kill Belinda?" I asked.

"I didn't know I was killing Belinda." Grief resonated in each word.

My mind flashed to the night I discovered Belinda, who I had originally thought was Hazel. In the dark, I couldn't really see the colors of the outfit. Belinda and Hazel had dressed identical except for which color was the prominent one and which the accent.

"You meant to kill Hazel," I said, pressing the gas.

The car surged forward. I eased off the pedal.

Leonard cursed and fumbled for the gun.

"Are you trying to kill me!" Darlene squealed.

"What the hell are you doing?" Leonard punched the back of the driver's seat.

"Sorry. Something rolled under the pedals." I leaned forward, grabbing the cell phone. I hit speed dial option number one. *Help me.* I texted. "I got it."

"What?" Leonard leaned forward.

Great. Now I had to toss the phone. Hopefully that got Eliza worried and had her call the cops or come over to Darlene's house. I threw the phone to the floor of the front passenger seat. "Women stuff."

Leonard made a sound of disgust and settled back into the seat. "Be careful or someone could get shot."

"I thought someone was getting shot." I clenched the steering wheel.

Keep it together. You can do this. I hoped she heard the words I spoke in my mind and heart.

"Hazel was harassing Belinda," I said.

"Shut up, Faith," Darlene said.

"I thought the matching hairstyle was a little over the top," I said.

"Belinda was okay with the hair cut but not the dye job." Leonard draped an arm on the seat and pressed the gun into my ribcage. "I told her Hazel was nuts but she didn't believe me. The same clothes. Coming over and doing her laundry. Folding her clothes and putting them away. Belinda said it was always a little smothering. It got real bad when Belinda moved out."

"Was Hazel jealous of you guys?" I leaned away from the gun and made sure I didn't inch the car over at the same time.

"Belinda never told her about us. I told Belinda no ring if she couldn't detach from her mom."

"So you killed Belinda. How did that help her?" Darlene asked.

"I didn't know I was killing Belinda. Belinda said she was scared of her mom. Afraid she'd really go crazy. I told her to get a restraining order. She decided not to. Thought just taking her mom's keys would give us some privacy. Nope. The night before Belinda's big day, Hazel goes and sneaks in through the back door when Belinda was in the shower. Belinda found her mom in our bed. The woman had got them matching pajamas and said they were having a slumber party."

"We always had slumber parties," Darlene defended her family.

"You all sneak into each other's houses?" Leonard asked.

"No." So much shame filled the small word.

"The police wouldn't help my girlfriend. So I did." The anger left Leonard's voice. "Thought I did anyway."

"Did Belinda know?" I wished with all my being Belinda didn't die knowing the man she loved killed her.

"That I was going to kill her mom for her? It was her plan." Leonard pressed the gun further into my ribs. "She forgot to tell me she planned on showing up to watch. Sure wished she would've changed out of that stupid outfit first. Now how about you shut up and drive."

At that moment, I decided silence was much better.

I pulled into the driveway.

"Park inside." Leonard pointed the business end of the revolver at the button for the garage door.

"No!" Darlene snapped. "My studio is in there. The backdrops. The lighting. I just spent four thousand dollars putting down hardwood floors."

"You'll be dead. Why do you care?"

"You'll be alive so you should care. I never park in my garage. No one will buy I decided to park in my garage tonight. Just park here in the driveway. When we get out, put your arm around Faith's shoulder, people will think she and Steve came here for engagement photos."

Darlene opened up the passenger door.

I refrained from pointing out that was I driving.

"If you're trying anything funny." Leonard tugged her back into the car then dragged her out with him. He yanked open the driver's door and jabbed the gun into my ribs.

I winced. The sharp pain increased as Leonard inched the gun further into my skin. I remained still, afraid any movement, even a breath, might set him off. The image outside the window blurred.

"Trust me. I do *not* do funny." Darlene glanced into the map holder.

Her gaze slid to mine for a moment. She knew. For better or worse, we were in this together. We'd either both get out alive, or neither of us would.

"Back away from the car, Ms. Not Funny. You get out." Leonard dug his fingers into my waist and hauled me out. "I ain't stupid. You two are planning on overpowering me together."

"Stupid isn't a word I'd use for you." Darlene stood on the small front porch.

"Get up there." Leonard released my waist and prodded me.

"That hurts," I said. "The police are going to think it's weird I have all these round bruises in my side if Darlene shot me in her house."

"It'll be because she poked you to make sure you were dead."

"She poked me numerous times to make sure I was dead, yet killed herself over the grief of having killed me."

"Shut up." Leonard grabbed my right arm, squeezing tight and shaking. "Just get up there. It's time to get this over with."

I was fine with prolonging the inevitable.

Half-dragging me to the door, he glanced around. I also scanned the area, hoping to spot a make-do bat for use on Leonard's head. A soft light bathed the small area entrance into her house. Rose bushes flanked either side of the door. A metal mailbox hung underneath the porch light. It might work.

Darlene held the door open.

"Get inside." Leonard motioned with the gun.

Darlene entered.

Movement behind the rose bush caught my attention. I halted.

Leonard tugged my arm as he walked inside the house. "Get in here or I'll shoot her."

I glimpsed a shadow on the wall coming downstairs.

"Sweetheart! No." Darlene's panicked voice grabbed Leonard's attention.

He loosened his grip on my arm and aimed the gun toward the stairs.

A cold object was shoved in my hands. I looked down. Eliza squatted behind the rose bush.

I tightened my grip on the stun gun. Quickly, I jabbed it into Leonard's side and squeezed. "Duck!"

The revolver went off. Darlene screamed. Eliza bellowed and launched her small, compact body into the house.

With limbs twitching, Leonard went down. The gun shook loose from his grasp.

Blocking back tears, I stepped into the house. Please, let Darlene be alive.

TWENTY-SEVEN

Darlene huddled near the stairs, arms wrapped tightly around a russet Great Dane. The dog lifted its head from her shoulder and woofed at the still form of Leonard.

Did I kill him? I glanced down at the stun gun.

Hazel, who had hid behind the other rose bush, nudged the man with his toe. He made a small moan. "Not dead."

Good he was alive. At least I think it was good. I kicked the weapon away from his hand. "We should call the cops and restrain this creep."

"Get tape." Darlene shooed Hazel up the stairs. "In my craft studio there's a plastic storage case labeled 'tape' and then a drawer marked 'fun times.' Bring both. I store my washi tape in there."

"Don't you have duct tape?" I held Leonard's no longer twitching hands behind his back.

"They'll work. Sweetheart, mean man."

The dog lumbered over like an angry father intent on chasing off the biker dude wanting to date his daughter.

Eliza flattened herself across Leonard's back. Sweetheart plopped down, using the man's legs and backside as a pillow.

Hazel raced up the stairs.

"The tape is thin. It won't hold," I said.

"It will. Trust me."

Hazel scurried back down holding the drawer. Darlene took it from Hazel and brought it over to me. Darlene selected a roll and went to work on the man's ankles.

I wasn't nearly as picky and grabbed a roll. Quickly, I wrapped the entire roll of daisy print decorative tape around Leonard's wrists. I reached into the storage case and yanked out another.

"No!" Darlene screeched.

I lunged backwards, planting my hands behind my back, setting myself to give Leonard a proper pounding to his head with my feet. I wouldn't be able to knock him out cold with a punch, but a well-placed kick would accomplish it.

Darlene lurched forward and snatched the roll of tape in my hand. "Do you know how hard the Hello Kitty tape is to find?"

It had to be a joke. I gaped at Darlene. For the love of scrapbooking, she wasn't joking. She lovingly and protectively clutched the pink tape decorated with red hearts and a white cat face to her bosom.

"I need another one. One roll isn't going to hold him." I stretched out my arm.

Hazel threw one toward me. It fell short, bonking Leonard on the head and then cavorted to the other side of the room with twists and turns across the spectacular bamboo floor.

Another roll whizzed past my head.

"Give me those." Eliza rushed over and grabbed the whole drawer from Hazel. She dumped it over Leonard. A plethora of washi tapes rained down upon Leonard and me. I snagged hold of a black and white plaid I knew we carried at the store.

I peeled back a tiny corner then whipped the whole row of tape around the man's wrists. I grabbed another roll. The tape had never been tested as a method of tying someone up. Or at least not that I knew about.

Eliza joined in the wrapping. She tore a new roll out of cellophane and got to work on the man's ankles.

"I want to help, too." Hazel glanced over the offerings and chose a beige roll with inspirational sayings written on it.

"Not that one." Darlene tore it from her aunt's hands. "I paid ten dollars for it."

She got ripped off.

I picked the closest roll and wrapped it speedily around Leonard's wrist. I had quite a collection decorating his wrists.

"How about this one?" Hazel held out another roll.

Darlene shook her head. "I know what project I want to use it for."

Hazel plucked out another. "This?"

"Nope."

"Grab one and tape." I shoved a roll at Hazel. "We need him bound before he regains consciousness."

Darlene drew in a displeased breath.

"I'll buy you some of the new sexy cowboy tape to replace it," I said. "Just keep taping."

"Sexy cowboy?" Darlene's eyes widened with interest.

"It's a new line. Sexy Santa. Sexy cowboy. Sexy fireman," I recited the ones I remembered as I continued to tape. "If there's a profession or a hobby they could make a man look sexy doing, they have a tape for it."

"Use them all." Darlene dumped an armload of tape into Hazel and her mother's lap. With a wide grin, Darlene set to work mummifying Leonard.

By the time we were done, every inch of Leonard was covered in some style of decorative tape.

Sweetheart woofed his approval. A large bead of drool dripped onto Leonard's face.

"Someone should call the police." I shoved a wad of hair from my face. I grimaced as I touched the knot on the side of my forehead.

"Oliver went to get him," Eliza said. "We were at our knitting group when he got Darlene's message. We came right over and he went for the police."

Went for? Wouldn't calling them have worked better? I think Oliver needed to read a few more mysteries. "Hopefully they get here soon. We might not have enough to hold this killer."

"The four of us can take him." Darlene cracked her knuckles. "I hope the detective is a little late. I have a lesson for Leonard."

"He's here," Ted's voice echoed through the house.

A rumble echoed from Sweetheart. Darlene snagged the Great Dane's collar. "He's good."

Sweetheart lowered himself into a sitting position, keeping his dark soulful eyes on Ted.

"What took you so long?" Darlene stood, dusting off her pants. "I thought you were a runner."

"I had to lock Oliver in my bathroom first. He wanted to come over and help me defend you ladies," Ted said. "I thought it was best he stay put. I didn't need another person who doesn't like listening to police. He should've called 911 instead of wanting to keep his line open in case you texted again."

Darlene tsked. "That's what I forgot to tell Leonard. Detective Roget lives down the block. Good thinking on using my phone to get backup."

Oliver filled her number one spot? No wonder she got worked up about the necklace. That was a huge step in a relationship.

Ted knelt beside me on one knee. "You okay?"

I nodded.

His finger drifted under the lump on my forehead. He pressed his lips together. I had a feeling I knew what he wanted to say but wouldn't in front of an audience. He handed me his cell phone. "Call the station. Tell them I need some officers and an ambulance."

"I'm fine."

"Maybe this has knocked some sense into you." Ted cuffed Leonard. "Mrs. Watson, you can't kick the prisoner again."

"I'm clumsy," Hazel said, firing off another kick. "Sorry."

"Me too. Clumsiness runs in the family." Eliza reared her foot back and booted the killer in the butt.

"Ladies..." Ted used his warning tone on them.

I placed the call. "There's a guy trussed up like a Thanksgiving turkey at Darlene Johnson's house."

"Not again," Bobbi-Annie moaned. "You tell Darlene, Oliver's aunt said the next time things got like that between her and her nephew she'd make her marry the boy."

Gaping at Darlene, I muttered something about sending the police and an ambulance. Bobbi-Annie's response of 'Darlene's mother can explain it this time' barely registered in my head.

Darlene carefully deposited the few remaining tape rolls back into the drawer marked Fun Times. "I told you they'd work for re-straining a guy."

Shivering, I wrapped my grandfather's afghan around me and curled into the chair. So much hatred combined with so much love. What drove people to that place? I not only thought about Belinda and Leonard, but Adam and me. In a way, our relationship had been the same; one person in each couple was being used. In my case the user was obvious—Adam. With Belinda and Leonard it was a toss-up.

I guess in a way Belinda got what she aimed to give. The thought unsettled me. It wasn't right to have those feelings about someone, especially the deceased. Guilt wormed through me. I needed comfort. I needed chocolate. I also didn't want to move.

Maybe I shouldn't have been so quick to insist to Steve I need-ed to be alone. Having company who liked waiting and doing favors for you was lovely when you were soul tired.

A loud thud sounded from outside my kitchen door.

I shot up in the chair. The blanket slipped from my shoulders. A loud yowl shattered the quiet outside. I knew that sound. Some-one stepped on the tabby tomcat stray I named Ol' Yowler's tail. Ol' Yowler had taken up residence on my back porch.

I lurched to my feet and ran for my cell phone I left in my purse. I needed to start wearing it around my neck.

"Don't call the police, Faith." Ted's muffled voice came from my deck.

"Give me one good reason." I wasn't in the mood for any un-expected, unwanted company. Especially anyone who thought I was a senseless, aggravating woman who didn't display the good sense God granted a toddler.

"I am the police."

Okay, it was a good one. Still, I wasn't quite ready to let him off the hook.

"If I wanted to be read the riot act again, I'd invite my grandmothers over. At least that way I'd get some cookies along with the lecture."

"You're going to get your wish," Ted grumbled. "Hello Mrs. Greyfield and Mrs. Hunter."

This I wanted to hear and see. Gleefully, I tugged the door open and eased out on the porch.

Grandma Cheryl stood on the outskirts of the beginning of my yard, a shotgun aimed at Ted. "Hope is calling the chief. You better have a good explanation for lurking around my granddaughter's backyard."

He had his hands reaching for the stars. "Patrolling."

I decided to sit on the nice comfortable lounge chair in the corner. I wished I had some popcorn. Once I got comfortable, Ol' Yowler jumped up beside me.

Cheryl snorted. "Without a flashlight?"

"I could use some help," Ted said.

"I'm too senseless to figure that out." I scratched Ol' Yowler behind the ears. He purred, adding a nice soundtrack to the evening's entertainment.

"You know what I meant," Ted said.

"Precisely. I don't know enough to keep out of things I ought to. So, I'm showing you I do." I stuck out my tongue, knowing my grandmother couldn't see me. "Happy now?"

"I was referring to playing private detective. You and Darlene were lucky Leonard was possibly the world's dumbest criminal. One of you could've been killed and I don't see Darlene being the self-sacrificing type."

"I have to agree with him, Faith." Cheryl lowered the gun. "Just what in the world were you thinking getting into the car with that man? Hope and I taught you to never get into the car of a stranger."

"We kind of didn't have much a choice, the whole at gunpoint thing." I forced lightness and snark into my voice even as a shudder ripped through me.

"I'm bringing back-up!" Hope shouted. "He's hot and bothered and itching for a fight."

"Do I want to know?" Ted threw a look at me, a cross between bewildered and terrified.

"I'd say she's bringing her handgun or else she told Mr. Murphy that Grandma Cheryl was in danger and he's coming over to use his karate moves on you."

Ted moaned. "Not Clive."

So, Detective Roget had a few run-ins already with Clive Murphy.

Seventy-five year old Mr. Murphy was our neighborhood's self-appointed Citizen Watch group leader and one of the two members of the team. Mrs. Barlow was the other. Much to Mrs. Barlow's irk, Clive had a thing for Cheryl.

The word "charge" echoed from down the block.

Cheryl ran for the safety of her home. While my grandmother loved shoving Steve at me, insisting I needed a man, she wanted nothing to do with one. I wished she'd find someone, but Clive didn't inspire me to do any matchmaking. He was nice. Cute in the old, grandfather kind of way, but the man came with four ex-wives and twelve children who were already fighting over who'd get his belongings once he died.

Grandma Cheryl wasn't into drama which is why my insistence on jumping into it to help friends, and especially frenemies, confused her.

"Can I come in?" Ted reached down for a heavy case placed on the ground near the deck.

"Planning on fingerprinting the place or setting up a wiretap?"

"Now there's an idea." Ted smiled at me. "I came to return some items to you."

"By jumping over my fence." I made myself more comfortable on the lounger.

"I was hoping to avoid your grandmothers, and Mrs. Barlow's binoculars."

"Epic fail on your part. Maybe God should've given you more sense."

"You sure don't like letting anything go." Ted hissed out a frustrated breath. "I was worried. Scared to death for you and I let my emotions get the best of me. Give a guy who cares about you...and is returning your secrets...a break."

"Forgiven." I jumped to my feet. Ol' Yowler mewed pathetically. I scooped him up. "Tonight you can come inside. Just tonight."

"Fine. I wasn't requesting to move in."

I rolled my eyes. "I was talking to the cat."

"Okay, but I think we're moving kind of fast." Ted lugged the metal box inside. "I'd be okay with dinner."

"Behave or I'm going to tell my grandmothers you're being fresh."

"I found your Army information when we searched Leonard's car." Ted placed the lock box on top of my table. "I made the call these documents aren't necessary to try the case. Consider the secure storage a gift."

"Thank you." I ran my hand over the cold metal. "Who else knows?"

"The Chief, Jasper, Prosecutor Harlow."

I nodded, clenching the fabric of my sweatshirt. I felt sick.

Ted stood behind me and kneaded my shoulders. "All they know is these were family pictures stolen from your house. They were important to you and I didn't feel it was necessary to solve the crime. Everyone agreed. We have enough real evidence for cataloging, no sense adding in hundreds of photographs."

I spun around and hugged him. Tight.

"Stop torturing yourself." Ted whispered into my hair.

"I'm not." I put some distance between my ear and his chest.

He tipped my chin up, making me look into his concerned green eyes. "You fell in love with a man who wasn't worth your heart. Don't let him still have it."

"He doesn't." I tried stepping away from Ted, but his gentle touch on my waist kept me nearby. "I want nothing to do with him. Ever."

Ted tucked a lock of hair behind my ear then trailed his fingers up and down my cheek. "As long as you're too scared and feel too unworthy to allow someone else to love you, he still has it. He doesn't deserve it."

The intensity in Ted's eyes and anger in his voice sent a curl of heat through me. This time, I did leave the zone Ted and I created together. I needed space. Boundaries. I needed to think.

"I'll go." Ted rapped his knuckles on the box. "While I'd like it to be me you're willing to let go of the past for, I'd be okay if it was Davis. He's a good guy. The bad guys shouldn't win over the good guys."

"They won't," I whispered.

"Then I'll be waiting to see which good guy gets a real chance."

All I managed was a nod.

Ted strode over to the front door. He twisted the knob. "If you're ever in the mood to roast something, I have a fireplace."

I shut the door and Ted's words swirled around me. I leaned against it, my gaze traveling to the metal box lurking in the background.

Ted was right. Not about needing to roast something but the fact Adam still controlled my life. As long as I continued, in a way, living from that moment I'd never totally be over him. He lurked in all the decisions I made...and didn't make. It was time to do some ghost-busting and get rid of the one I carried around with me.

There was only one way to banish the last remnants of Adam from my life. Declare my new one.

I took in a deep breath, squared my shoulders, and marched out the door. I tromped through my grandmothers' front yard. The porch light blazed on, bathing me like I walked under an interrogation spotlight. Might as well get this decision out in the open.

Grandma Cheryl raced out her front door. "Faith, what are you up to now?"

"Formally claiming my man."

Cheryl beamed and inched her way back into her house. "I think I should just let you be."

I rapped my knuckles on Steve's door. My heart beat against my chest harder than I knocked. Sweat popped up on my brow. My hands and knees shook. I hoped I could get to say the life changing words before I swooned, or worse puked on Steve.

He answered the door. Fully clothed.

Disappointment shot through me and chased away the nausea. Here went everything. I looked him in the eye. "Okay."

Steve's eyebrows' quirked up. "Okay?"

Apparently, I wasn't very good at this. I tried again. "You and me. I want to give us a try. A real try."

He crossed his arms. His kissable mouth set in a straight line. The sleeves of the t-shirt bunched up, revealing a smidge of his tattoo. "An actual relationship."

This wasn't quite as easy as I'd imagined. I placed my hands on his toned arms and leaned closer, hoping he'd wrap them around me soon. "A commitment. I tell people we're dating. You tell people we're dating. My grandmothers start buying wedding themed scrapbook supplies."

"Even without knowing..." His gaze drifted toward my hand resting near the sleeve of shirt and now covering the tattoo.

"Knowing everything is overrated." I fluttered my eyes and moistened my lips. I wasn't quite ready to form them in the international signal of "kiss me" as a girl didn't want to invite that bold of a rejection.

"Are you sure?" His hands drifted to my waist.

"Whatever it is isn't going to break my heart?" My heart pounded.

"No. A decision I made that was the first wedge between me and my father." Pain crept into his eyes.

I wrapped my arms around Steve. I knew that kind of pain and hated that he lived with it also. Maybe we were meant for each other?

Maybe? I marched over to declare my intentions. There was no maybe about it. Ted flashed into my mind. I tightened my hold on Steve. No. I wanted Steve. I cared about Steve. I could count on Steve and knew he wouldn't hurt me. He stood beside me. Behind me. Whatever I needed and whenever I needed it. He never argued against me, always for me.

Steve untangled himself from my arms. His eyes locked on mine. "Faith..."

"Kiss me." A slow and sexy smile curved his lips. Steve obliged, happily and quite heartily with my request.

TWENTY-EIGHT

A golden-yellow ray of sunshine dipped down from the sky and highlighted the church. Hazel stood by the front door and tipped her head up, a soft serene smile on her face. The perfect day she planned happened. Sadly, it wasn't the wedding she envisioned for her beloved daughter but a funeral.

I gulped down a lump knotting my throat.

Steve and Ted headed up the stairs. They walked side-by-side and looked almost like twins in their dark suits and dress shoes. They had offered to act as pall bearers for Belinda's funeral along with Gussie's sons, Wyatt and Wayne. Neither Belinda nor her mom had many true friends in Eden. I knew everyone, yet didn't know anyone.

Almost like me.

Moisture built in my eyes. I blinked the tears away and shut off my pity-party.

This day wasn't about me or my woes. My self-created heartache. There were two decent and honorable men in my life. A handful of friends who stood beside me even when I annoyed the everloving daylights out of them and kept them walled off from parts of my life. My adoring grandmothers loved me in spite, despite, and because of who I was and yearned to be.

"Aunt Hazel is going all out isn't she?" Darlene stood beside me. She wore a vintage style black dress paired with a black birdcage style hat. A black veil stuck straight up into the air.

My eyebrows rose.

Darlene smiled sadly. "Belinda had a matching outfit. We planned on wearing them to the other's wedding."

I didn't know what to say, so I remained quiet.

"It's our family's nature. The way we bond. We compete with each other. Belinda would've loved me showing up in this getup. Just like I would've loved it if she did when I got married. Nothing more heartwarming than knowing you caused your cousin to feel a whole lot of green."

I guess jealously worked for some relationships. In a strange way, the sisters and daughters had been happy with their lives. They fought, supported, plotted, and loved each other. Who could ask for more?

No one did, until Leonard stepped into the picture and wanted more for Belinda. He gave her confidence to want more for herself. While admirable and understandable, their way of achieving the goal was horrific.

The motive for Belinda's murder, that it was supposed to have been Hazel's, weaved around me. Belinda meant to kill her mother.

My gaze rested on Karen staring at Hazel and Eliza. She had the truth in the palm of her hand, ready to launch at Hazel. The truth was the end all in her world of needing to expose ugliness for sales. I loved that my job now was about preserving the preciousness of memories. Some people wrote the good and bad in their albums.

Like Darlene. If someone was going to reveal the devastating news, it should be Darlene. At least she'd have the best interest of her aunt in mind.

"Are you going to tell Hazel what Leonard said?" I whispered.

Darlene looked up the stairs. Her mother enveloped her grieving sister in an embrace and led her into the sanctuary. Darlene motioned for Oliver to follow after her family. "Aunt Hazel's heart already broke once. I don't see any need to break it again."

"Belinda was trying to frame you for Hazel's murder with that necklace. They stole the hammer and planned to use it to frame you."

"She's dead. It doesn't matter now. I have to live with it, why should Aunt Hazel."

"She'll find out when the trial takes place." I knew Hazel would take up a front seat vigil when her daughter's murderer stood before the court. She'd hear the truth.

"I'll tell her I don't believe a word that man is saying. He's a murderer. A low life. Of course he doesn't want to take full responsibility for his actions. He's just the kind of man to blame a woman. We know all about those types of men."

I sure did. "Won't you be lying?"

"Not every truth needs documentation in a scrapbook." Darlene tugged the black veil over her face.

Or to be kept in a locked box on the top shelf of a closet.

Faith's Scrapbooking Tips

How to Tweak a Scraplift to Fit Your Style

When scraplifting a design, remember pages are to showcase your memories for you and your loved ones' enjoyment, not to submit to contests or as a means to get on a design team.

Scraplifting helps croppers find a way out of the too familiar scenario of scrapbooker's block. That frustrating place where you have stunning photos, galore of fantastic supplies, but no idea on how to use any of the awesomeness at your fingertips. Designers, and hobbyists who post their layouts, love to see how their designs inspired others so feel free to share your pages on messages boards. Just remember to credit the scrapper who inspired you or at least mention the design is a scraplift.

1. Play with the elements of the design. Instead of placing all the embellishments, pattern paper, cardstock, and photos in the exact position as in the inspiration layout, move them around. Place the title at the bottom of the page. Line the strip of photos on the opposite side or place it horizontal instead of vertical.

2. Add a twist. Instead of following the design down to the last brad, substitute a product you love for one the designer used. Add in an extra photo or a larger photo than on the inspiration page. Exchange the strips of pattern paper for cardstock. Washi tape instead of ribbon.

3. Don't be afraid to eliminate. If your style is more minimalist, don't think you have to keep embellishment clusters or use all the techniques showed on the page. Remove some of the clusters. Take out one or two of the techniques from the inspiration page. Strip the layout down to the basic design. Only use the parts that help you create a page pleasing to your eye.

4. Control the Chaos. If you like a linear style, and would love to incorporate some element from a less structured design, use the technique in a more "organized" method. Do your splatter in a line instead of free form. Make embellishment clusters with lines, squares, rectangles, and any other shapes that have strong lines.

5. Shop your stash. An inspiration layout is not a recipe that has to be followed. Use what you have on hand, product that caught *your* eye, instead of purchasing the exact products the designer used. Using the items you love will show your style. Do you have a preference for bold colors over pastels? Whimsical designs instead of geometric shapes? Let your layouts showcase your inner designer by using the scrapping goodies already filling your scrapbooking studio and cropping totes. (I can't believe I'm sharing this one.)

And remember every page you make is beautiful, a work of heart. Don't worry about following trends, what is deemed hot by the scrapbooking Divas, and compare your page as lacking if it doesn't look like the layouts published. Your love of scrapbooking makes them beautiful. Each and every one. Enjoy your hobby! No matter what Darlene says, it's not a competition.

Photo by KD Images

CHRISTINA FREEBURN

The Faith Hunter Scrap This Mystery series brings together Christina Freeburn's love of mysteries, scrapbooking, and West Virginia. When not writing or reading, she can be found in her scrapbook room or at a crop. Alas, none of the real-life crops have had a sexy male prosecutor or a handsome police officer attending.

Christina served in the JAG Corps of the US Army and also worked as a paralegal, librarian, and church secretary. She lives in West Virginia with her husband, children, a dog, and a rarely seen cat except by those who are afraid or allergic to felines.

Don't miss the FIRST book in
The Faith Hunter Scrap This Mystery Series

CROPPED to death
by CHRISTINA FREEBURN

Former US Army JAG specialist, Faith Hunter, returns to her West Virginia home to work in her grandmothers' scrapbooking store determined to lead an unassuming life after her adventure abroad turned disaster. But her quiet life unravels when her friend is charged with murder, and Faith inadvertently supplied the evidence. So Faith decides to cut through the scrap and piece together what really happened. With a sexy prosecutor, a determined homicide detective, a handful of sticky suspects and a crop contest gone bad, Faith quickly realizes if she's not careful, she'll be the next one cropped.

Available Now
For more details, visit www.henerypress.com

IF YOU LIKED THIS HENERY PRESS MYSTERY,
YOU MIGHT ALSO LIKE THESE...

Lowcountry BOIL
by Susan M. Boyer

Private Investigator Liz Talbot is a modern Southern belle: she blesses hearts and takes names. She carries her Sig 9 in her Kate Spade handbag, and her golden retriever, Rhett, rides shotgun in her hybrid Escape. When her grandmother is murdered, Liz hightails it back to her South Carolina island home to find the killer.

She's fit to be tied when her police-chief brother shuts her out of the investigation, so she opens her own. Then her long-dead best friend pops in and things really get complicated. When more folks start turning up dead in this small seaside town, Liz must use more than just her wits and charm to keep her family safe, chase down clues from the hereafter, and catch a psychopath before he catches her.

Available Now
For more details, visit www.henerypress.com

ARTIFACT
BY GIGI PANDIAN

Historian Jaya Jones discovers the secrets of a lost Indian treasure
may be hidden in a Scottish legend from the days of the British Raj.
But she's not the only one on the trail...

From San Francisco to London to the Highlands of Scotland, Jaya
must evade a shadowy stalker as she follows hints from the hastily
scrawled note of her dead lover to a remote archaeological dig.
Helping her decipher the cryptic clues are her magician best friend,
a devastatingly handsome art historian with something to hide, and
a charming archaeologist running for his life.

Available Now
For more details, visit www.henerypress.com

DINERS, dives & DEAD ENDS
by Terri L. Austin

As a struggling waitress and part-time college student, Rose Strickland's life is stalled in the slow lane. But when her close friend, Axton, disappears, Rose suddenly finds herself serving up more than hot coffee and flapjacks. Now she's hashing it out with sexy bad guys and scrambling to find clues in a race to save Axton before his time runs out.

With her anime-loving bestie, her septuagenarian boss, and a pair of IT wise men along for the ride, Rose discovers political corruption, illegal gambling, and shady corporations. She's gone from zero to sixty and quickly learns when you're speeding down the fast lane, it's easy to crash and burn.

Available Now
For more details, visit www.henerypress.com

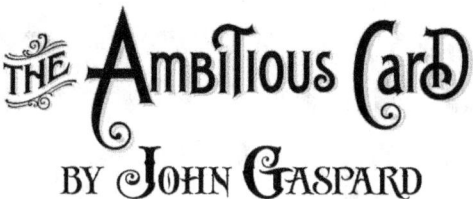

THE AMBITIOUS CARD

BY JOHN GASPARD

The life of a magician isn't all kiddie shows and card tricks. Sometimes it's murder. Especially when magician Eli Marks very publicly debunks a famed psychic, and said psychic ends up dead. The evidence, including a bloody King of Diamonds playing card (one from Eli's own Ambitious Card routine), directs the police right to Eli.

As more psychics are slain, and more King cards rise to the top, Eli can't escape suspicion. Things get really complicated when romance blooms with a beautiful psychic, and Eli discovers she's the next target for murder, and he's scheduled to die with her. Now Eli must use every trick he knows to keep them both alive and reveal the true killer.

Available Now
For more details, visit www.henerypress.com

BOARD STIFF

by Kendel Lynn

As director of the Ballantyne Foundation on Sea Pine Island, SC, Elliott Lisbon scratches her detective itch by performing discreet inquiries for Foundation donors. Usually nothing more serious than retrieving a pilfered Pomeranian. Until Jane Hatting, Ballantyne board chair, is accused of murder. The Ballantyne's reputation tanks, Jane's headed to a jail cell, and Elliott's sexy ex is the new lieutenant in town.

Armed with moxie and her Mini Coop, Elliott uncovers a trail of blackmail schemes, gambling debts, illicit affairs, and investment scams. But the deeper she digs to clear Jane's name, the guiltier Jane looks. The closer she gets to the truth, the more treacherous her investigation becomes. With victims piling up faster than shells at a clambake, Elliott realizes she's next on the killer's list.

Available Now
For more details, visit www.henerypress.com

PORTRAIT of a DEAD GUY
by LARISSA REINHART

In Halo, Georgia, folks know Cherry Tucker as big in mouth, small in stature, and able to sketch a portrait faster than buck-shot rips from a ten gauge -- but commissions are scarce. So when the well-heeled Branson family wants to memorialize their murdered son in a coffin portrait, Cherry scrambles to win their patronage from her small town rival.

As the clock ticks toward the deadline, Cherry faces more trouble than just a controversial subject. Between ex-boyfriends, her flaky family, an illegal gambling ring, and outwitting a killer on a spree, Cherry finds herself painted into a corner she'll be lucky to survive.

Available Now
For more details, visit www.henerypress.com

DOUBLE WHAMMY

by Gretchen Archer

Davis Way thinks she's hit the jackpot when she lands a job as the fifth wheel on an elite security team at the fabulous Bellissimo Resort and Casino in Biloxi, Mississippi. But once there, she runs straight into her ex-ex husband, a rigged slot machine, her evil twin, and a trail of dead bodies. Davis learns the truth and it does not set her free—in fact, it lands her in the pokey.

Buried under a mistaken identity, unable to seek help from her family, her hot streak runs cold until her landlord Bradley Cole steps in. Make that her landlord, lawyer, and love interest. With his help, Davis must win this high stakes game before her luck runs out.

Available Now
For more details, visit www.henerypress.com

FRONT PAGE FATALITY
by LynDee Walker

Crime reporter Nichelle Clarke's days can flip from macabre to comical with a beep of her police scanner. Then an ordinary accident story turns extraordinary when evidence goes missing, a prosecutor vanishes, and a sexy Mafia boss shows up with the headline tip of a lifetime.

As Nichelle gets closer to the truth, her story gets more dangerous. Armed with a notebook, a hunch, and her favorite stilettos, Nichelle races to splash these shady dealings across the front page before this deadline becomes her last.

www.ingramcontent.com/pod-product-compliance
Lightning Source LLC
Chambersburg PA
CBHW060521260626
47161CB00003B/714